DEAD
SILENT

SHARON JONES

ORCHARD

ORCHARD BOOKS
338 Euston Road, London NW1 3BH
Orchard Books Australia
Level 17/207 Kent Street, Sydney, NSW 2000

This edition published in 2014 by Orchard Books

ISBN 978 1 40832 756 2

A CIP catalogue record for this book is available
from the British Library.

1 3 5 7 9 8 6 4 2

Printed in Great Britain

Orchard Books is a division of Hachette Children's Books,
an Hachette UK company.

www.hachette.co.uk

For my mum, Denise Jones.
Happy Birthday!

PROLOGUE

It had to be here.

The soles of his shoes squeaked from marble to wood as he ran between the choir stalls, swinging the torch beam like a whip that could beat back the night.

How could he have been so stupid as to lose the book? If he didn't find it he was dead.

A faint scuffling noise brought him to a halt. *Shit!* His fingers fumbled to shut off the torch. The light died and he stood frozen, holding his breath. Slowly, his eyes adjusted to the gloom. He could pick out strange shapes in the darkness, but none of them moved.

He was being an idiot. There was no one there. The noise was probably just a mouse or a rat. Places like this had to be teeming with vermin.

He sucked in a deep breath of cool air that smelled of snuffed-out candles and damp stone, switched on the torch and resumed his search.

Soon the college porters would start their rounds – unlocking doors and doing security checks. The last thing he needed was to land in the crapper for breaking into the chapel. Not that he'd needed to break in: he had a key – but he could hardly tell that to the proctor.

Quickly, he found the choir stall where he'd been sitting earlier that evening. He kneeled down and felt beneath the bench. No, nothing there but grit and dust. Maybe he'd kicked it further along.

He stretched as far as he could reach. Suddenly something tickled against his face, almost as if a spider had run out from its secret hiding place and made an escape across his skin. He shot to his feet, wiped his cheek with the sleeve of his dinner jacket and spat away the clinging stickiness from his cold-cracked lips.

As he ran a hand over his face to check that the thing had gone, the torch beam caught something startlingly white, falling like a snowflake onto the oak choir stall.

A feather.

Large, white and downy. A goose feather? Where the hell had that come from?

He swung the torch at the beamed ceiling but there was no bird. Of course there was no bird. The only thing in here with wings was the Archangel Michael slaying the red-faced devil in the twenty-feet-tall painting above the altar, and he very much doubted *that* old bastard was moulting. It must have blown in, got caught somewhere.

He sighed. There was no bird in here. And no book.

Maybe he'd left it in the Old Kitchen…or the bar. Yeah, he could have left it in the bar, which meant anyone could have it. Damn it!

His shoes, still wet with melting snow, squeaked

against the marble floor as he marched towards the door, the torchlight bobbing in front of him. He'd go back to the bar. With any luck someone would have had handed it in without realising what it contained.

There was a soft clunk somewhere just behind him and to his left, like someone had banged into something.

He froze.

'Hello?' He swung the torch beam in the direction of the noise.

The chapel was silent again. But there was someone there, watching him. He could feel it, like icy fingertips tracing down his spine.

Probably someone saw him coming in here and thought it would be funny to put the frighteners on him. Bastards!

Even if it was someone having a laugh, it didn't stop his pulse thumping against the collar of his high-winged shirt. 'I'm about to lock up,' he said, hoping the threat would draw out the prankster.

The only reply came in the form of a loud clinking noise that echoed around the chapel as if someone was dragging chains across the floor.

He spun around, cutting through the dark with the beam of light. What the hell was going on?

Nothing. He couldn't see a damned thing. He forced himself to be still and listen.

Nothing moved. But he could hear something. Something that sounded like…breathing.

Adrenaline burned like acid through his veins and he ran.

He hadn't gone far when a blow to the side of his head sent him reeling. He crashed to the floor, grunting in pain as his shoulder crunched against marble. He rolled onto his back. The torch beam swung up to the painting, illuminating the Archangel Michael; his golden breastplate and metal-tipped spear. A spear that looked like the very real one pointing at his chest.

'What the…?'

The torch slipped from his hand, there was a scuffling noise and the next second the beam was blinding him.

'What are you doing?' he gasped, squinting into the light. 'Who are you?'

He pushed himself onto his elbow but a foot to his stomach pinned him to the floor.

The pain that struck his chest didn't seem real. And as he lay there spilling hot blood onto the floor of the chapel, he didn't think about dying. Didn't think about all the things he would never get to do…the places he would never get to see.

Instead, he thought about the book he had lost.

And the oath he had broken.

CHAPTER ONE

'Are you sure you're holding the map the right way up?'

Poppy tried glaring at Michael. Instead, a guilty smile inched across her face as she kicked at the pile of slush that had collected in the gutter.

Snowflakes the size of cotton wool balls drifted out of the night sky with haphazard elegance. Clumps of them caught in Michael's dark hair and for a moment she could imagine that there was just the two of them, in some magical snow globe.

Michael stared at her, his face deadly serious and his gaze so steady that she knew the game was up. 'Poppy, have you – by any chance – been taking us in the wrong direction?' Before she could answer, Michael rolled his eyes. 'You can't put off seeing your dad forever. In case you haven't noticed the cold white stuff, it's snowing, and I'd rather not spend the night out here.'

'But don't you think it's pretty?'

Michael turned his face to the heavens as a smile tugged at his lips. He shook his head. 'You're unbelievable. Where are we?'

'Not in Kansas any more.'

He grinned. 'Where are we?'

'Somewhere in Cambridge?' Poppy said, shrugging and taking a step back.

Michael advanced on her. '*Where* are we?' He made a grab for the map. Poppy just managed to dodge him and set off running down the cobbled street. Her foot hit a patch of ice. She skittered to a stop as the weight of her backpack combined with gravity to tug her towards the ground. A hand grabbed her arm just in time to stop her from toppling over and, before she could object, the map was snatched from her grasp.

Michael's smile was victorious and just a little bit cocky. Oh, how she'd love to wipe that smile off his face – and maybe she would…*tonight.*

There was no room for them to stay at Dad's so he'd arranged for her and Michael to stay in guest rooms at the college where he worked. Student rooms. Where there would be no parental supervision. And that presented them with certain…*possibilities.* A shiver of nervous energy tingled up her spine.

Michael looked at her strangely. 'What is it?'

'Nothing.'

He smiled and brushed away a flake of snow that landed on her upturned cheek. 'Please tell me you know where we are.'

Time to put him out of his misery. 'That's King's College,' she said, nodding down the alleyway.

Michael's eyes widened. 'Really?' Her transgression was instantly forgotten. He stared open-mouthed like she'd just told him they'd found Atlantis. She grinned, grabbed his jacket and pulled him down the alley, past a church with a squat golden-brick tower that looked like it had been squeezed in between other buildings, and a pub where people had spilled out onto the pavement, smoking and stamping their feet against compacted snow. The street opened onto a wider road, lined with shops on one side and King's College on the other.

Poppy and Michael stopped.

Carefully placed streetlamps lit the stone façade. The college looked more like a film set than an actual building, let alone a place where teenagers drank, partied and occasionally picked up a book. Everywhere, the bone-coloured stone was adorned with archways, chimneys and intricately carved turrets that seemed to have been chiselled out of the billowing snow clouds.

She'd seen the pictures in the prospectus – Michael had kept it open on his desk for the last two months so it had been hard to miss – but the photographs hadn't done the college justice. And for the first time she felt a small pang of jealousy that Michael might be living here in just over nine months' time.

She glanced up at him. His lips were parted, and his eyes clouded with dreams of his future. She was happy for him – she really was. Going to Cambridge had been his ambition since he was six years old. But a nagging, selfish voice couldn't help complaining that after all the time it had taken for them to admit to each other that they were more than just good friends, he was going to leave. And come here. Without her!

'It's certainly impressive,' she forced herself to say.

Michael nodded. 'It's only a building, but...' He shrugged.

'There was an article in the *New Scientist* that said that listening to Bach can actually make you smarter – something to do with the structure and the intricacy of the patterns. I wonder if it's the same with architecture. Because I'm pretty sure that just looking at that college could make you smarter.'

'What about kissing smart girls? Does that make you smarter?' Despite his smile, his brow creased and she wondered whether he too could hear the clock ticking down on their relationship.

'I don't know. I've never tried it.'

'Nahh. Me neither.'

Poppy whacked the back of her hand against his stomach.

'Oof!' Michael groaned, doubling over like she'd lamped him. 'Right, that's it!' He looked up and grinned from beneath the sodden fringe that flopped over his eyes.

Poppy set off, dodging between the groups of students huddled together, holding each other up after a night in the pub, their college scarves wrapped around faces and hoods, weighed down with snow. She could hear Michael's feet pounding the road behind her, and a disgruntled someone shouting, 'Hey! Watch where you're going!'

She kept running, despite the way her feet were sliding off cobbles, and took the road she thought would lead to Trinity, her dad's college. With every step, the straps of her backpack cut deeper into her shoulders and the freezing night air stabbed her lungs with icy little daggers. She wished she had left her Mac at home, and a couple of the books weighing her down. She was almost relieved when a hand grabbed her arm and yanked her to a stop. She giggled as her legs wobbled dangerously.

Michael's cheeks were blotched red and he puffed out clouds of steam like a racehorse that had just won the Grand National. He grinned, and before she knew what was happening, he'd pushed her up against a shop window, his lips were on hers, and his hands seeking her body through the padded waterproof.

All the breath that was in her disappeared, creating a vacuum; a need stronger than she'd ever felt for anyone or anything. It made her head whirl and her heart dance. *Don't stop*, she wanted to tell him. *Don't ever stop*. But he did.

Michael broke the kiss and stepped back. His eyes were wide and just for a second, she thought she saw that same need in him, and like a black hole it sucked her back towards him.

He looked away, took a deep breath and brushed his sopping hair out of his eyes. 'Come on,' he said, with an almost shy smile. 'It's this way, isn't it?'

She took his warm hand and they walked up the winding street in silence, as if neither one of them knew what to say about what had just happened.

When they'd first started going out, the kissing had been a bit awkward. They'd been so careful with each other, as if after years of being best friends they were frightened of breaking this new thing that they had. But three months later that fear had melted away. And now after four months it had been replaced with something dangerous and even more scary: need.

The snow was falling heavier now, whirling around them so fast that it was hard to see beyond the dance of the flakes. They tingled against Poppy's cheeks and cooled her kiss-bruised lips but she felt dizzy, like she was falling with them; tossed around on waves of wanting that seemed to creep up on her and then drown her. Would tonight stop her from feeling so overwhelmed by all of this? If they just *did it* would she feel less out of control?

'It'll be OK,' Michael said, softly. And for a second she thought he was talking about tonight. Oh God, did he know? Had he guessed why she'd really wanted to come with him?

'Terms here are really short. And then when you go to Manchester we can see each other at weekends.'

Oh. He was still thinking about that. 'Yeah,' she agreed, although she doubted it would be that simple.

He squeezed her hand. 'Hey, I think this is it.'

Ahead of them was a strange building of red brick and golden stone. Between two turret-like towers was an arched oak door and above that a statue of a king who had gained a few extra pounds where the snow had clung to his waistline. The scene reminded Poppy of something from a book: the gateway to another kingdom, another world. A world she knew nothing of.

Dad's world.

She sighed. She'd almost forgotten that she was about to see Dad.

Tension knotted in her spine. Her feet stopped moving. Michael had just turned to her – no doubt with a be-nice-to-your-father lecture – when a smaller door to the right of the main entrance opened and that Other World spat out three of its creatures.

The first was a dark-haired guy dressed in a tuxedo and bow tie that was partly undone, like someone had tugged on it, but not quite managed to unknot it. He tripped out of the door, turned and held his hand out for the next: a girl with ice-blonde hair and a red dress that, although floor-length, was slit almost to her waist and left very little to the imagination.

The last guy had on a dinner jacket similar to his companion, but this guy had finished the look with a black gangster hat and two bottles of wine that swung from his hands like he was about to juggle with them. Instead, he took a swig from one and handed it to the girl.

She put the bottle to her lips, threw back her head and drank. She shuddered.

'Was this from the dining room? Tastes like cat's piss!'

The guy laughed as she turned the bottle upside down. The yellowy white wine poured out onto the ground and where it met a patch of white snow it did indeed look like something, or someone, had taken a leak.

As the last drops drained, the girl's gaze connected with Poppy's. She threw the empty bottle back to the gangster and walked slowly and unsteadily towards Poppy and Michael.

'Well, what do we have here? Tourists?'

Poppy exchanged a wary glance with Michael.

'I'm here for an interview,' Michael piped up.

Snowflakes sparkled in the girl's long, straight blonde hair, making it appear almost as white as her bloodless skin. She had the face of a doll; wide blue eyes, sweetheart lips framed by flawless porcelain.

The girl stopped in front of them and those large blue eyes examined Poppy's face like someone would a painting. Her expression remained fixed: inquisitive, almost perplexed. Then her gaze slid over to Michael.

She was almost as tall as him and seeing this beautiful and unworldly creature toe-to-toe with her boyfriend made Poppy slightly nauseous.

The girl reached up a hand and caressed his cheek.

'The face of a poet,' she murmured, as if lost in a dream.

Michael swallowed, but said nothing.

Suddenly she whirled around. 'Snow!' she squealed excitedly, as if noticing the weather for the first time.

'What are you doing?' one of the guys called to her, as the girl ran to a roped-off triangle of ground that Poppy imagined had once been grass before becoming a snowdrift. She hopped over the chain-link barrier and, without hesitation, flung herself backwards into the drift. Not worrying what she might be showing to the world, she began flapping her arms and legs, carving out the wings and gown of a snow angel. But her skin and hair were so pale that she seemed to disappear into the white, leaving only the red dress, a bloodstain against the snow.

The guy with the gangster hat laughed, but the other swore under his breath and bolted over to her.

'What the fuck do you think you're doing?'

'I'm going to be an angel!' she said, grinning and crunching snow between her fingers like it was warm sand.

The guy grabbed her arm and yanked her to her feet.

'Where's Danny? I want my Danny,' she said.

The guy brushed the snow from her skin and dress, hastily took off his dinner jacket and put it around her bare shoulders. 'He's meeting us at the club. He had something to do.'

She smiled contentedly. 'Oh Danny boy-o-boy-o-boy.'

As the two guys helped her over the chain fence and back onto the icy pavement, the girl smiled in Poppy's and Michael's direction.

'Goodnight, sweet poet,' she said, blowing Michael a kiss before being dragged, stumbling, down the road.

'OK, this place is *seriously* weird. Are you sure you want to come here?' Poppy said, watching them go.

Michael didn't reply. His eyes were fixed on the students who stumbled down the road like characters from one of the old movies he and Poppy used to watch when they were kids.

For a second he seemed so very far away, as if a little bit of him had gone with them.

Michael swallowed and suddenly turned to her. 'We should get inside and find your dad.'

'Yeah,' she agreed, and forced her lips into a smile.

As they headed for the open door, Poppy heard the girl's voice singing: '*I'm lovin' angels instead*'. Michael turned to look in their direction, and Poppy couldn't help wondering if, in his head, *Poet Michael* was waxing lyrical about the angel in the red dress.

CHAPTER TWO

'You wait here, miss, and I'll give your dad a call,' the porter said, giving Poppy a kind smile and edging back around the polished wood counter.

Michael caught her eye. 'It's going to be fine.'

She couldn't see how it could be. The last time Dad had visited she'd made a point of telling him that it would never be all right between them ever again. It was true, she'd been a bit on the dramatic side, but she was angry with him. He'd shown up for a visit after changing the date twice, expecting everything to be like it used to be. Just because Mum had married Jonathan didn't mean everything was OK now. Didn't change the fact that he'd bailed to the other end of the country, and for what? So he could prance about in a black cassock? Surely he could do that closer to home. Unless he just didn't want to see her any more.

She fingered the flat, smooth stone that hung around her neck – the piece of obsidian that a Lakota medicine woman had given her. It was supposed to keep away negative energies. Maybe it worked on pesky parents too.

The snow came down so heavily that the world beyond the arched doorway looked to be shrouded in a heavy lace curtain. She almost didn't recognise the

21

figure that ran into the porter's lodge. Then again, she'd never seen Dad in a dinner suit and bow tie before.

He brushed the snowflakes from his shoulders and reddish-brown hair and nodded to the porters before turning his gaze on her. He hesitated. The eyes that were practically the mirror of her own searched hers, as if trying to judge her mood, then he smiled, leaned down and kissed her cheek.

'Hey, Pops,' he said, squeezing her shoulder as if they'd seen each other earlier that night, rather than three months ago.

His sideburns bristled against her cheek. She swallowed back the tight feeling in her throat and caught Michael staring at her. He was holding his breath as if praying that she wouldn't screw this up. And she wouldn't. She'd be civil to Dad. Not because he deserved it, but because Michael's interview was important and she didn't want him worrying about it.

'Hi, Dad,' she forced herself to say. 'Sorry we're late, Michael got us lost.'

'Easily done,' Dad said, before Michael could protest. 'Good to see you, Michael.'

As they shook hands, Michael narrowed his eyes at her over her dad's shoulder.

Poppy allowed her lips to smile. A smile that died on her face the second Dad turned back to her. Just being in the same room as him seemed to stir such a ferocious mixture of emotions that she felt seasick.

'So...er...what's with the penguin suit?' she asked.

Dad glanced down at himself. 'Just a dinner – formal thing – you know what this place is like.'

'No, I don't,' Poppy said, before she could stop herself.

Michael cleared his throat – a gentle reminder. *Yeah. C'mon, Poppy, get it together!* She swallowed and forced her face back into an expression she hoped resembled that of an attentive and forgiving daughter.

Dad gazed steadily back at her and then nodded. He was far from stupid; he could see through the little charade she was trying to put on for him.

'Right, do you want to go straight to your rooms or would you like to come back to my place for a coffee?'

'I'm tired,' she said, in case Michael tried orchestrating a bonding session. She really couldn't cope with any more tonight. And besides, she had plans.

'OK. We can meet in the morning for breakfast and then I'll take you on a tour of Cambridge, if you like?'

'That'd be great,' Michael said, leaping in.

It was weird seeing the two of them together. She always thought of Dad as this towering giant of a man, who had somehow produced a Hobbit-sized daughter, but now Michael was just as tall as him.

Dad put a hand on Michael's shoulder. 'What time's your interview?'

'I have to be at King's by twelve. There's a lunch.'

'You must be nervous.' Dad gave Michael his serious

look. 'Don't be. Any college would be lucky to have you. Don't be intimidated by this place. It's just another university. Right?'

Michael sucked in a deep breath and nodded. 'Right.'

Dad smiled, and then turned to her. 'I thought we could hit the Fitzwilliam, Pops?'

Great. Another museum trip. That's all their relationship consisted of these days. But maybe that's where their relationship belonged – in a museum along with all the other extinct creatures and civilisations. The tightness in her throat was back.

'Yeah, OK. That sounds great.'

Dad insisted on taking Poppy's backpack from her before leading them out of the porter's lodge. The storm was worsening. Howling gusts of wind chased thick flakes of snow around the domed fountain at the centre of four blanketed lawns like a flock of circling birds. Cold yellow light flooded out of doorways and upper windows, and by it Poppy could just about make out the whitened roofs surrounding them on all sides. To her right a tower, framed by turrets and topped with ramparts, caught her eye. It reminded her of the picture of a knight's castle contained in one of the fairy tale books she'd read over and over again when she was little.

Dad followed her gaze. 'That's the chapel,' he

shouted, his voice barely audible over the howl of the wind.

Dad pointed out various other places, but it was hard to hear him above the wind. Besides, she couldn't help staring at the place where Dad spent much of his time. Beneath the ramparts a line of two-storey tall windows were black against the stone, as if they were made of enchanted mirror that sucked light in rather than reflecting it. Poppy buried her hands deep into her coat pockets. That's what it felt like the church had done: sucked Dad away, changing him into someone she didn't really know any more.

Realising Dad and Michael had started walking again, she hurried to catch up. They dodged past a group of drunken students just as one stuffed a snowball down another's neck and the whole group went pelting off towards the main gate. She turned to watch them go, but again her gaze was drawn to the chapel and she shuddered.

Dad stopped under an archway marked 'M'.

'This is it.' He led them up a few flights of worn stone stairs and unlocked a door that opened onto a short, narrow, dimly lit corridor lined with yet more doors. Poppy rubbed her stinging hands together as the blood returned to her fingers and took in the institutional brown carpet and peeling paintwork.

'There are a couple of bathrooms. One here and...' Dad pushed open another door. 'Yup, one there. But I think that's just a toilet. The guest rooms were booked so I'm afraid we've had to put you on what is normally a girls' corridor, Michael. But the student who lives in the other set said that she didn't mind as it was only for a couple of nights.'

'Oh, he won't mind sharing with girls,' Poppy said, suppressing a smile and shaking melting snowflakes from her hair.

Michael rolled his eyes at her.

'I imagine not. Try to keep him under control, will you?' Dad winked at her. For a second it was just like before he'd left: the two of them winding Michael up. It was so easy to fall back into old ways. But times had changed. Their relationship was different now, as was hers and Michael's. And it was about to change again, if everything went to plan.

Poppy pressed a hand to her chest, glad they couldn't see how hard her heart was beating.

After pacing the small bedroom until she was dizzy, Poppy shoved a hoodie and jeans over her nightclothes, pushed open the bedroom door and stepped into in the study that the set of rooms they were staying in shared. Staring at the door of Michael's room for a moment, she chewed her thumbnail.

Maybe it was too soon. God, it would be awful if he said no. But he was a guy being offered sex. It was a no-brainer, right? Yeah, but this was Michael. There was a reason why her parents trusted him. Mum and Dad hadn't even questioned whether it was a good idea for them to stay so close… She'd expected Dad to put Michael in a totally separate part of the college, but no, there they were, in two rooms isolated from prying eyes by the shared study.

Maybe Dad was testing her, or trying to show how much he trusted her – there would be a reason. But she would bet the reason wasn't so she and Michael could…

Poppy swore under her breath. This standing around wasn't going to make it any easier. And besides, she wanted this, didn't she?

She knocked quietly on the door. No reply. Poppy took a deep breath and blew it out between pursed lips. *Calm down*, she told herself. It wasn't like they'd never been in the same room before. The kissing might be new but, hell, they'd practically lived in and out of each other's houses since they were five. She knocked again, louder this time.

There was a clicking noise – the door being unlocked. She stepped back as Michael appeared in the doorway.

His pale cheeks were still reddened by the wind and his hair, damp from the snow, fell over his eyes, making him look more than ever like one of his 1970s punk band idols. He smiled. 'What are you doing here?'

Was this the time to tell him the real reason she'd come to Cambridge?

'Umm – I – er – couldn't sleep.' Obviously not.

Michael stepped back and Poppy scooted past him into a room that looked exactly like hers, except everything was the opposite way around. She gingerly sat on the edge of the bed and shoved her hands in the pockets of her hoodie, kicking herself for not thinking to wear something slightly more alluring. Her Winnie the Pooh nightie, over jeans, topped off with a Fat Face hoodie, didn't exactly scream *come and get it!*

When she looked up, Michael was leaning against the door, observing her with a slight smile.

'What?' she asked, warily.

'Exactly what I was thinking.'

Poppy shot to her feet. 'If you're tired I'll just go, I can listen to some music or something.'

Michael stayed where he was, blocking the door. And his slight smile had turned into a full-on heart-stopper that made her insides melt like ice cream left out on a summer's day. It wasn't fair that he could do that to her with a look.

'We could watch a film,' he said, still guarding the door.

'OK.' She felt like the biggest dope in the world. What the heck had made her think that she could pull this off?

Michael peeled himself away from the door and went over to the chair where he'd deposited his backpack. While he set up his laptop, Poppy wandered

28

over to the window. She couldn't see a damned thing because of the reflection from the ceiling light, but she pretended to admire the view just to give herself a minute. She pressed her hand to her stomach. There weren't just butterflies in there, but a whole menagerie of fluttering and squirming creatures. Was that normal? The ceiling light flicked off and she spun around, bumping right into Michael.

'Better?' he asked, running a hand down her arm.

A long, slow shiver worked its way up her spine. 'The light, you mean?' The warm glow from the bedside lamp softened everything. Was he trying to be romantic? 'Oh, yeah – we'll be able to see the screen better.'

Michael looked away, not quick enough that she didn't catch his smile. 'Yeah, I suppose so. Why don't you pick a film? I just need to...' He nodded to the sink in the corner of the room.

'Sure you trust me?' She flopped on the bed and opened iTunes. Her attention was drawn away from the screen by Michael yanking his shirt over his head.

'Not normally,' he said, dumping his shirt on the chair and running his hand through his hair. 'But seeing as your choices are limited to what's on my hard drive, I'm pretty confident you're not going to force me to sit through any more of that vampire crap. I like my vampires slain, preferably by a blonde.' He went over to the sink, carefully took out his contact lenses, dumped them in the bin and then scrabbled around in his wash bag before loading his toothbrush with paste, turning on the tap and beginning to brush his teeth.

She watched his shoulder blades moving beneath his skin, the muscles in his back tensing and releasing as he brushed vigorously. He had a really nice back. Not that she'd made a study of backs, but his was...*nice*. Suddenly he turned.

Poppy shifted her gaze to the screen as the heat rose in her cheeks.

'Found anything you fancy?' he asked, through a mouthful of toothpaste.

'Not yet.' Not film-wise anyway.

Poppy took a deep breath and tried to concentrate but it was hard to ignore the nervous buzzing sensation in the pit of her stomach. She scrolled through the list of films. None of them were what you'd call romantic. In fact, most of them were dominated by car chases, exploding buildings, gangs or gangsters.

She was about to click on *The Godfather* – at least it was a classic – when she heard a zipper being pulled down. She nearly choked.

'You OK?' Michael asked. 'Do you need some water?'

Poppy shook her head. 'I'm fine.' She cleared her throat. 'Just a tickle.' She forced her gaze back to the screen while silently screaming at herself to get a grip.

She clicked play and the sad trumpet theme swelled

out of the speakers. Out of the corner of her eye she could see Michael pulling off his jeans, leaving him wearing nothing but his black boxer shorts. He was getting ready for bed.

Bed.

'Is that your nightclothes you've got on under there?' he asked, coming to stand in front of her.

'Yeah.'

'Then why don't you take off the jeans? You might as well make yourself comfortable. You're going to be here half the night if we're watching *The Godfather*.'

'OK,' she said, without moving.

Michael grabbed the zipper of her hoodie and pulled her to her feet. Slowly, he inched it down.

Poppy's breath hitched in her throat. 'I can do that,' she said, stepping around him.

'Ooookay.'

She quickly undid the hoodie and shucked it off while Michael pulled back the covers on the bed and lay down.

Nearly naked. In bed. With Michael. The words whizzed around her head, as dizzying as the snowstorm outside. She turned away from him, kicked off her shoes and yanked down her jeans. She tried to step out of them but her foot caught in the leg and she pitched over. She only just managed to save herself from crashing to the floor by catching hold of the sink.

'Do you need some help?' he asked. She could hear the laughter in his voice.

'No. *Thank you.*' She took her time folding her jeans then turned back to him.

He patted the mattress. 'Come and get under the covers before you get cold.'

Her legs took some persuasion to move, but somehow she managed to force herself over to the bed. She perched on the edge and Michael's arm hooked around her waist and pulled her back against his chest. He yanked the quilt over them both and wrapped his arm around her, locking her in place.

'Comfy?' he asked.

'Yeah.'

After a moment punctuated by gunfire and screaming – and that was just what was happening in Poppy's head – he squeezed her. 'Is there a reason why you've turned monosyllabic?'

'What?'

She heard him shuffling, the mattress rocked, and a hand on her shoulder rolled her onto her back. Michael propped himself up on his elbow and gazed down at her.

'What are you doing here? Really?'

When she didn't answer he placed a soft kiss on the end of her nose and grinned. 'Let's watch the film.'

The film?! 'Yeah – er – sure.' Poppy rolled over onto her side and Michael slipped an arm around her waist.

This was not going to plan. Didn't he know what she was saying by turning up at his room? Really, did he not get it? Maybe he didn't want to. She'd assumed that like any teenage male of the species, he barely thought about anything else. But maybe there was a reason he didn't want to go there.

As the killing started on screen she replayed the last few months in her head. She was so caught up in trying to understand his behaviour that she didn't notice that Michael's hand had slipped under the covers and was edging its way over her hip. His fingers stroked her stomach, catching a ticklish spot. She squirmed away from him.

He snorted. 'Poppy, is it going to take all three Godfathers for you to tell me what you're doing here? Because personally, I think the third one's a bit of a snooze.'

She twisted her head so she could see him. 'Are you really going to make me say it?'

His gaze burned into her and suddenly there wasn't enough air in her lungs. He took a deep breath, swallowed and whispered: 'Now? Are you sure?'

Was she? This had seemed like a good plan when she was alone in her room at home. Now…

But when else were they going to be together for a whole night? Logistically, this was probably the best opportunity to be together and it was bound to happen at some point, right?

She nodded.

Michael seemed to hesitate before he leaned across her so that he was half lying on her and closed the laptop.

'You shouldn't do that, you should stop the programme,' she said, disapprovingly.

Michael grinned. 'You're always telling me off.'

'Because you have no respect for technology.'

As he rolled onto his back, he pulled her on top of him, kissing her. He tasted of toothpaste and... wanting? Did he want her as much as she wanted him?

His hands slipped around her and stroked down her spine. He smiled.

'Why, Miss Sinclair, I do believe you're not wearing a bra.'

She rolled her eyes. 'Do you wear a bra to bed?'

'Only on weekends.'

Poppy laughed but she felt breathless and lightheaded.

Michael spun them around. He sat up, straddling her legs, and pushed off the covers. He stared down at her, his eyes wide and questioning. Taking hold of her hands, he wove his fingers through hers, pressed them onto the pillows beside her head and leaned down and kissed her, gently at first, then more urgently. Whoa! So she wasn't going to have to *not* ask twice, then? He'd always been so cautious before, but just recently the control had slipped and it was like she was seeing a different side of him. It was exciting and nerve-wracking all at the same time.

She felt a tugging on her nightie. Michael grinned and shifted himself so he could pull it up around her hips. *Oh!* He was going to take it off. Suddenly she felt shy and not at all sure of anything. She grabbed the fabric and held it over her stomach.

Michael stopped pushing. Then he leaned over and switched off the bedside lamp, plunging them into darkness.

'Poppy, are you sure about this?' he asked.

Her heart was hammering so hard that she could barely speak. 'I'm sure.'

When he kissed her again, his lips were gentle, testing, as if he didn't quite believe what she'd said. She slid her hands into his hair, deepening the kiss. Michael drew her to a sitting position and slowly slid the nightie off over her head.

The chill of the room tickled over her chest and she felt goose bumps prickling her flesh. But then Michael was kissing her again and warmth flooded her skin, as though they had slipped into a hot bath. The familiar wave of wanting crashed over her, and for a time all the words disappeared from her head...until Michael's hand strayed once more to her ticklish spot.

'No!' she squealed. She squirmed away from him and collapsed back onto the mattress. She felt the tremble of Michael's laughter.

'I can't help it,' she giggled.

He shuffled down the bed and blew a raspberry on her stomach. She screamed and tried to push his head away.

'Oh, that was too good, I'll have to do it again,' he threatened.

'Don't!'

His hair tickled her stomach and she sat up trying to push him away. He was killing himself laughing and the sound of his laughter made her relax...a little. Two could play at that game! She sat up and made a grab for him but Michael caught hold of her hands.

'I wouldn't if I were you,' he warned. 'You've never won at that game yet.' He leaned down and nipped her shoulder. It was so unexpected that she gasped. She tried to wriggle away from him, but a hand swept down her back and didn't stop when it reached her one remaining piece of clothing.

As he untangled her underwear from her legs everything quickened...her breathing, her heartbeat.

Suddenly Michael got up. She heard him moving things about. What the heck was he doing now?

Poppy sat up and took the opportunity to grab one of the papery cotton sheets and pull it over herself. The fabric was cold and scratchy and only served to remind her that she was naked.

That had happened *fast*.

'What are you doing?' she asked, trying to see what he was up to.

'Just getting something.' He wandered back to the bed and put the something on the bedside table. The moonlight coming in around the curtains reflected against a silver foil packet. Oh...protection. She'd almost forgotten about that. That could have been disastrous.

'Hoping to get lucky, were you?' she asked, her throat tight again.

Michael sat on the edge of the bed and leaned his hand on the other side of her.

'Yeah,' he replied, quietly. 'I didn't think it would be you, though.'

Poppy gasped and pushed him. 'You pig!'

Michael laughed, lifted the sheet and crawled into the bed beside her. She had to roll onto her side to create room for him and ended up with her back pressed up against the cold wall.

She wondered how many of these encounters these stones had seen over the centuries. She wondered if all those girls had felt the same heart-pounding, stomach-clenching mixture of fear, fascination, doubt and longing.

Michael kissed her again, so intensely that she forgot about the wall, forgot everything. She even forgot she was naked until Michael was touching her in a place she'd never been touched before.

'Bugger!' she whispered.

Michael laughed, hoarsely. 'Told you I'd win at tickling.' He kissed her gently on the lips and got up. He turned away from her and she heard the ripping of the foil packet.

OK. This was it. She was actually going to have sex...with Michael.

'Are you still there?' Michael whispered.

She heard herself reply, but wasn't entirely sure what she'd said. Everything in her head sounded distorted...even Michael's voice. The only thing she could hear clearly was the hammering of her own heart and the murmur of doubts whispering in her ear.

'Are you sure about this?' he asked, stroking her face.

She was sure, wasn't she? This was Michael. She loved him more than anyone in the world and this was what people who were in love did, right? 'I want to.' The words slipped past the objections.

He kissed her again, and took up where he had left off. For a time she was lost in the sensation and fear and complete sensory overload. Her skin felt like it had developed a whole new set of nerve endings that zinged and tingled. His hands left hot trails wherever he touched. She was losing sense of herself, focused only on what he was doing. But it felt right – to be lost in him.

Then he was on top of her.

She squeezed her eyes shut and held her breath. Would it hurt? Everything with her and Michael had been going so well, what if sex spoiled it? What if she was no good at it? She had no idea what she was supposed to do. Every time Mum had tried talking to her she'd brushed her off. And now she wished she'd listened, or at least read a few more issues of *Cosmo*. What if the condom didn't work? She could get pregnant like Mum had. That would be terrible for both of them, it would ruin everything...all their plans...and then he'd hate her. She could lose him. She could really lose him.

The worries clogged her lungs like smoke, choking and suffocating her. She couldn't breathe.

'No...no...' she said, pushing on Michael's shoulder.

She untangled her legs from his and leaped out of bed. Her heart pounded her ribs. She felt too exposed...too vulnerable.

'Poppy?' Michael was up too. He grabbed her hand. 'What's wrong, did I hurt you?'

'No. I'm sorry. I just can't.'

'It's OK.' But he didn't sound all right; his voice was gruff and strained.

She pulled her hand out of his and scouted around in the darkness for her clothes. He touched her shoulder, awakening all the nerve endings that had gone to sleep the minute panic had hit. She spun around and Michael handed her the nightdress he'd not long removed.

'Thanks,' she whispered, and pulled it over her head. She yanked her hair out of the neck and began looking for the rest of her clothes. What the heck had he done with her pants?

'So...what? We're not going to talk, you're just going to leave now?' he asked, quietly.

Poppy stopped the hunt for her underwear and turned to face him. She noted he wasn't getting dressed. She levelled her gaze at his face but she couldn't see his eyes in the shadows, couldn't tell what he was thinking.

'I thought you'd want me to go.'

'No. I don't want you to go! I want you to tell me what's going on in your head. And if you can't do that...well...we can watch the damned film. But I don't want you to walk out and turn this into something bigger than it is.'

He leaned down and snatched his boxers from the floor. As he sorted himself out she turned away and ran a hand over her face.

This was horrible. Not at all how she'd imagined it.

'Come back to bed,' she heard him say.

She really wanted to go back to her room so she could bash her head repeatedly against the wall, but then how would she face him in the morning?

Michael had already got back into bed and pulled the covers over himself. She slipped in beside him. He tucked the duvet around her and hugged an arm over her stomach.

For a while they lay there in silence. She wished he'd say something. She couldn't hack silences, she'd prefer that he shouted...anything just to know what he was thinking. Seconds stretched into minutes, but felt like hours. She couldn't take any more.

'Are you angry with me?' she whispered.

'No.'

Now who'd turned monosyllabic? 'You sound angry.'

'I'm confused. It's different.'

'I'm sorry.'

'Shit, Poppy, you're trembling. Stop apologising and tell me what happened.'

She wrapped her arms around herself. He was right, she really was trembling. 'I just... I... I got...'

'Scared?' Michael shifted until he had both of his arms wrapped around her and he could turn her to face him. He kissed her forehead and murmured, 'It's OK to be scared.'

She felt sick with – what? Embarrassment? 'God, I'm such a baby.'

'Nahh.'

'So much for *feel the fear and do it anyway*.'

'You live in a house with too many self-help books.'

Poppy snorted. 'Maybe I should have read some of them.'

'Your problem is—'

'—I have just one problem?'

'OK, *your main problem* is, you push yourself too much. You end up doing things that you don't want to do.'

'That's not true.'

'Oh yeah? You want me to list the times I've seen you do it – tonight being a classic example?'

'No.'

'You even did it at the fair the other week. You don't like going upside down…it's hardly a big deal, but because someone called you on it you did it anyway.'

'It's not the same. I wanted to…tonight.' Poppy nestled her head into his shoulder. She *had* wanted to. She'd thought about nothing else for weeks. In school, at the cinema, every time he kissed her…so why had her mind gone into overdrive like that? On top of that, she'd ruined things the night before his flipping interview. Talk about rubbish timing.

'You should sleep. It's your interview tomorrow,' she whispered, squeezing the arm he'd hugged around her. She couldn't talk about this any more. Her head was too full of noise and thoughts about what they'd be doing right at that moment if she hadn't backed out.

'You sure you're OK?' Michael asked.

'I'm fine.'

He nuzzled his face against her hair. 'I don't believe you.'

She didn't say anything. She just lay there listening to Michael's breathing and the noise of the storm howling through the ancient steeples and towers.

'Morning.'

A tickling sensation danced on Poppy's cheek, tugging her into consciousness. She opened her eyes and stretched. The sight of the unfamiliar bedside lamp and Michael's laptop disoriented her. For a second she wasn't sure where she was, until she saw the empty condom packet, and the events of last night came flooding back. Slowly, she turned her head.

Michael was propped up on his elbow. She examined his eyes for any sign of anger or resentment about last night, but they were as calm and blue as a clear winter sky.

'I thought you were never going to wake up,' he said, with a smile. Only then did she notice the blood pooling in his cheeks.

An ache pulled at her shoulder. She tried to rub it away.

'Stiff?' Michael asked.

Poppy nodded. 'You?'

Michael laughed and ran a hand through his hair.

'Oh my God!' Poppy felt the heat rush to her own cheeks. She rolled onto her front and buried her face in the pillow.

Michael rubbed her back. 'I'm kidding. Ish. Come on, we need to get up if we're going to have breakfast with your dad.'

'And just when I thought life couldn't get any more awkward,' she mumbled into the pillow.

'It's just a couple of days.'

'Yeah, I know.' She glanced back up at him. 'I'm sorry. About last night.'

He shrugged, his lips twitched into a side-smile and he shook his head like she didn't know what she was talking about. 'Nothing to be sorry about.' His hand travelled down her back and stopped where her nightdress had racked up around her bum. Bugger! She wasn't wearing any pants!

'Seriously, Poppy, you'd better get up before I get ideas again.'

Poppy turned over, casually pulling down her nightie. 'Maybe I want you to.'

Michael leaned down and kissed her but his hand stayed very firmly on her waist.

'Y'know, half the fun is the anticipation,' he whispered. Suddenly he was up and taking the sheets with him.

'Hey!' Poppy gasped, half protesting his whispered promise and half the removal of her warm cocoon.

'Up!'

Reluctantly, Poppy dragged herself from the single bed that really wasn't big enough for two people to sleep in, especially when one of them was Michael. She hunted around for the rest of her clothes and pulled them on.

'I should go and shower,' she said, zipping up her hoodie.

'Yeah, sure, you go first. Give me a knock when you're done?'

She nodded, turned the lock on the door and opened it.

'Hey, Poppy?'

She stopped.

She felt Michael close behind her, but she didn't turn around.

'We are OK, aren't we?' he asked

'Yeah, of course.'

'Just checking.'

Poppy slipped out of the door and closed it behind her, wondering if they really were OK or whether her freak-out last night had damaged something. Before she had time to mull it over, movement caught her eye.

Sitting in one of the battered brown armchairs, dressed in full vicar uniform, was Dad.

CHAPTER THREE

'Oh, hi. You're here, that's…great,' Poppy said, words tripping over each other as they fell from her lips. 'I was just making sure Michael was awake.' She knew the burning in her cheeks was giving her away and she had no idea how long he had been sitting there.

Dad blinked and looked away. He wasn't even pretending to smile. 'I came to say breakfast in an hour.'

'Great. I'll have a shower and then…'

'That's fine. I've got Morning Prayer. Why don't you come and meet me at the chapel when you're ready. Will you find it OK?'

'Yeah, I think so.'

He nodded, got up and turned to leave.

'Dad?'

He spun around. His mouth opened and closed, but no words came out. He swallowed, flipped his jacket back and rested his hands on his hips. 'Poppy, I don't think now is the time to talk about this. But later we *are* going to talk because you are only sixteen. Does your mum know about this? Are you on the pill? Didn't anyone think to tell me you and Michael were seeing each other?' He held his hand out to stop her answering, squeezed his eyes shut and took a deep breath. 'Later.'

He turned and bolted.

She felt sick. Dad didn't know. That's why he'd thought it OK to set them up in their own little Cambridge love nest. How could he not know that she and Michael were together? Surely she must have mentioned it last time he visited...or Mum? Hadn't she said anything when she and Dad spoke on the phone?

Behind her the door opened. 'What was that?'

She turned and, seeing her face, Michael frowned and reached for her hand. 'What is it?'

'Dad. He thinks we're... Crap!'

'Oh.' Michael's face drained of colour. 'I'll talk to him.'

Poppy couldn't help laughing at the thought of that scene. '*Noooo!* You are keeping out of the way until I've talked him down. You know what he's like; he'll go off the deep end. He's probably already on the phone to the local convents to see if they've got a room for tonight.'

Michael swore under his breath, bit his lip and shook his head.

It was his interview today and as much as he was trying to appear calm about it, she knew he wasn't. He was the only person from their school applying to Oxbridge and everyone knew it. If he didn't get in, everyone would know that too. The last thing she wanted him worrying about was her dad. Poppy squeezed his hand. 'Don't worry. Focus on your interview. I'll sort this out, I promise.'

'You shouldn't have to. It's not like we *did* anything.'

Something about the edge of anger in his voice made Poppy take a step back.

Michael's jaw fell slack. 'I didn't mean...' He licked his lips and glanced away. 'I just mean it seems a bit unfair for you to get done for something you didn't do.'

Somehow, the explanation felt worse, but she wasn't sure why.

She shrugged, feeling like a small child who'd been caught trying to walk in her mother's high heels. 'I'll talk to him now. I'll sort it out.'

Morning had barely broken through the cloudbank but the storm had left behind a fresh blanket of white that hugged the roofs, chimneys and towers of the college that seemed to have got bigger overnight. Over by the main entrance, porters in bowler hats and overcoats chatted with a couple of students, their laughter echoing around the walls of the otherwise eerily silent courtyard. Poppy tripped down the steps into Great Court, past two girls returning from their morning run. They shot her a quick smile that she tried to return despite the sick feeling in the pit of her stomach.

Dad catching her and Michael *not at it* wasn't

something she'd factored in. And now she wasn't sure how to play this. Did she play innocent, *outraged*, even, that he could think she and Michael would be doing anything that a God-botherer would be ashamed of? Although it was the truth, knowing that she had fully intended on doing something her father really *would* disapprove of meant that going on the defensive probably wouldn't work. Dad had a built-in lie detector, always had. The only option available was to go on the offensive – fight her corner. She was nearly seventeen. It was legal. His right to have an opinion on this disappeared the day he chose to follow his calling to the other end of the country.

Snow had compacted where someone had walked what looked like a central pathway between the lawns, past the fountain that was topped with an elaborate stone crown, right to the door of the chapel. But after all Michael's warnings about not walking on the grass she daren't risk it. This place was so full of weird rules and customs that you were probably only allowed to use the shortcut if you were Stephen bloody Hawking. Instead she zipped up her waterproof against the chill and followed the path round the outside of the quad.

Despite dawdling, Poppy reached the chapel steps far too quickly. She should have taken a detour...via Wales. She stopped and glanced back at the side of the quad where she and Michael were staying. What a huge mess she'd made of last night. After all the planning...

she'd really thought she was…well…ready.

She took a deep breath of frozen air. One problem at a time. First she'd deal with Dad, then she'd try to figure out what had happened last night.

Poppy had no idea what to expect from a college chapel, but she hadn't expected a room of polished stone and wood panels, empty except for a collection of bigger-than-life-size white marble statues staring down at her from their stone plinths. Not recognising any of the names, she wandered around them until she got to the statue at the far end. The detail in the carving was amazing. From the waves in his marble wig to the wrinkles in his marble stockings. Then she noticed the inscription. Isaac Newton. It was a statue of *Isaac Newton!* Of course, he'd been a student here.

Cambridge was something that she associated with Dad's past. The past he'd admitted running away from. He was the public school boy who'd got a first class degree from this place and then pissed off his parents by running away to a peace camp in the middle of Gaza in order to find himself. That's where he'd found Mum. Poppy had always loved that about him. He'd rebelled against all of this – so how the hell had he ended up back here, snuggling up with Isaac *frickin'* Newton?

'No offence, Isaac,' she murmured to the statue.

The doors that looked to lead into the rest of the chapel were closed. Damn! The service must have begun. She daren't just barge in there, even if Dad did deserve a bit of ritual humiliation. Poppy folded her arms and blew the hair out of her eyes. Her gaze darted around – drawn by the ghostly statues whose sightless eyes stared down at her as if Dad wasn't the only one who had an opinion on her recent behaviour.

'Ha! You can't tell me none of you had sleepovers.'

Maybe she'd wait outside.

A couple of feet away, on the white marble floor, was what looked like a polished glass bead. She stooped down to pick it up, then realised it wasn't a bead at all. It was liquid – dark and red. Blood.

She couldn't imagine why there would be blood on the chapel floor…unless someone had hurt themselves.

'Dad?' she called out, before she could stop herself.

Her feet moved swiftly to the oak doors. She grasped one of the brass handles and yanked it open.

As soon as she stepped into the carved wood archway it was as if the chapel had closed in around her, squeezing the air from her lungs. The chandeliers hanging from the high ceiling, which looked like the skeleton of a boat, cast a hazy light over everything, almost as if there was fog. Her gaze followed the black and white marble tiles to where the boxed oak seating began.

There, in the centre of the aisle, Dad was kneeling with his back to her, his head bowed over like he was praying. Poppy sighed. He was probably praying for her soul. She was about to march over there when he turned his face to her. His eyes were wide and his skin pale except for what looked like bloody finger marks scratched down his cheek. He scrabbled to his feet, holding out his hands as if to chase her out of the chapel. And his hands...his hands were covered in blood. She took a step back, but stopped when the clawing metallic smell hit the back of her throat.

It was then she saw him.

Lying on the marble floor smeared with blood was a body. Poppy edged forward, her gaze fixed on the motionless form. It was a guy. His eyes were wide open; as if he was staring into heaven.

'Poppy, stop,' Dad said.

Her feet stopped moving, but she couldn't stop looking. The guy's black dinner jacket had fallen open, revealing a shirt that was no longer white, but had merged with the gaping wound in the centre of his chest.

He'd bled so much that the blood had pooled around him and somehow his arms had smeared through it, creating bloody wings beneath his outstretched arms.

A little way from the body was what looked like a javelin or a spear.

'Poppy,' Dad said.

She tried to tug her gaze away, but she couldn't stop looking. His skin, so bloodless that his chiselled features could have belonged to one of the white marble statues, was framed by curling dark hair and set with eyes so blue that for a second she thought it was Michael that was lying there cloaked by bloody wings.

Poppy's hand flew to her mouth as a scream scratched at her throat.

'Poppy, listen to me. *Poppy!*'

Her gaze flicked up and connected with Dad's.

'I need you to go to the porter's lodge and tell them that we need the police and an ambulance.'

Poppy nodded, but she couldn't move her feet. It was like they'd sunk through the marble, trapping her there. And she couldn't help looking at those wide blue eyes. This time she could see that it wasn't Michael. This guy was a bit older. There was the beginning of stubble around his jaw, and the mouth that hung open as if in a scream wasn't anything like Michael's.

'Poppy, look at me.'

Dad's voice seemed a long way away, as if he was talking to her from the other end of a long, dark tunnel. Black passed between her and the body, like a curtain being drawn across the scene.

'Poppy!'

She swallowed and looked up to see Dad standing there, staring down at her. His eyebrows scrunched together. The blood smeared across his cheek looked like someone had tried to scratch his eyes out.

'Yeah, the porters,' she said. 'I'm going.'

She turned and ran, through the oak doors, into the

antechamber. Her foot hit something and she skidded, almost losing her balance.

Blood. She'd slipped in blood, smearing it across the white marble. She stumbled back, bumping up against one of the statues. But when she turned around, it wasn't a statue at all, but a guy with black hair and heartbreakingly blue eyes. He reached out a hand to her as if to steady her and she saw the blood pouring from the wound in his chest. She blinked and he was gone. Poppy bit back a scream.

She ran, through the doorway into the freezing morning air that smelled of blood and death. Across the virgin snow, ignoring whether she was running over pavement, cobbles or the sacred grass that Michael had warned her about. She ran so fast that she was barely able to stop when she charged into the porter's lodge.

Three startled faces looked up.

'What the blazes is the matter?' the old guy from last night said.

Poppy tried to gulp back enough air to get the words out, but her lungs were sore and her mouth couldn't seem to form words.

'Hey now,' the porter said, rushing around the desk and putting an arm around her shoulder. 'You're safe here.'

Safe? She almost laughed.

'Nothing's going to happen to you while we're here

to look after you. Rodger, nip over to the chapel, will you, and get Miss Sinclair's dad.'

'That's where it is. The body,' she managed to force out.

The younger porter who'd been dispatched to get her dad stopped in the doorway. 'What did she say?'

Poppy pulled out of the older man's arm and grabbed hold of the reception desk to steady herself. 'In the chapel. Dad's with him. He said you need to call the police and an ambulance.'

'Rodger, you stay here with Miss Sinclair. Poppy, isn't it?' he said, grasping her shoulder.

Poppy nodded.

'You stay here with Rodger. He'll make you a cup of tea.' He looked at the other. 'Call 999 then radio Bill to meet me at the chapel. Tell him to stay on the door. People will be heading over for Morning Prayer any minute. Then call the Master and the Junior Bursar. I imagine the Dean will be along soon enough.'

With that he squeezed Poppy's shoulder and bolted out of the door. She watched through the frosted window. Instead of taking the route she had, he turned right and for a second disappeared from view. Then he appeared again, running along the path that bordered the snowy lawns. Seemed that even in the case of murder, he couldn't bring himself to walk on the grass.

CHAPTER FOUR

Through the oblong panes of mottled glass, Michael watched Poppy walking the path towards the chapel on the other side of Great Court, her long coppery-blonde hair tucked into the collar of her army surplus all-weather coat. She was dragging her feet – not surprising, really. He wouldn't want to be in her shoes. He felt guilty about letting her talk to her dad alone, but she was probably right about needing to let Jim calm down.

Michael ran a hand over his face and let out a long slow breath.

This was not how it was supposed to happen. He'd been so damned careful to not let things go too far. He'd promised himself that they'd wait at least a year – she deserved that. He wanted her to have the whole dating experience...the crap nights out...the silly presents...the crazy moments when a touch or a word makes you fall just a little bit harder. He wanted her to have it all.

He had a plan. *He should have stuck with the plan!*

There was just one problem with the plan: it was based on the firm belief that Poppy was kind of shy about these things. The last thing he'd expected was for her to show up in his room, wearing her best Winnie the Pooh sleepytime nightdress, asking him to…

He snorted and shook his head. What other girl would show up to seduce her boyfriend wearing that little outfit? She was so fucking adorable and she really didn't know it.

That was beside the point. He should have put a stop to it the minute she'd shown up, but he was weak and selfish.

He'd let it happen because, as they'd walked through the snowy university town he'd dreamed about for as long as he could remember…all he could think about was her. Right now she felt like the only unwavering constant in a life full of *ifs* and *buts*.

Beyond the window, Poppy had reached the steps that led up to the chapel door. She paused for a second and looked back. He had the strange urge to wave, but there was no way she could know he was standing there watching her…wanting her more than he'd ever wanted anything in his whole life and scared that the wanting would be the thing that would destroy them. He should have known that she wasn't ready. He knew Poppy – really knew her – he should have been able to tell that it wasn't just nerves…that she was scared. He was so angry with himself for getting it wrong.

God, he hoped she was OK.

Michael squeezed his eyes shut and ran a hand over his face. He had to get ready in case she brought her dad back here. If he was going to have to talk to Jim about what he had and hadn't done with his daughter, he didn't want to do it in boxer shorts and a T-shirt. Turning up to his interview in his underwear probably wouldn't go down too well either.

What if he was on a roll? What if he screwed up that as well? Everyone seemed so sure that he'd get in but what if he didn't? What if he didn't get in anywhere? It was entirely possible that he was going to wreck his whole future in the space of twenty-four hours... Poppy...Cambridge...everything.

He scrubbed his hands over his hair and rolled his shoulders, trying to stretch out the twitchy feeling in his muscles. It didn't work. Maybe a shower would clear his head. He grabbed his towel from where he'd thrown it on the armchair, stopped at the sink to clean his teeth, and then headed out of the door.

Passing through the shared study, he eased open the main door onto the corridor and peeked through the crack. He could hear people moving about on other floors, but this corridor appeared to be empty. He pushed open the door and headed for the bathroom. Would have been useful if Jim had mentioned that he had a key to get into their rooms, Michael thought, blanching at what could have happened, if last night had gone differently.

The door to the right of him swung open, and out walked a yawning figure with long blonde hair that wasn't quite as smooth as it had been the night before.

She opened her eyes and stared at him. Then a slow smile spread across her make-up-stained face.

'Did Father Christmas come early?' she asked, her voice still gravelly with sleep.

She slid her hands behind the small of her back and lounged against the doorframe.

She wore a long black silk robe patterned with red and gold dragons, tied with a bow at the waist. And he was pretty sure that was the only thing she was wearing.

Heat rushed from under his T-shirt and filled his cheeks.

'I was just looking for the bathroom,' he stuttered, not quite sure where to put his eyes.

'I was heading that way too. Should we toss a coin? We could always share.'

Michael tore his eyes away from the girl and rubbed the back of his neck. 'I'm not sure that would be such a good idea.'

'No?'

'You look like the kind of girl who would steal the soap.' Among other things.

She laughed. 'You're a good judge of character. I'm Ria, by the way. Hope you enjoy your time on the girls' floor. It's certainly a treat to have you here.'

The door behind her was yanked open. The person who pushed past her was not a girl.

'Out of the way unless you want me to piss all over you,' he said, clutching his boxer shorts like a three-year-old rushing for the potty.

'Morning.' The guy nodded to Michael as he barged past, into the bathroom. The door slammed shut.

'That was Conal. He's generally more verbose but it was a late night for all of us.'

Michael smiled.

'I'm guessing he might be in there a while. Will you join us for tea?' she asked, beckoning him towards the open door.

He should say no. There was something weirdly dangerous about this situation, but he couldn't help being curious.

Before he had a chance to answer, the other guy he'd seen last night appeared behind Ria. He was still wearing the black trousers of his dinner suit, but his shirt was open over a white T-shirt.

'Oh, hello.' The guy looked Michael over, like he was something unexpected, and gave him a broad smile. 'Devon Dewitt,' he said, thrusting his hand out.

Michael shook the guy's hand, struggling to keep a straight face. 'Michael Quinn.'

'Hate to break up the party,' Devon said, fingering his short brown hair as if rearranging it, hair by hair. 'But there's something going on in Great Court. The fuzz have arrived. It's all *terribly* exciting.' Devon wiggled his eyebrows before disappearing back into the room.

Ria raised her eyebrows, her smile never faltering. 'Well, you'll have to come in now.' She slid around the doorpost. 'Come along, Michael Quinn, hoarder of soap.'

Michael could do nothing but follow...like a dog chasing after a bone.

The room he entered wasn't anything like the bare and slightly moth-eaten set he and Poppy were staying in. This room looked like it had been in the hands of a decorator. Tall bookcases were crammed with leather-bound texts. A psychedelic screensaver swirled around the massive screen of a new Mac, but he couldn't see the keyboard for the mounds of papers covering the desk. The institutional brown carpet was almost entirely covered by heavy rugs and the whole place smelled of stale alcohol and musky perfume. In one corner a low table was covered in a black cloth that at the centre had an embroidered silver pentagram. It was like something Poppy's mum would have.

'What do you think's going on?' Ria asked Devon, kneeling on the window seat and resting an arm on his shoulder.

'God knows. Looks like something's happened in the chapel.'

'Where?' Michael asked, darting over to the window. Michael stared over Ria's shoulder, through the leaded window to where several police officers seemed to be herding people away from the chapel entrance.

'Paramedics have just gone in there.'

'Poppy,' he murmured.

'Who?' Ria asked, swivelling to him.

'My girlfriend. She just went over there to see her dad.'

'Who the hell's her dad?'

'The chaplain.'

Ria and Devon exchanged a look.

Devon smirked. 'She's Jim Sinclair's daughter?'

Michael nodded. The three of them looked out of the window as a police officer stabbed a metal pole into the lawn and began taping off the area with blue and white striped tape.

'Fuck me,' Devon muttered. 'Looks like someone died.'

Michael didn't wait to see any more. He ran through the corridor, passing a bemused Conal on the way, back through the unlocked door, through the study, into his room. He grabbed his jeans, yanked them on and shoved his feet into his best shoes, laid out ready for his interview.

She'd be OK. Not even Poppy could get into trouble in the ten or fifteen minutes she'd been gone. Oh, who was he kidding?

His heart hammered in his throat as he grabbed his keys and dived back out of the set, down the corridor and through the main door. His feet clattered on the stone staircase as he dodged the people drawn out of their rooms by the commotion.

He ran out onto the icy pavement and the cool winter air hit him like a slap with a wet flannel. He sprinted towards the chapel. A porter in an overcoat and bowler hat stepped out in front of him, holding out his hands, barring the way.

'I'm sorry, sir, but you can't go that way.'

'What's going on?'

'Nothing for you to be concerned about. We're asking everyone to go back to their rooms.'

'My girlfriend went in there. Is she OK?'

'Miss Sinclair?'

Michael nodded.

'She's in the lodge. She's being well looked after.'

'Looked after? Why does she need looking after? What happened?'

'Afraid we're not at liberty to discuss the situation at the moment, but if you go along to the lodge, I'm sure she'd be happy to see you.'

Michael jogged back the way he had come, his new shoes pinching his bare toes and sliding on the odd patches of ice the grit had failed to melt. He followed the path around the building, towards the door they'd entered through last night. She was OK, he told himself over and over again, but he couldn't stop the creeping feeling that he was losing control and that the cold

Cambridge air was so frozen that his lungs couldn't take it in.

When he reached the porter's lodge a uniformed policeman stopped him.

'We're asking everyone to go back to their rooms,' the officer said, before he could get a word out.

'My girlfriend's in there. One of the porters said I could see her.'

The policeman, who wore an expression that he clearly reserved for pain-in-the-arse students, folded his arms. 'Well he told you wrong. Now please, go back to your room.'

'I'm not going anywhere until I know that she's all right! Poppy!' he shouted over the guy's shoulder. '*Poppy!*'

The policeman's hand gripped his arm.

'Sir...'

Poppy appeared in the doorway. She looked around until her eyes met his, except she didn't seem quite there. She looked spaced out.

Michael yanked his arm out of the copper's grasp and dodged past him. 'Are you all right? What's going on?' He took hold of her icy-cold hand and had to stop himself from wrapping his arms around her and never letting go ever again.

She looked past him, towards the chapel, her face expressionless. 'Someone died.'

'What?'

'Can't you smell it?' she whispered.

'Smell what?'

'The blood. I can still smell the blood.' She buckled forward.

He slid one hand around her waist to stop her from falling, and with the other he held back her hair as she began to retch.

CHAPTER FIVE

The back office of the porter's lodge was no quieter, and no warmer, than where the crowd were gathering in Great Court. Poppy couldn't seem to fight the shivers that shook her over and over again. The constant ringing of the phone hurt her ears, but everyone was too busy to answer. And when the phone wasn't ringing there was the relentless chatter of porters talking to one another through the control deck for the walkie-talkies; instructions being barked and calls for assistance going unheeded.

She hadn't seen Dad since she'd left him in the chapel. The porters had said that he was busy. They'd told her and Michael to wait there until he'd finished with the police.

Poppy shivered again. She felt frozen, despite having on the warmest coat she owned. And she couldn't get the image of her dad's red-stained hands out of her mind.

'There was blood all over him.'

Michael leaned closer and cupped her hands within his. Even though he didn't have a coat on, his hands were warm. The feel of his skin should have been comforting, so why did it make her shivering worse?

Michael shrugged. 'He probably tried CPR.'

'There was too much blood for him to have survived. Dad must have known he was dead. Why did he go anywhere near him?'

'Because you Sinclairs can't help yourselves from getting involved.' Michael gave her a small smile. He was trying to be calm for her.

'I suppose so.'

She took a deep breath and looked him in the eye for the first time since being ushered into the office. But the eyes she saw were the dead guy's as he'd stretched out his hand to her. He'd looked so frightened. She squeezed her eyes shut, willing away the image. No. It hadn't been real. She was in shock, that's all.

'Hey.' Michael squeezed her hands. 'Try not to think about it.'

When she opened her eyes he held her gaze for a moment before looking down and smiling. 'So...when did the blue happen?'

'Huh?' She followed his gaze to her fingernails that she'd painted in alternate blue and green. 'Oh. Yesterday morning.'

'Couldn't decide on a colour?'

Poppy shrugged. 'You know me, I'm always changing my mind.'

Michael took a breath as if about to say something, but before he could speak the door creaked open. The woman who entered looked like a lawyer. Her blonde hair was pulled into a smart chignon, and she wore a black skirt suit over a crisp, white, high-collared blouse. Despite being a head shorter than the guy who followed her in, she exuded a *don't mess with me* air. Police. They always seemed to travel in twos.

'Are you Poppy?' the woman asked, her eyes examining Poppy from behind the square black frames of her glasses.

Poppy nodded.

'I'm Detective Inspector Dalca and this is Sergeant Lachlan.' The tall guy nodded a hello, his shaven head and single hooped earring offset by a friendly enough smile.

'How are you feeling?' the inspector asked in an accent that sounded kind of Russian.

'I'm fine.' Poppy straightened her spine and tried to pull her hands out of Michael's but he grabbed onto one and held on tight. 'When can I see my dad?'

The inspector wheeled a swivel chair away from the desk opposite and sat down. 'Your dad's very concerned about you but I'm afraid we're going to need to talk to him for a bit longer yet. I hoped that if you felt up to a few questions you could help by telling us about what happened this morning.'

Poppy glanced at Michael. He stared back at her, unblinking, and squeezed her hand.

She turned back at the inspector and nodded.

'Thank you. I'll try to be as brief as possible. Your father tells me that you live with your mother in

Windermere. Why are you in Cambridge?'

It was a simple enough question, but all the words had disappeared from her brain.

Michael seemed to realise. 'I've got an interview this morning,' he said. 'Poppy came along to support me. And to see her dad.'

'I see. And you are?'

'Michael Quinn. I'm Poppy's friend. Boyfriend.'

'And when did you both arrive?'

'Last night. It was late.' Michael looked to Poppy for confirmation. 'About eleven?'

She nodded.

'You went straight to your rooms?'

'Yeah.'

'Did you go out at all?'

Michael shook his head.

'What happened this morning?' The inspector turned her gaze on Poppy, making it clear that she'd heard enough from Michael and it was her turn to step up to the plate.

'When I got up Dad was already in the study of the rooms we're staying in. We talked for a bit – arranged to meet in the chapel after his service to go for breakfast. Then I got dressed and went over to the chapel.'

'You arranged to meet after the service?'

'Yeah.'

'So why did you go over earlier?'

'Umm...' Bugger! She was already tripping herself

up. Now she was going to have to explain to a complete stranger how Dad caught her *not at it* with Michael. 'We kind of had an argument. I didn't want to wait to sort it out.'

'So your dad wasn't expecting to see you until after the service?'

'I suppose.'

The detective smiled, kindly. She was didn't look old enough to be in charge of the bouncer dude standing in the doorway. 'What did you argue about?'

The heat rose in Poppy's cheeks. Her gaze sank to the floor.

'Poppy?'

'Jim caught Poppy coming out of my room and he didn't approve,' Michael said, plainly, like there was no problem.

Poppy glanced up to gauge the woman's reaction. For a moment, the policewoman stared steadily back, and Poppy couldn't work out what she was thinking.

'I see,' she said, eventually.

'I'm sixteen, nearly seventeen. It's legal,' Poppy blurted, and then immediately felt like an idiot.

Inspector Dalca smiled, unable to keep the amusement out of her eyes. 'You're not in trouble. Not with me, anyway. I'm only interested in the facts in so far as they help me make sense of what happened.'

'Yeah. Sorry,' Poppy murmured, feeling like a complete idiot. Again.

'So, how long did you wait after your father left before you followed him over to the chapel?'

'I'm not sure. Maybe ten minutes. I had to get dressed.'

Poppy stared at the detective. Why was she so interested in timings? Surely between Dad and the porters they could nail down when everything happened.

Then it struck her. The questions she was asking... the detective was trying to work out whether Dad had had enough time to kill the guy before she got there. That was crazy! Dad couldn't hurt a fly. 'He didn't do it,' she said, trying to keep her voice even, and failing.

'I'm sorry?'

'My dad, he couldn't have killed that guy! Michael will tell you: there is no way that my dad could kill anyone. He's a pacifist. He'd rather die himself.'

The inspector exchanged a glance with her sergeant.

'No one's accusing your dad, Poppy,' the sergeant said. 'We're just trying to work out what happened so we can find who did this. You're not in any trouble and neither is your dad.'

'You wouldn't be asking these questions if you hadn't thought about it.'

'Poppy, we'll be interviewing everyone who has access to the chapel. Your father happens to be the first person we're talking to. At this point we're not making any judgements, we're just trying to establish the facts. OK?'

Did this woman think she'd come down in the last shower? They'd jumped to the simplest and most obvious assumption – that she had walked in before her dad had had time to dispose of the body.

'Tell me about when you entered the chapel.'

Poppy squeezed her eyes shut as memories invaded her mind. Wings drawn in blood. The gaping wound that looked like something from a butcher's window. The guy's staring eyes, as unseeing as the milky-white eyes of the marble statues. Poppy swallowed and forced her eyes open. She didn't want to see that scene ever again. She could still smell the blood like it had coated her nostrils. Metallic, clawing. Like raw steak…

'Take your time,' the inspector said, softly.

'I went into the part with all the statues but the doors to the chapel were shut. I wasn't going to go in. I thought the service might have started. But then I saw something on the floor. Blood.'

The policewoman reached up and touched the arm of the sergeant. 'Make sure they've got that.'

He nodded and stepped out of the room.

'Sorry, go on, Poppy. You say the doors were shut?'

Poppy nodded. 'I thought Dad might have hurt himself…or someone was ill…and I couldn't hear anything, so I went into the chapel. Dad was kneeling over the guy. At first I thought there'd been an accident. Then I saw all the blood. Dad said to go to the porter's lodge to ask for them to call for the police and an ambulance.'

Detective Inspector Dalca nodded. 'That's just what your dad said happened.'

'That's because it's the truth.'

The policewoman seemed oblivious to the bite in Poppy's tone. 'If you can, Poppy, can you describe to me what you saw?'

'What?'

A uniformed copper stuck his head around the door. 'Sorry to disturb you, ma'am, but you're wanted on the phone.'

She dismissed him with the wave of a hand. 'I'll call them back.'

'But—'

'—I'll call them back.'

'But it's the Chief Constable, ma'am.'

'What?'

The uniformed officer held out a phone. 'He needs to talk to you. Now.'

Detective Inspector Dalca frowned. 'Excuse me for a moment,' she said, getting up and taking the phone. 'Sir? Yes, sir – I understand that – but, sir – yes – yes – we'll be as discreet as we possibly can, sir, but there's no doubt this is a murder inquiry – of course – thank you, sir.' She ended the call, took a deep breath and squeezed her eyes shut. Then she handed back the phone to the constable and sighed.

'Sorry for the interruption, Poppy. Go on. It helps for me to have all the details.' She sat back down.

Poppy glanced at Michael. The corner of his mouth twitched in an almost encouraging smile.

He squeezed her hand. 'Go on.'

Poppy turned back to the inspector. 'The guy was lying on the floor, with his head towards the door. I think he'd been stabbed in the chest. That's the only wound I could see. And it looked like he'd…almost like he'd…'

'What?'

'Like he'd drawn wings in the blood.'

The policewoman nodded. 'Does that mean anything to you?'

Poppy shrugged. 'What do you mean?'

She shook her head. 'Nothing. Forget I asked. Can you remember anything else? Small details could turn out to be very important.'

Poppy closed her eyes again and forced herself to look at the memory. 'There was spear or something a few feet away, but I didn't really get a good look at it.'

'And the dead man. Did you know him?'

She saw his face – his mouth open in a silent scream. Had he been calling for help? 'No.' She opened her eyes.

'You're sure?'

'Yeah. I'd have remembered seeing him.'

'Thanks for going through that. I know it's not easy. Just one last thing. We'd like to take away the clothes you're wearing.'

Poppy's head snapped up. 'What? But I didn't touch him. I didn't get that close.'

The inspector's expression remained neutral. 'It's just routine.'

'You're looking for blood, aren't you? You want to know if I was there when it happened. You do think it was Dad.'

'You must be Poppy,' a voice said from the door.

The woman standing in the doorway had thick silver hair that curled at her shoulders, and tanned skin. She had on a thick purple wool coat and a long black scarf, and a pair of glasses was hanging around her neck by a gold chain, above which was the collar of a priest.

'I'm Beatrice Barclay-Tillman, the Dean of Trinity College,' she said in an accent that made Poppy think of country music and cowboy boots. Holding her hand out to the inspector, she forced the younger woman to stand. 'Call me Bea.'

The inspector got to her feet and shook the Dean's hand.

'I'm sure any questions you have for Poppy can wait until I've at least given her and her *friend* a cup of tea.'

'Actually, I've just about finished with Poppy. I was just explaining to her that we need the clothes she's wearing so they can be taken away by our forensics team.' The detective turned back to Poppy and raised her eyebrows. 'It'll help us rule out any fibres that may have contaminated the scene.'

Poppy pulled her hand out of Michael's and pushed herself to her feet. 'I'll go and get changed.'

'Actually, I'd rather you stayed here. Perhaps Michael could run back to your rooms and get you a change of clothes?'

Amidst the fuzziness that had filled her head, a small voice screamed *noooo!* They wanted Michael to go through her bag? That was the last thing she wanted. There was stuff in there that she did not want him to see.

'No problem. Anything you want in particular?' Michael asked, turning to her.

'Umm – err – whatever you come across first. Whatever's on top.'

Michael nodded. 'OK, I won't be long.' He kissed her cheek before manoeuvring around the Dean and the detective.

'Your dad's going down to the station to help the police,' the Dean said. 'I'll look after you while he's gone.'

'The station? Why does he need to go there?' Poppy glared at the policewoman.

How could she really expect her to believe that her dad wasn't a suspect?

CHAPTER SIX

Michael fished the keys out of his pocket as he waded through the crowd that had gathered in the quad. He'd almost made it to the staircase when Ria, still wearing nothing but the black silk gown, ran out of the entrance, heading straight for the chapel.

Conal appeared behind her, calling her name. Spotting Michael, he shouted, 'For God's sake, stop her!'

Michael stepped in front of the girl.

Ria's face was marked by black tearstains. She tried to push him away.

'Is it Danny?' she asked, her eyes pleading with him. 'Is it?'

Conal and then Devon appeared at their side, both gasping.

Conal swore under his breath. 'You have to come inside.'

Ria glared at him. 'You told them, didn't you? After we agreed not to, you told them.'

Conal shook his head. 'No, I didn't.'

The sound of Ria's hand slapping Conal's face cracked through the murmurs of the crowd, drawing the attention of nearby students.

Ria pressed the hand to her mouth, her eyes wide

with shock, as if she'd just witnessed someone else's violence.

Conal turned his gaze to the ground. He bit his lip and looked like he was mentally counting to ten. When he turned back to Ria, his expression was neutral but there was no masking the anger in his eyes. 'You have to come inside. *Now*,' he said, his voice quietly menacing. 'You're making a scene.'

'What's going on?' a porter asked, edging into the group.

Ria sniffed, visibly trying to compose herself before taking the porter's weathered, red hands in hers. 'Bill, you have to tell me. Who was it in there? Who died?'

'Miss Mansey, we're not allowed to talk about this. Please don't ask me.'

'Was it Danny? Was it? Please – *please*, Bill. Was it him?'

The old porter's face crumpled. The sadness in his eyes was enough to confirm everything Ria needed to know.

She shook her head as more tears flowed down her cheeks.

The old porter took off his bowler hat. 'Let's get you inside, miss. You haven't even got any shoes on. Come on, now.'

Michael followed the strange group back into the staircase and up to the first floor where the porter unlocked the door and ushered them all inside.

'I'm sorry about your friend,' Michael said quietly to Conal.

For a moment Conal clung to the doorframe of Ria's room like a man who'd been kicked in the guts. He squeezed his eyes shut and butted his forehead against the wood with a force that made Michael wince. Then the guy turned, and without a word, shut the door behind him.

Michael rubbed the nagging pain in his neck before forcing his feet down the corridor to his and Poppy's set. For a second, he couldn't think what he was there for. Clothes. Poppy needed clothes.

Thankfully she hadn't locked her room, as he hadn't thought to ask for her key. On the bed that hadn't been slept in were Poppy's nightdress and the jeans and hoodie she'd worn last night. Jeans and a hoodie was a start, but it was freezing out there, she'd need something else. Michael spotted her backpack on the armchair and dug inside until he found the long-sleeved Ramones T-shirt that was one of her favourites and a pair of mismatched socks, but there didn't seem to be any other shoes. Michael shoved his hand further down to the bottom of the pack. Definitely no shoes. He'd have to grab his walking boots – they'd be too big, but they were better than nothing. As he pulled out his hand, his arm caught something and sent it flying onto the floor.

His jaw dropped open. What the hell? He picked up the square red box. Condoms.

Well, well. Maybe last night hadn't been a whim. Just when he'd about convinced himself that all the talk of them being apart had scared her into it, it looked like Poppy hadn't just thought about sleeping with him; she'd planned for it.

He sighed as the tension in his shoulders eased. She'd wanted it to happen. Even if she had got scared, she'd wanted it.

He tucked the packet back in her bag, quickly gathered up the clothes, ducked into his own room and grabbed his walking boots, and headed out onto the corridor. As he passed Ria's door he could hear her shouting.

'It's because he said no, isn't it? It's because he didn't want Yaser at the embryo party.'

A male voice replied, too quiet to make out what he was saying.

'You tell me, Conal!' Ria screamed. 'You're the one who's working for them.'

There was the sound of scuffling, heavy footsteps. The door burst open.

'I hadn't even told them that Danny had blackballed Yaser. You're being completely paranoid.' Conal spun around and froze when he saw Michael.

'Shit!' Conal cursed, before storming off down the corridor.

CHAPTER SEVEN

The Dean's study appeared to be built out of books. Elaborately carved floor to ceiling bookcases covered every wall but one. Despite still feeling shaky, Poppy couldn't help being impressed. There was even one of those old-fashioned library stepladders to reach the top shelves.

'Come on in,' the Dean said, heading behind the large mahogany desk.

Poppy scrunched her toes inside Michael's walking boots, desperately trying to keep them on her feet and not fall over. On the one wall without bookcases there was a huge poster of Martin Luther King Jr, his mouth open and his hands reaching out, as if to emphasise a point. Down the side were printed the words of his *I have a dream* speech that Poppy remembered reading in school.

'You're a fan of Dr King?'

'Hmm?' Poppy said, turning to find the Dean watching her.

'I was there when he made that speech. I was, of course, very young. Very, *very* young.'

'Wow,' Poppy murmured. 'It must have been incredible.'

'He was a true inspiration. A man driven by a thirst

for God's justice. But of course, you're not a Christian, are you?'

The question sounded loaded with judgement. Poppy shook her head, unsure whether admitting to not sharing Dad's beliefs would get him into trouble. 'I'm not really anything.'

The Dean slipped on the glasses that were hanging around her neck and looked at Poppy over the top of them. 'Oh? I hear that you were brought up a Pagan.'

'Yeah...but...'

'Please don't get her started,' Michael said, shooting her an amused grin. 'She's an atheist. Richard Dawkins's biggest fan.'

'No, I'm not!' Poppy hit back, before she could stop herself.

'You named your dog after him.'

That much was true. Dad had not long moved out when he'd turned up with the cutest bundle of fluff she'd ever seen. It was the same day he told her that he was going to train to be a vicar, and he was going to the other end of the country to do it. It was stupid, but it had felt like the church – or maybe God – was stealing him away from her.

Michael was staring at her.

'I was thirteen. I didn't understand the nuances of the argument.'

'But you do believe in justice, don't you, Poppy?'

the Dean asked. The woman's eyes were alight with more than interest...it was almost...zeal? 'Even atheists believe in justice, so I am told.'

'Agnostic,' Poppy corrected. 'I'm agnostic.'

'Really?' Michael's face took on a puzzled expression. 'Someone's changing their tune.'

'To say definitively that God doesn't exist makes about as much sense as claiming that God does exist,' she said. 'There's no evidence either way.'

Michael folded his arms. He looked like he was about to argue the point with her, but then, smiling, he shook his head. It wasn't like him to concede a point so fast. But when he glanced at his watch, Poppy realised why.

Hell, with everything that had happened she'd almost forgotten: there was only an hour and a half before he had to be at King's for his interview and the police still weren't letting people out of the college. What would happen if he didn't get there – would they reschedule?

'Umm, do you think the police will let people go soon?' she asked, turning to Bea. 'It's just, Michael's interview is soon.'

'Mmm. We should talk to someone just in case. Come and take a seat, Michael. Do you know who's interviewing you?'

'Professor Madigan.'

The Dean sat down, tapped some keys on her

computer then picked up the phone and dialled a number.

'Hi, Fiona? It's Bea Barclay-Tillman over at King's… yes, it's terrible…no, we haven't had confirmation on who it was yet…thank you for that, I'll pass on your well wishes to the fellows…I'm actually calling about a young man you're due to interview this morning, Michael Quinn? Yes, well he was staying here and so has gotten caught up in everything that's going on… they're not allowing anyone out of college yet, but we'll get him over to you as soon as we can. Thank you, Fiona. Goodbye.' Bea put down the receiver. 'There, all sorted. No problem at all. This won't count against you one little bit. Now come and sit down and tell me what madness led you to apply to King's and not Trinity.'

Michael flashed Poppy a smile before sitting in one of the modern red chairs that were arranged in a semi-circle facing Bea's desk.

Poppy wandered from bookcase to bookcase, admiring the eclectic mix of titles while Michael attempted a rational explanation of why he wanted to go to King's. Wow, he could come out with some crap when he wanted to. She was tempted to tell the Dean that the real reason he'd applied to King's was that when he was six his grandparents had sent him a postcard of the college and he had decided there and then that King's was where he was going to study when he was older. Even now, the curled and faded postcard was still stuck to his pinboard.

She glanced at him as he switched to talking about some history of Russia he'd just read, totally at home talking to this woman who probably had a million letters after her name. She smiled; she loved that he was such a nerd.

On one of the shelves, in front of the books, was a photograph of three students with shaggy hair and disarming smiles – one of whom she knew very well.

'You found the picture of your father,' the Dean said, as the conversation reached a lull.

'Yeah.' She turned to Bea. 'Did you know him back then?'

'No. But the boy on the right is my son, Lance.'

'They're friends?' She'd never heard Dad mention someone called Lance.

'They were. For a time. Then your father fell in with another group.' The Dean's tone grew decidedly frosty as she said, 'But I suppose that's what happens when you're young. Friendship is as disposable as fashion.'

'I don't think that's true.'

'No?'

'No.' She glanced at Michael. He'd been her best friend for as long as she could remember. He smiled and her chest tightened just a little. 'A true friend is someone who grows and changes with you. Anyone who doesn't do that isn't really a friend at all. What's that quote? *A friend's someone who gives you total freedom to be yourself.*'

Bea's brow wrinkled. 'Seneca?'

'Jim Morrison.' Michael laughed.

The Dean turned to Michael. 'I don't know him.'

'Lead singer with The Doors.'

'Oh. Afraid I'm not very up to date with music. I wouldn't have a clue about new bands.'

Poppy shared a grin with Michael before the Dean ushered her to sit down too and have a cup of tea.

Half an hour later, there was a knock and Dad peered around the door. In place of his clothes was a blue papery boiler suit. The police must have taken his clothes too.

'Hi. How's everyone doing?' He nodded to the Dean. 'Bea.'

'Jim. They let you go. What a relief,' Bea said.

Poppy shot up and, tripping over her own feet, landed heavily in Dad's arms. Dad held her tightly. A lump rose in her throat and a wash of tears blurred her eyes. Of course they'd let him go. He hadn't done anything wrong.

'It's OK, Pops,' Dad murmured, stroking her hair. 'It'll be OK.'

After enough deep breaths to force back the tears, she cleared her throat and stepped out of his arms.

Dad's lips tugged into a side smile, but as his gaze moved from her to Michael his expression darkened. Heat crept into Poppy's cheeks.

'Michael, they're letting people out. You should just about make it to your interview on time.' Dad's tone was flat and ominous.

Damn! She'd been hoping he'd forgotten about this morning.

Michael stared back at Dad, his gaze not wavering. 'Thanks,' he said, his voice equally flat. 'I'll get going.'

Bea got up out of her chair, distracting everyone from the glaring match. 'Why don't I walk you there, Michael – we can swing by your rooms and you can get changed, and Jim can spend some time with Poppy.'

'No, I want to walk Michael,' Poppy said, going to stand next to him. She felt his hand close around hers.

'Why don't you meet me afterwards?' Michael said. 'They reckoned I'd be done by three.'

'Sure?' she asked.

'I'm positive.' He smiled, but she could tell it was forced. After all the distraction, nerves were finally creeping in. And why shouldn't he be nervous? His dream depended on the next few hours. Her own heart quickened in sympathy. She leaned down and pressed her lips to his.

At the sound of Dad clearing his throat, Michael's hand touched her cheek, gently pushing her away.

'Good luck,' she whispered. 'I'll be keeping everything crossed.'

He smirked. 'You might want to reconsider that, given how hard you're finding it to walk in those boots.'

'Poppy, let's go. You'll make Michael late,' Dad said, gruffly.

OK. She was back to being angry with him again. He was treating her like she was a kid. When was he going to realise that she was no longer the child he'd abandoned? She glared in his direction and then smiled at Bea.

'Thanks for the tea.'

'You're welcome *any time*,' the Dean replied, shooting Dad what looked like a smile of triumph. Poppy was getting the feeling that they didn't really get on. And there she was thinking that priests were meant to love everyone.

Dad's rooms were no bigger than the set she and Michael were staying in. And this was where he lived – full time. There didn't even appear to be a kitchen, only a sideboard with a kettle and cups. Poppy gazed around. Every dark nook and cranny had been jam-packed with mismatched bookcases and CD racks crammed with Dad's extensive music collection.

On one wall was an oil painting of an ageing cleric

with steely grey hair and a gaze to match. She couldn't imagine Dad choosing that, it must have come with the rooms, but lining the mantelpiece and windowsills were woodcarvings from the various parts of Africa Dad had visited in his youth. They were the only things to disappear from the house after he had left. Them and his CD collection.

Poppy remembered the pile she'd found left on her bed after he'd gone. The Clash. Velvet Underground. The Cure. Siouxsie and the Banshees. Bowie. Anything he'd thought essential to her musical education. She hadn't listened to any of them. She'd flung them across the room, splintering cases and ripping the accompanying booklets. She had been so angry that he could think that a few CDs made up for the lack of him in her life.

Dad stood in the middle of the room and stared at the wall. Poppy shoved her hands into her jeans pockets and waited.

After a minute or so, he seemed to remember she was there. He turned to her, his eyebrows raised in a question.

'Would you like a drink?'

Poppy shook her head. 'Think I drank about a gallon of tea in Bea's office.'

Dad nodded. 'Was Bea OK with you?'

'Yeah, fine. Why shouldn't she be?'

Dad shrugged. 'Sometimes she can be a bit funny.

It's so dark in here, you'd think it was the middle of the night.' He dashed around putting on various lamps. It didn't make any difference. The room still felt dark and gloomy.

'The guy that died, was he a student?' Poppy asked.

'Yes.'

'Did you know him?'

'Yeah. Not well, but I knew him.'

'I'm sorry.'

'Thanks.'

'Why didn't you call for the police when you found him?'

'What?' Dad looked at her.

'You got there well before me, why didn't you call for help?'

'I didn't get there long before you. I stopped to talk to one of the kitchen staff after I'd seen you. Why do you ask?'

Poppy shrugged. 'I was just wondering.' She was pretty sure that the police had wondered that too. 'You should probably get changed.'

Dad looked down at the blue suit the scenes of crime officers had given him to wear. 'And I though paper was all the rage.' He went into what Poppy thought must be his bedroom and closed the door behind him.

Poppy wandered over to the desk, switched on the green reading light and fingered the books there. She picked up one entitled *Dante in Love*, and flicked through it. The book was filled with margin notes in Dad's careful, neat handwriting. Although he'd finished his training and had been ordained, he was still hard at work on his PhD. She replaced the book and worked her way around the room, squeezing between one of the battered old leather sofas and the polished wood coffee table, towards the fireplace. There – amongst the strangely shaped, half-animal, half-human sculpted figures that Dad had once explained to her had been carved by shamans from one of the tribes he had stayed with – was a photograph of her and Dad. It was from a few years ago, before she'd discovered mascara and before he had left them.

She knew her parents had problems – Dad had gone and found Jesus and her Goddess-loving mum hadn't been happy about it – so the divorce hadn't exactly come as a surprise. And maybe splitting up was for the best – Mum seemed happier with Jonathan than she'd ever been with Dad. But the way Dad left, without even talking to Poppy about what was going on with him – that had hurt. And she still didn't understand why he had to move to Cambridge. There were other vicar schools. There was one less than two hours' drive from home – she knew, she'd checked. Why did he have to come all the way here? And then stay, even after he'd finished training?

Poppy reached up to take hold of the photograph and as she did, something fluttered to the floor – what looked like a blank postcard. She leaned down, picked it up and turned over the thick cream card. On the other side was printed:

11th December
Whales & Sherry from 7pm
Old Kitchen

An invitation, but from whom? And why the hell would they be eating whales – she thought that was pretty much banned unless you were Japanese. The 11th December was yesterday – was that why he'd been all dressed up last night?

A clunk from behind the bedroom door sent Poppy scrabbling to put the photograph and invitation back where she'd found them. She turned away, just as Dad appeared from his bedroom wearing a black suit. No dog collar, thank goodness, just a plain white shirt. He still didn't look like himself, though. She was used to him in Bermuda shorts and faded T-shirts sporting the names of bands most people had never heard of.

'You look smart.'

'Yeah. Afraid I think there'll be a couple of meetings to talk about what's happened. I hate to…'

'It's fine. I need to go and buy some shoes. And then I'll meet Michael from his interview.'

His jaw tightened and one of his hands squeezed into a fist. Bugger. He really was angry.

But then he looked at her properly for the first time since walking through the door and his face softened. 'How are you doing?'

She shrugged and tried to sound bright. 'I'm fine. There's no need to worry about me. It's not like I haven't seen…blood…before.' Images of the boy and his bloody wings flashed before her eyes.

She clutched her stomach as the three cups of tea she'd had in the Dean's office staged a comeback and her head felt so light it might float away from her neck.

Dad guided her onto one of the leather sofas and pushed her head down until it was between her knees.

'Deep breaths,' he said, rubbing her shoulder.

'I'm OK,' she muttered, trying to sit up. Dad's hand kept her where she was.

'I'd be worried if you didn't feel sick about what you saw this morning.'

'Did you?' Poppy asked.

'Fuck, yes. I nearly threw up twice on the way to the police station.'

She glanced up, and this time he let her straighten up.

He ran a thumb over her cheek and pressed the back of his hand to her forehead as if checking for a fever. 'Feeling better now?'

'Yeah.'

A knock at the door set his face into a frown. 'Sorry, I'd better get that.' He got to his feet and opened the door.

'Hi, Jim, I hope you don't mind me coming over, but I thought with Zoe being away we'd better talk about what to do about choir practice and the services,' said a soft voice with the hint of a Geordie accent.

'Of course, Chrissie, come on in,' Dad said. 'This is my daughter, Poppy. Poppy, this is Chrissie Sharrock, our junior organ scholar.'

The girl was dressed in jeans and a navy blue Paddington Bear duffle coat and had a college scarf wrapped around her neck. She had shoulder-length nut-brown hair and her pretty face was pink with the cold, but bore no visible make-up.

'Oh, I'm sorry. If I'd known you had company…' she gasped, touching Dad's arm with a familiarity that made Poppy flinch inside. 'I'll come back.'

'No,' Poppy said. 'Don't go on my account.'

The girl glanced up at Dad. 'Sure?'

'We're sure. Sit down.'

Chrissie sat on the opposite sofa. Poppy was about to shuffle over to make room for Dad on her sofa, but just as she moved, he slumped down next to Chrissie.

Poppy swallowed, a sudden dryness in her throat.

'What a time to visit,' Chrissie said. 'I'm so sorry that you've come in the midst of all of this. Jesus, Jim, I hope you're going to work hard to make this up to her,' she said, giving him an accusatory look.

'It's true, I have a lot of making up to do.' Dad smiled sadly.

'What's an organ scholar?' Poppy asked, speedily changing the subject. 'Did they give you a kidney, or something?'

Chrissie laughed. 'I get a scholarship and private music lessons in return for playing the organ. It's not a big deal, but certainly helps pay the bills. There's no way my parents could afford more organ lessons *and* pay for little luxuries like food and clothing. Don't know what I'd have done if I hadn't got the scholarship. So, what are you going to do while you're here?'

'I'm not sure,' Poppy said. 'Things are all a bit up in the air.'

'I suppose they must be. It's horrible, what's happened. It's not always like this, y'know? I mean, there are some completely spoilt dicks in Cambridge, 'scuse my French, Jim,' she said, touching his arm again, 'but they don't normally set about killing each other.'

Chrissie's easy manner made Poppy smile. She liked the girl, even if she did seem to have a bit of a crush on Dad. Wasn't like she hadn't seen that happen before. Some of her teachers had gone into mourning when he'd left.

'Danny was a nice guy,' Dad said, thoughtful again.

'Yeah. He wasn't like the others.'

'Others?' Poppy asked.

'He was one of those guys. You know: good at everything and everyone loves them?'

Poppy nodded. She was, after all, going out with one of 'those guys'.

'Rumour had it he was heading for a double first,' Chrissie continued. 'Most of that lot think they're better than everyone else, but Danny was pretty normal, even if he did have crap taste in friends.'

'He was a nice guy, and he'll be missed,' Dad said, firmly, giving Chrissie the kind of look generally reserved for Poppy.

Chrissie looked suitably chastised and Dad crossed an ankle over his knee and tapped his fingers against the black leather of his shoe. Poppy had seen him do that before. Normally it would have been a battered pair of Doc Martens, but it was what he did when he was worried about something. She got the impression that there were things the two of them wanted to talk about without her being there. She felt uncomfortable and in the way.

Poppy pushed herself up off the sofa.

Dad jumped up too. 'Where are you going?'

'I should leave you to talk about whatever it is you need to talk about.'

He shook his head. 'You don't have to go.'

Poppy looked down at her feet. 'I need to buy shoes.'

'Oh, right, yeah. OK.'

'Listen, I'll come back later,' Chrissie said, getting up. 'It was really nice to meet you, Poppy. If you need anything or fancy going for a coffee, my room's in Blue Boar Court. Just ask the porters, they'll point you in the right direction.'

'Thanks. Nice to meet you too.'

'Talk to you later,' Dad said, as she disappeared out the door. 'You really don't have to go,' he said, turning back to Poppy.

'I can't wear these all day.'

Dad sighed. 'I could come with you.'

'Don't you think things are bad enough? I still have the mental scars from the last time you took me shoe shopping.'

He snorted and smiled. 'Fair comment. OK. We'll talk properly later, yeah?'

'Yeah.'

'Got your phone with you?'

Poppy nodded.

'I'll give you a call when I'm done. You're sure you're all right?'

'I'm fine.'

Dad went to the door, pushed aside the black academic gown that hung there and took down a blue scarf that had two gold-coloured stripes running either side of a red one. He hooked it over Poppy's head and looped it around her neck. It smelled of him.

She'd almost forgotten his smell – the warm, spicy aftershave he'd worn since she was a kid.

'What's this for?' she asked, pressing the scratchy wool to her neck.

'If you want to walk through any of the colleges you're less likely to get stopped wearing one of these. Porters will assume you're a student.'

'Think I can pass for eighteen?'

'Scarily, yes.' He brushed a hand down her hair. His eyes became watery as he looked at her and he took a deep breath as if about to say something. He closed his mouth and shook his head. 'I should go and see what's happening.' He leaned down and kissed her forehead. 'Do you know the way?'

'I think so.'

Dad grabbed his keys off the coffee table and opened the door for her. They walked in silence, down the uneven stone steps of the stairwell and into the columned cloister of Nevile's Court. To the right was the library he'd pointed out on the way over. It seemed to float above arched pillars, as if it had been built on stilts to keep the books safe.

'This is where Isaac Newton first measured the speed of sound,' Dad said, stopping beside her.

'Really?'

'Listen.' Dad clapped his hands together. The sound echoed, almost as if unseen people were sending the clap back to him.

Poppy smiled. 'That's really strange.'

'And Lord Byron, the poet?' Dad continued, seemingly enjoying his new role as tour guide. 'He lived over there with his bear.'

'His bear?'

'Yeah. Although the college allows cats, they have never allowed dogs. And Byron got a bit annoyed about that and so got himself a bear.'

'That's a bit of an extreme way to prove a point.'

'By all accounts, Byron was a bit of an extreme character.'

'Did you live here when you were a student?'

'No. This is the inner sanctum of the college. You need to be a senior fellow to get a room here. That, or a humble chaplain. Oh, and Winnie the Pooh's in there,' Dad said, catching Poppy looking back at the library.

'Dad, I hate to break this to you, but Winnie the Pooh isn't real. He's a fictional character.'

'Ha, ha. I meant the original manuscripts.'

Poppy and her dad smiled at each other and she could tell they were both remembering playing Pooh sticks down at the river and reciting nonsense rhymes to one another. Her lungs contracted painfully. It took all her willpower not to throw herself into his arms and tell him how much she missed him.

Dad's smile faded and his brow crinkled.

'Poppy, I'm really —'

The wind changed directions and whipped through the columns, filling the cloister with the sound of whispers. Poppy shivered as the cold slid between every gap in her clothing and, in among the whispers of the wind, she thought she heard someone calling Dad's name.

A guy appeared from behind one of the columns on the opposite side of the courtyard and waved. He was tall with dark hair, cut into almost the same style as Michael's – slightly long at the front so that his fringe flopped over his eyes. He wore stone-coloured trousers, a dark wool sweater and a scarf wrapped several times around his neck so that it almost covered the bottom half of his face. Even so, he was vaguely familiar.

Dad looked over his shoulder and sighed. 'I have to take care of this. Do you know where you're going? Head through that passageway there and you'll be in Great Court, and then you can go out through the main gate. Turn right, and keep going. You'll eventually hit King's.'

'I'll be fine.'

The guy who'd called to Dad had stopped at the corner. He bobbed up and down, obviously trying to keep away the cold. He glanced up and his gaze connected with Poppy's.

That's where she knew him from: he was one of the guys from last night.

He began walking in their direction but was cut off by a tall girl who was wrapped up in a quilted jacket. She had hair so red there was no way it was natural. And even from this distance, Poppy could tell that her eye make-up had smudged. She guessed they were friends of the guy who'd died. Glancing at the two people waiting for him, Dad put an arm around her shoulders and steered her towards the stone steps that led to the passageway into Great Court.

His pace was brisk, and he practically pushed her up the first of the steps. 'I'll call you later.'

'Yeah, OK.' Poppy looked between him and the approaching guy.

'Bye.' With that, Dad marched away, as if to head off the students before they made it any closer to her. Was he ashamed of her or something?

Poppy slowly mounted the steps, surreptitiously glancing at them from behind the curtain of her hair. As she reached the top step, Dad turned and waved at her. She got the feeling he was just making sure she was leaving. She waved back, put her head down and ducked quickly into the shadow of the passageway. There she stopped, stepped closer to the wall and edged back to where she could just about see Dad and the students.

Dad had his hands on his hips. The guy was waving his hands around. He was whispering so she couldn't hear what he was saying, but his expression was furious, as if he'd really like to be shouting. Dad glanced back towards where she was hiding. Poppy flattened herself against the wall, waited a second and then dared another look.

Dad was pointing his finger at the guy. He only did that when he was really angry. She'd expected to be on the receiving end of that finger herself, but the dead body in the chapel seemed to have got her out of that so far. But why would Dad be getting so angry with a guy who only looked old enough to be a student? Was that really the way chaplains were meant to behave with students?

The guy pushed past Dad and headed in Poppy's direction, shouting, 'No, Lucy! I won't do that.'

'You need to talk to Messenger. If you don't, I will,' Dad shouted after him.

Footsteps echoed on the stone steps. Poppy pretended to be taking a great interest in the notice board and the guy carried right on past her, his clipped footsteps echoing like whip cracks.

CHAPTER EIGHT

'So you think espionage stopped the Cold War from turning hot?'

Michael shifted in his chair. Why the hell had he said he was interested in Cold War politics? He barely knew a thing about the subject. His A level didn't even cover that period...but it had just somehow slipped out. And now they expected him to be an expert. What an idiot!

Professor Madigan leaned back in her chair and observed him from behind steepled fingers. She was younger than he'd imagined, probably in her thirties, and despite her rounded cheeks and jovial manner, the amusement in her dark eyes was disarming. He got the feeling that she knew he didn't have a clue what he was talking about and was going to enjoy teaching him a lesson about overreaching.

OK, all he had to do was steer the conversation onto safer ground – something he actually knew about. Until then, he would roll out everything he could remember from that documentary he'd watched last year. Thank God for the History Channel!

The professor crossed one leg over the other and let her black high-heeled shoe dangle from her foot. 'That's an interesting argument to make,' she continued thoughtfully. 'Most people would want to argue the exact opposite: that every time a spy ring was discovered on either side of the Iron Curtain, relations between East and West became more fraught.'

Michael cleared his throat. 'I think politicians on both sides would have been more paranoid if they didn't think they had some insight into what the other side was doing. They might not have trusted all the information that they received, but without it their imaginations alone would have escalated the paranoia.'

Scratching noises drew his gaze. The other lecturer, Dr Holden, a hulk of a man in a worn-out suit, was furiously scribbling something on his pad. Probably the word REJECT over and over again. After meeting a couple of the other people they were interviewing today, Michael realised he didn't have a chance in hell of getting in.

'You sound like you admire the work done by our security services,' Professor Madigan said. 'Is that a career path you yourself are interested in?'

What? Seriously? Was that a trick question? She really wanted to know if he was interested in being a spy? Oh yeah, she'd definitely made up her mind to reject him and now she was amusing herself by making him squirm.

Michael tightened his grip on the arm of the chair. 'I'm not interested in working for the Russians, if that's what you mean,' he said, his tone a little sharper than he'd meant.

Professor Madigan's cheek twitched, turning the corner of her lips into a horrifying smile. She'd riled him, and she knew it. 'Not all spies educated in Cambridge have turned traitor. Besides, you shouldn't believe everything that was written about Guy Burgess – our government was just as capable of producing disinformation as the Russians.'

He cleared his throat. 'No. I didn't mean to imply...'

The two tutors glanced at each other.

'Leaving the Cambridge spy ring to one side, in your opinion, if the Americans hadn't instituted the Marshall Plan, do you think the Cold War would have taken the same course?'

What?

They wanted his opinion on that? He didn't have an opinion on that.

Shit.

He was opinion-less.

As Michael passed out of the main gate of King's College, it felt as though the doors had slammed shut behind him. Permanently. There was no way they were going to give him a place after that little performance. Ugh! He'd sounded like a complete numbskull in there.

His parents were going to be gutted. Mum had been blabbering on and on to her golf cronies about how her son was going to Cambridge – she'd hate having to take that back.

Michael spotted Poppy standing by the low wall that ran around the edge of the snow covered lawn, hopping from one foot to the other with her phone pressed to her ear. She wore an exasperated expression.

'No, Dad didn't know. Didn't you tell him? No, I do not want Jonathan to come and pick us up – *Mum!* Seriously. I can't just leave.' She glanced up and, seeing him, smiled.

He raised a hand in greeting, forced a smile onto his face and shoved his hands into his trouser pockets.

'I've gotta go, Michael's here.' She rolled her eyes. 'I'll ask him – Mum says, how did it go?'

The truth didn't seem warranted. He shrugged and turned away. He didn't want her to see the big F for failure stamped between his eyes. Poppy had enough on her plate after what had happened that morning.

'It went great, Mum,' Poppy said, before launching into all the reasons why they couldn't immediately jump on a train home to Windermere. Good. He didn't want to go home just yet. He couldn't face people knowing how badly he'd screwed up.

He watched groups of students hurrying by, heavy bags tugging at their shoulders, loaded with books from the libraries he'd never get to use. Tiny snowflakes drifted out of the leaden sky making the whole scene appear fuzzy and slightly unreal. Cambridge *was* unreal. A stupid dream that was never going to happen.

A hand on his arm brought him back to reality. 'Oh, hey,' he said. 'Sorry, I was miles away.'

'Reliving your triumph?' She dumped a plastic bag on the floor, tucked her hands into the ends of his scarf and pulled him against her. He felt the contours of her body mould to his and the briefest memory of her stretched out beneath him slid through his mind.

He shivered and forced a smile. 'Something like that.'

She reached up on tiptoes and pressed her icy lips to his and for a moment he didn't care about screwing up the interview. When she tried to step away he wound his arms around her and leaned into the kiss. Poppy wasn't having any of it. She pushed her hand against his chest and frowned up at him.

'What's wrong? It went OK, didn't it?'

Shit! He sometimes wished she were a little less observant. He shrugged. 'I'm not sure. Do you mind if we don't talk about it?'

Her forehead wrinkled. 'Really?'

He nodded.

'OK…well, Dad's got meetings and stuff, so I think we'd better stay out of the way. What do you want to do?'

After an actual slaughter in the morning and

metaphorical slaughter in the afternoon, there was only one thing he wanted to do, and given how wrong that had gone last night, he'd just have to settle for the pub.

The Eagle was full to bursting with students and people taking a rest from Christmas shopping. The noise of laughter, chatter and Christmas songs was overwhelming after the strange muffled quiet of the snowy streets. Most importantly, though, it was warm. Poppy stamped her feet on the entrance mat, trying to dislodge some of the snow that clung to cheap pumps she'd bought to replace Michael's boat-like boots. They weren't exactly suitable attire for the weather, and her toes stung with the cold, but at least they made her feel less like a big-footed hobbit.

They made it halfway to the bar before Michael stopped and turned to her.

'Why don't you go and find us a table?'

In other words, *if you're expecting something other than a refreshing orange juice, you'd better not get any closer to the bartenders.* Poppy rolled her eyes and pushed out an exaggerated sigh. 'Dad says I look eighteen.'

'Fine. You go for the drinks then.' He raised his eyebrows in a challenge.

A slow smile inched across his face when she didn't move.

Poppy glanced across the sea of people, then back at Michael. She tried not to return his grin, but the muscles in her face betrayed her. '*Fine*, I'll go and find a table.'

He leaned down and kissed her. It wasn't the usual brush of lips normally reserved for public places, but a full-on, God-was-I-breathing?-Can-I-remember-how-to-breathe? kiss. Her limbs softened and suddenly her head was filled with memories of all the places he'd touched her...and kissed her. What the hell was he doing to her? Too intense. *Way* too intense. She broke from his lips and gently pushed him away.

'Michael...'

He didn't look at her, instead his gaze was focused somewhere over her left shoulder. He grinned.

Was that clapping? OK, that was some kiss, but she didn't think it called for applause.

Poppy spun around to see three guys clapping their hands above their heads, whistling and saying things like 'very nice' and 'encore'. Blood rushed to her cheeks.

Michael laughed, put his hand on his chest and bowed.

'Stop it!' Poppy punched his shoulder. 'Oh my God! You are just begging to be punished.'

'Promises, promises.' Michael grinned. 'Cider?'

'Yeah. Thanks.' Spotting people getting up from a table in the far corner, she made a dash for it. She skirted the table of guys just as one of them shouted,

'Moose!' and all five of them slammed their glasses on the table and downed their pints in one.

Poppy shook her head. This Cambridge lot might be wicked smart, but it didn't stop some of them from acting like complete tossers. She dumped the plastic bag containing Michael's boots on the floor and flopped into a squeaky chair that wobbled as she sat down.

Poppy put her elbows on the table and rested her head in her hands. She watched Michael as he edged his way through the crowd at the bar. There had been something a little too brittle about his laugh…and too desperate in his kiss. He was trying to be cool, but she could see through him better than he thought she could. That stuff about messing up his interview wasn't him being his usual modest self. He really did think he'd screwed up.

For the last couple of weeks he'd spent more time with his head in the books than ever before. He'd read so much in preparation for this interview that she was half-convinced he'd given up sleeping.

Michael arrived back at the table and dumped two pints of cider down. He slumped onto a stool opposite her and quickly swigged back a quarter of his pint.

'What happened?' she asked. 'Why do you think you screwed up?'

He stared into his drink and shook his head. 'Made an arse of myself. Don't really want to talk about it.' He picked up the glass and his Adam's apple bobbed as another quarter of a pint disappeared down his throat.

Poppy sipped at her own drink while Michael picked strips of paper from a torn beer mat. She grabbed his hand and squeezed it.

Michael glanced up. 'I'm fine,' he said, quickly. He smiled, but too soon his gaze slid back down to his pint and she knew he was lying.

A loud voice from the neighbouring table broke into Poppy's thoughts.

'Did you hear what happened at Trinity?'

'Oh yeah, that's what I was going to tell you,' another voice said. 'I was talking to one of our porters and he said that the dead guy was posed, like someone was trying to send a message to someone. Sounds really creepy, if you ask me.'

The porter was right. The body had been posed. With an hour or so to herself, walking around the packed Cambridge shops, the image of the bloodstained marble floor had invaded her mind over and over again, and there was one thing she was sure of: either the guy had dragged his arms through his own blood to leave a clue to the identity of his killer, or the murderer had cold-heartedly watched the blood drain from the guy's body and then taken the time to create bloody wings. Both scenarios were horrifying. And both meant that the key to the murderer lay in those bloody wings.

Michael must have been listening to the girls too. He raised his eyebrows at her. 'How was your dad?'

Poppy shrugged. 'He's…weird. I mean, he's fine, but he's acting strange.'

'In what way?'

'Like he's hiding something.'

Michael screwed up his face. 'I know he's being an arse, but you can't think he had anything to do with…'

'I'm not saying that. I saw him arguing with one of those guys we ran into when we got to the college last night. It seemed a bit odd.'

'Really?' Michael's expression shifted to one of curiosity. Poppy had to stop herself from rolling her eyes. He was thinking about that bloody girl in the red dress again. She knew he'd fancy her – she was just his type. Tall…blonde…gorgeous. 'What were they arguing about?'

Poppy took over picking at the beer mat where Michael had left off. 'I don't know. I couldn't hear. I was too busy hiding around the corner.'

Michael snorted. 'You were hiding around the corner?'

'I got the impression it was about the murder.'

Michael chewed his bottom lip as if deciding whether to tell her something. 'It could have been. The girl from last night…'

Ha! She knew it! He was still obsessing about her.

'…She's on the floor we're staying on,' Michael continued. 'And the guy who was killed was her boyfriend.'

'How do you know all that?' Poppy's brain whirred like a computer processing data. The girl in the red dress was the dead guy's girlfriend? That same girl who'd run bare arms through the snow, carving out the wings of a snow angel...just like her dead boyfriend had done with his own blood. That couldn't be a coincidence. She blinked when she realised Michael was still talking.

'...And when I went to get clothes for you I ran into them. I think they might know who did it.'

'What?'

'I overheard them arguing and it sounded like Ria thought that Danny had been killed because of something that they'd done. Or not done. Something to do with a party.'

'A party?'

'That's what it sounded like. Something to do with whether they should invite someone to a party. They called it something weird.' Michael squeezed his eyes shut and rubbed his forehead. 'Nahh, I can't remember.'

'Why would you kill someone for not inviting you to a party? That's crazy. There must be more to it than that.' And what was with the wings? The angel thing was bugging her – it had to mean something. 'What do you know about angels?'

'They have wings.' Michael's mouth dropped open as soon as he realised what he'd said. 'The policewoman asked you if you knew what the wings were about.'

She nodded. 'The girl in the red dress – who you so obviously fancy – d'you remember what she did?'

'I don't fan...oh, shit.' His eyes widened as he made the links.

'They were dressed like they'd come from a party.' Just like her dad. Had they been at the same party? She remembered the weird invitation on the mantelpiece in Dad's study – the date matched.

Poppy felt in her pocket for her phone and opened the web browser. It was predictably slow.

Michael pulled out his phone too. 'What are we searching for?'

She shrugged. 'Angels, I guess.'

'I don't think that'll get us very far. That'll bring up millions of websites.'

True. 'OK. How about if you look up *angel* and *Trinity College*? I'll have a look at angels on Wikipedia.'

When the page eventually loaded, she scanned the article on angels and gathered that they were messengers of God and occasionally they acted out God's vengeance. There was a list of individual angels, at the top of which was the Archangel Michael. She glanced up grinning. 'Hey, did you know your name means "kindness of God"?'

'Vaguely,' he murmured, not even looking up. 'Did you see this?' He handed over his phone.

Poppy stared at the screen. It showed a painting of a terrifying angel, dressed in what looked like the uniform of a Roman soldier with golden breastplate and red skirts. In his right hand he held a long spear, drawn back, ready to strike a red-faced man who was staring up at him with a mixture of anger and fear. Then she noticed that the body of the red-faced man coiled into that of a serpent. He was the devil.

'What is it?' she asked.

Michael took the phone from her and after a few swipes of his finger, handed the phone back.

Poppy looked down at the screen and the air stuck in her throat. Familiar black and white marble floor tiles zigzagged between the boxed oak seating towards an altar, above which hung the painting. She blinked, and for a second saw the body stretched out on the chapel floor, his bloody wings, his eyes fixed on the angel towering over him, arm drawn back ready to drive the spear through his chest. It would have been the last thing the guy had seen.

For a second she saw eyes, staring down at her, so full of hate and anger...

She blinked and they were gone. Nausea hit her so suddenly she gasped. The phone slipped from her fingers and clunked onto the table just as the lead singer of Slade screeched out of the pub's speakers: '*It's Christmas!*'

'Are you OK? Poppy?'

'I'm fine.'

'You didn't see the painting, did you?' Michael

asked, grabbing her hand.

She shook her head. With his free hand, he took back his phone and shoved it in his pocket.

'Poppy —'

'— I need another drink,' she said, tugging her hand out of his and shoving her own phone back in her pocket. Michael didn't move. He just watched her for a moment. She pulled out her best *I'm completely normal* smile. 'What?'

'Cider?'

'Yeah.' She managed to keep the smile in place until he was halfway to the bar, then she slumped back in her seat and rubbed the ache in her forehead. What the hell was happening with her head? Maybe it was shock...teamed with an overactive imagination. It didn't mean anything.

She couldn't believe that she hadn't noticed the painting. Of course the police would have seen it. And Dad. But why would someone re-enact a painting like that? And why reverse the symbolism so that the angel had ended up dead on the floor? Surely the killer didn't think he was the devil?

A pint of cider appeared in front of her. She took hold of it and smiled up at Michael. 'Thanks.'

He plonked his own pint onto the table and slouched down on the stool. 'Change of subject?' he asked.

She nodded. 'I think that would be good.'

'Excellent,' Michael twisted his glass, creating

smudged wet circle patterns on the dark varnish of the table. 'Because I have one in mind.'

'Oh yeah?'

'I have some questions about the contents of your backpack.' He looked up at her and grinned.

'What?' It took a second for Poppy's brain to switch tracks. Her heart thudded in her chest.

Michael straightened up and pointed a finger at her. 'Ah ha!' He grinned. 'So you know what I'm talking about. Where the hell did you get them?'

Poppy's cheeks burned so hot there was a possibility she'd melt all the snow in Cambridgeshire. There were several things in her bag she wasn't keen for him to see. Which one of them was he talking about? 'I'm not telling you.'

Michael bit his lip, in a pathetic attempt to hide the big stupid grin on his face. 'Did you go into a shop and buy them? Because I'd really like to have seen that.'

Bugger! He'd found the condoms. Her cheeks flared hotter. 'No, I didn't!'

He arched an eyebrow. 'If you don't tell me, my imagination will run wild.'

She sighed. It was going to be a long night.

CHAPTER NINE

'Poppy!'

Just as she was about to step into the road a hand hooked around Poppy's elbow and yanked her to a stop. She staggered back into Michael's arms as a blur of light and metal whizzed by. 'Oops. Sorry!' she called to the cursing cyclist who just about managed to stay upright after having to swerve around her. 'What kind of nutter cycles in snow?'

Michael's arm slid around her and he grinned. 'We should get you a sign: dangerous when drunk.'

What? 'I'm not drunk. This isn't drunk.'

'Uh huh.'

'This is...tipsy.'

Michael stepped in front of her. He raised an eyebrow and nodded slowly. It was the expression he gave her when he was trying to appease her while making it quite clear that he thought she was off her rocker.

She opened her mouth, ready to give a verbal beating, when something caught her eye. Two lines of choristers were weaving their way down the street towards the entrance to King's College, dispersing tourists and students in their midst. With their ruffled white collars, red cassocks and black cloaks, the kids looked like a regiment of angels trooping through the snow. Either that or the cast of Harry Potter.

'They're so cute! Look how little that one is,' she said, watching a little blond-haired kid with a solemn expression. 'I just want to hang him on a Christmas tree.'

Michael smiled and shook his head at her. 'I think that might get you into trouble.' He glanced at his watch. 'Must be time for evensong. We could go if you like?'

'Hmm. Go to church...go to church...' she mused.

Sitting through a church service wasn't something she would normally be interested in, but she was a little curious. She wanted to know what Dad saw in the damp stone buildings, dreary hymns and long lists of *thou shalt nots.*

On the other hand, if they went back to their rooms they could have another bash at breaking a commandment or two. Her stomach tensed and her heart fluttered at the thought.

'Poppy? Hello, Earth to Poppy?'

'Hmm?' She realised that she was gripping Michael's arm like she was holding onto the hull of the *Titanic.*

He brushed the hair back from her face. 'What was all that about?'

'Nothing. I was just thinking.'

'About what?'

'About...fracking.' *Fracking?!* That's all she could

come up with. She really must be drunk.

'Fracking? As in, drilling for shale gas?' His eyes narrowed ever so slightly and she felt his muscles tense beneath her fingers. 'I see.'

'It's an important issue.'

His gaze caught hers. His expression was deadly serious. 'I agree.'

'I mean, no one knows what effect it'll have on the environment. They could just go and frack away and although it might be good in the short term, it could have disastrous consequences. I mean what if something went wrong? We'd have to live with that. For a long...time.'

Michael nodded slowly. 'That's what you're worried about? Consequences?'

'Well, yeah.'

He took a deep breath and hugged her closer. 'I get that. You think maybe we should wait, until more... *precautions* have been put in place?'

'Yeah. *I don't know*. I really want to—'

'—If you say frack I am going to lose it,' he said, grinning.

She snorted out a laugh and focused on untangling his scarf. 'I admit, the metaphor's been stretched about as far as it'll go.'

'I'd say so.' He lowered his lips to hers, kissed her gently 'So...do you think we should use real words now?'

She glanced up at him from under her eyelashes, wishing her cheeks weren't about to go supernova. 'You mean the S. E. X. word?'

He smiled. 'I think we're past spelling it out.'

'Michael?'

Michael's arms fell away from her and he took a quick step back like he'd been caught stealing alcohol from his dad's drinks cabinet. 'Professor Madigan, hello.'

Standing next to them was a woman drowned by a woollen hat, cloak-like black coat and a scarf the same colours as the one Dad had lent Poppy.

'Umm – this is Poppy, my girlfriend.'

The woman's gaze shifted to Poppy. Her eyes widened for a second before a bright smile lit up her face. 'You're Jim's daughter.'

Jesus! Was there anyone who Dad didn't know?

She shook her head. 'I can't get over how much you look like him.'

'I'm not sure that's a compliment,' Poppy said, stuffing her hands into the pockets of her hoodie.

The woman laughed. 'Oh believe me, it is. Your dad was quite the stunner when he was younger. What are you two doing out here? Shouldn't you be with him?'

'We were talking about fracking,' Michael said.

Poppy nearly choked. Damn him!

'Oh, gosh, yes. Terrible what they're doing. You know, I'm about to have some students for drinks.

Why don't you come along? Michael, it will give you a chance to meet some current students and ask all those questions you no doubt forgot to ask on the official part of your visit. And I can give Poppy all the gossip on her dad from our college days.'

'You were students together?'

'We were. Do come. Unless Jim's expecting you?'

Bugger! The last thing she wanted was to spend an evening with a load of teacher types. But if Michael really had stuffed up his interview as badly as he thought he had this might be a good opportunity for them to see him as he really was. Plus, she wouldn't mind putting off the conversation about last night for a bit longer.

Michael was already shaking his head when she jumped in and said:

'That would be great. Dad's stuck in meetings.'

'Of course, he would be. It's just terrible what happened. Danny was a very gifted young man. His death is a great loss.'

This place was worse than back home – everyone seemed to know everyone else.

'This way,' Professor Madigan said, setting off in the direction of the entrance to her college.

The professor led them through the main gate into King's College. Poppy had seen so many pictures of the place, but none of them had prepared her for how huge it was. Across the snow-covered lawn that had to be the size of a football pitch, spotlights lit up the line of turrets along the chapel roof that speared the night sky like bony fingers. She was about to comment on it when she glanced up at Michael.

His cheeks had paled and he looked at the grand old buildings like they had broken their promise to him. Poppy's chest tightened. As much as she hated the thought of him coming here and being so far away, she hated the thought of him not getting in even more. There had to be something they could do.

The professor led them through a smaller courtyard and into one of the buildings. Poppy had assumed this little gathering of students would take place in her office, but the room they were ushered into appeared to be some kind of function room. A few leather armchairs were scattered around the edges of an oriental rug and beside the white marble fireplace. Along one wall was a long table bearing various sizes and styles of glasses as well as at least twenty bottles of wine. At the centre of the table was a large bowl on a stand, underneath which a tea light burned. She guessed that was where the smell of cinnamon and orange was coming from.

'Oh good, they delivered the mulled wine. Would you like some? It might warm you up,' Professor Madigan said.

'Oh, uhh, I'm not sure I should,' Poppy said, glancing at Michael, who almost cracked a smile at her feigned abstinence. Almost.

The professor stripped off her coat to reveal a neat black suit that was tucked around a curvy figure. 'I'm sure Jim won't mind you having one glass.' When she took off her hat, long brown curls fell around her shoulders. She smiled, running fingers through her hair. 'That's better. So, mulled wine?'

As Professor Madigan set about ladling out the hot red wine, Poppy spotted a large print attached to a display board. It was a copy of a painting of a nativity scene. The Mary figure, who weirdly was dressed like a Jane Austen character, displayed her baby to grovelling wise men. Behind her was an old man who Poppy guessed was supposed to be Joseph. Two fat-armed cherubs hovered over the scene, held aloft by ridiculously tiny wings.

Unwrapping the scarf from around her neck, Poppy moved slowly towards the painting.

'That's a print of the Rublev that hangs behind the altar in the chapel,' Professor Madigan said.

'It's a bit less intimidating than the one in Trinity,' Poppy murmured.

'Ah, yes. You're talking about the Archangel Michael defeating Satan.'

She wondered how much the professor knew about angels. 'Satan was an angel too, wasn't he?'

'Yes, according to some mythology. A fallen angel.'

'So why is it Michael in the painting? Why not one of the other archangels?'

'It's meant to be a scene from the Book of Revelation,' Professor Madigan said, handing a glass of mulled wine to the not-so-angelic Michael, and one to Poppy. 'Michael is God's first lieutenant – the leader of the forces of good in the battle against evil. He's the one who is said to defeat Satan in the final battle. But Michael isn't always depicted as a warrior; he's also seen as being a mediator between God and his people. If you're interested in angels, you should ask your dad – he's the real expert.'

'He is?' She'd never known Dad be interested in angels.

'His PhD is on "Angels in Milton and Dante".'

They'd talked a little about what he was studying, but somehow she'd missed that. 'Oh, right, yeah. I knew he was studying Milton and Dante.'

The door swung open and in walked a red-haired girl followed by two waiters carrying silver trays of food. It was the girl Dad had argued with this morning.

'Please put the platters at that end of the table,' said the girl, directing the waiters.

'Lucy, you're here,' Professor Madigan said, rushing over and hugging her. 'I didn't know whether to expect you or not. How is everything?'

'Horrible,' Lucy replied with a shrug of her shoulder. 'Ria won't be coming.'

'Of course not. I wouldn't expect it. Come and meet some guests. This is Michael Quinn who's here on interview and Poppy Sinclair—'

'—Jim's daughter. I'd heard you were visiting. Hi. Nice to meet you,' she said, in a thick French accent. 'I'm Lucy Chantal. I'm a third year student at Trinity. It's so nice you could come. Is Jim also coming?'

'No, he'd already sent his apologies,' Professor Madigan said. 'In the circumstances we should have cancelled, but it was too short notice to get the word out.'

Dad was supposed to be here? 'Is tonight to celebrate something?' Poppy asked.

Professor Madigan and Lucy exchanged glances.

'No, it's just a get-together. For…Christmas,' Lucy said, making it sound like a convenient excuse.

The door swung open again and in walked three men, two of whom were wearing suit jackets and ties.

Lucy went over to welcome them and Professor Madigan excused herself to go and talk to the serving staff.

'That's the girl who was with the guy from last night,' Poppy whispered to Michael.

He screwed his face up. 'What?'

'The students Dad was arguing with. She's one of them. Isn't that weird?'

Michael deliberately looked away from her. 'What's weird is you accepting an invitation to one of these kinds of things, especially when you must have known I didn't want to come back here. Are you really that desperate to not talk about what happened last night?'

'No. That's not why I...'

His voice hardened. 'Then why?'

'I...' Shit! She couldn't tell him the real reason; then he'd be pissed off at her for interfering.

Thankfully Professor Madigan returned, saving her from having to come up with something to tell him. 'Poppy, Michael, may I introduce to you Yaser Al-Qahtani.'

'Yaser?' Michael asked. His eyebrows drew together, like the name meant something to him.

'Hi there.' The guy standing next to the professor smiled broadly and held out his hand to Michael. He was tall, dark and dressed in clothes that seemed peculiarly tweed-like for a guy who sounded like he'd grown up in the States. 'Do we know each other? Are you both students here?' Yaser asked.

'No, we're just visiting,' Michael said. 'You have the same name as a football player.'

The guy laughed. 'That's right. Captain of the Saudi team for a while. Myself, I'm more of a Man United fan. But don't tell my father.'

While Michael and Yaser talked football, Poppy

turned to the professor. 'You knew my dad when he was a student, Professor Madigan?'

'Fiona, please.' She smiled. 'Yes, we were good friends. There was a group of us that palled around. Jim kind of held us all together. He was the glue that stopped us from killing each other. Although he could be a little sod at times. He once threw me in the river.'

'Really?'

'I was panicking about a final and I think he got sick of me going on about it so he picked me up and dropped me in the Cam.' Fiona laughed. 'I was so furious that I chased him the full length of the Backs, all the way back to college. I totally forgot about the final, which was of course the point – as he argued at length.'

Poppy smiled. 'He doesn't talk about his student days much.'

Fiona's smile faded. 'You must miss him. I know he misses you.'

Poppy nodded. But this wasn't a line of conversation she wanted to pursue. Seeing Michael was deep in conversation with Yaser, she stepped away from them. Fiona followed with a puzzled expression.

'Umm…can I ask a question?' Poppy said, lowering her voice to just above a whisper.

'Of course.'

'It's just, Michael thinks he did really badly in his interview. Is there any way he could do it again? He

128

spent all of this morning looking after me. Y'see, I was with Dad when he found the guy, and believe me, the throwing-up part wasn't pretty and definitely not the best way to prepare for an interview. But this is Michael's dream. And he's so smart. Honestly, he's like the smartest guy I know. I'm sure he'd impress you if you just gave him another chance.'

Fiona smiled sadly. 'I'm afraid we can't do that. It wouldn't be fair on the other candidates.'

Poppy's heart sank. 'I guess. I'm sorry for asking.' She directed her attention to her glass; an oily sheen was developing over the surface of the mulled wine. When she heard an exasperated sigh, her gaze darted up in time to see Fiona shaking her head.

'So like your father,' she laughed.

'Sorry?'

She smiled. 'Look, I don't think Michael did nearly as badly as he thinks he did. In fact, I think he'll fit in very nicely around here.'

'You mean you're giving him a place?'

'I couldn't possibly tell you that.'

'No, of course not.' Relief swept through her. 'But he did OK?'

Fiona squeezed her arm and walked away.

While he discussed England's chances at the World Cup, Michael watched Poppy talking with Professor

Madigan. Not that he didn't trust her...but *he didn't trust her*. She was definitely up to something. She had that damned determined look in her eye. He just hoped she wasn't bending Fiona's ear about giving him a place – *that* would be humiliating.

More people had joined the party. The room hummed with conversation, and someone had put on music: a choir singing Christmas carols. The door opened again and in walked Conal. He stalked towards the drinks table and poured himself a glass of red wine before looking over the crowd. When his gaze settled on Michael and Yaser, Conal froze.

Michael had been pretty sure that the guy he'd overheard Ria and Conal arguing about had been called Yaser. Now he was definite. So this was the party...the one with the weird name he still couldn't remember.

After taking a hefty gulp of wine, Conal made a beeline for them.

'Conal, how are you?' Yaser asked, slapping him on the back and shaking his hand like they were buddies. Conal even managed to smile.

'It's good to see you, Yaser. Michael, isn't it?' Conal asked, turning to him.

'Yeah.'

Conal's gaze was unwavering, and Michael couldn't help feeling he was being given a warning. His spine stiffened and he gripped his glass tighter.

'So, Yaser,' Conal said. 'You still up for Monday night?'

'Definitely. Looking forward to it.'

'What's happening Monday?' Michael asked, drawing another icy glance from Conal.

'We're going to this club in London. A guys' club.' Yaser wiggled his eyebrows. 'You should come if you're still around.'

At that moment Poppy appeared at his side. Yaser looked her over like she might be the kind of girl he was hoping to find in the 'guys' club'.

Michael's jaw tightened. He took hold of her arm, just above the elbow. 'Excuse me,' he said. 'I just need to...'

He tugged her away from them, through the now busy room, and dumped his glass on the table. Before Poppy could protest, he snatched hers out of her hand and left that there too. Michael led her out of the door into the corridor. He kept walking, barely keeping his temper in check, until they turned the corner. There, Poppy stopped and yanked her arm away from him.

She brushed her hair out of her eyes and squared her feet. 'Now don't get all shouty.'

Ha. This was going to be good – *not*. 'What were you saying to Professor Madigan?' he asked, doing his best to follow her request.

She folded her arms and looked down at the floor.

Her hair fell over her eyes again. 'I asked if you could have a do-over.'

The bottom fell out of his stomach. Even though he'd been expecting something like this, he still couldn't believe she'd actually done it. 'Poppy!' He slouched against the wall. '*Shit!* What did you say to her?'

'I just told her what a bad morning you'd had. I thought they might interview you again. But apparently they don't do that kind of thing. It would be unfair to the other candidates.'

Michael snorted and shook his head. 'Do you have any idea how embarrassing this is? Having my girlfriend argue on my behalf. Don't you think it's bad enough that I made a complete arse of myself?'

'I know. It was a stupid thing to do. But I can't stand seeing you...'

'You're not flaming Bob the Builder, Poppy. There are some things you can't fix. You had no right to interfere.'

'I know. I'm sorry.' Poppy closed the distance between them. Her hands began to slide around him. He caught hold of her wrists to stop her. Her eyes, the bronze of autumn leaves, flashed up at him full of hurt. She hadn't meant to embarrass him – he knew that – but he couldn't shift the anger simmering in his chest.

'Fiona said you didn't do as badly as you think you did,' she said, softly.

Michael snorted a laugh. Even now she couldn't let it go. 'I don't want to hear it, Poppy.'

She pulled away and folded her arms. Even though he was mad as hell with her, his first instinct was to draw her back to him. He resisted.

'What the fuck are they doing here?' A male voice shouted, somewhere down the corridor. He thought it was Conal, but couldn't be sure.

Poppy's gaze flashed up to him. He pressed a finger to his lips, pushed away from the wall and popped his head around the corner.

Yup, it was Conal. He paced back and forth in front of the French girl – Lucy, was it? – who looked about as pissed off with Conal as Michael was with Poppy. Must have been something in that damned mulled wine.

'Never mind them,' Lucy seethed. 'Why is Yaser here? After what's happened to Danny...you still invited him?'

Michael flattened his back to the wall again. Poppy's arms were folded and she was listening hard.

'I didn't invite him,' Conal said.

'Someone did.'

'I don't know, Lucy!' Conal shouted. 'Right now, we have bigger problems to deal with.'

'What?'

'The book's gone.'

'The book?'

'Yes, *the book*. I've been through Danny's room and it's gone.'

'Maybe Danny had it with him.'

'No. I checked with Messenger. The police never found it.'

'You don't think... Could Ria be right? They've wanted information on the society for years.'

'No.'

'How can you be sure?'

'Because I already gave them a copy. OK? That's how I know.'

'*What?* You made an oath!'

'Some things are more important than oaths.'

A door slammed and there was silence. After a few seconds, Michael sneaked a glance around the corner. Conal was still there, standing side-on to Michael, in the middle of the corridor, shoulders slumped, staring at the floor. He took a phone out of his jacket pocket, pressed a button and held it to his ear.

'Yaser will be there,' was all he said before ending the call and shoving the phone back in his pocket.

CHAPTER TEN

'You're sure?' Poppy asked. Her damned hoodie was no match for the icy wind that sliced through the fabric like it was netting, chilling her to the bone. She shuddered and dug her hands deeper into her pockets. Fog had invaded the winding streets of Cambridge, swirling beneath the phosphorescent yellow glow of the streetlamps and turning every dark alleyway into a confusing tunnel of ghostly shadows.

Michael's arm slid around her shoulder. For a second she thought he'd forgiven her, but his arm felt stiff and awkward, and his body jostled against hers like they were walking out of sync.

'Yaser was the guy that Conal and Ria were arguing about. They said he'd been blackballed,' Michael said, quietly, as if he was afraid someone would overhear them.

'Blackballed? Do I even want to know what that means?'

'It's what happens in clubs where all the members have to agree to someone new joining. Happens at my mum's golf club. It only takes one of the committee to blackball you and you're refused membership.'

'That's harsh.'

Michael nodded.

'So they're in some kind of club? Conal...Ria...Lucy...and Danny?

'I think so.'

'And that would make the party we've just been to—'

'—A recruitment drive.'

'But I didn't hear anyone mention being in a club. And why would Professor Madigan be there? Why would Dad have been invited?'

Michael glanced down at her. 'Maybe they're members too.'

'But if Dad's a member, why hasn't he said something?'

Michael shrugged. 'There are all kinds of student societies. Some are the usual type, like the societies we have at school, but some are more exclusive. The Pitt Club's the most famous. It's men only and I think you have to have been to the right school to be asked to join.'

'I'm guessing Windermere Grammar doesn't count.'

Michael laughed. 'Nope. Some of these societies have been going for hundreds of years and the membership is a closely guarded secret.'

'Sounds like a coven. Makes you wonder what they're up to.'

They fell silent as they continued through the freezing fog, up the icy cobbled street towards Trinity. Michael's arm kept her pressed up against his side, but no warmth radiated from him. By the time they reached the gate of the college she was glad to have an excuse to draw away from him and talk to the porters.

'Should we find your dad?' Michael asked as they dawdled from the lodge towards their rooms.

'He'd have called if he was free.'

The fog seemed to play with the perspective of the place. Although she could see shadows of the roofs and towers, they seemed further away, as if the fog had forced the walls apart. It came as a surprise when they reached the corner of the court as soon as they did.

Poppy sucked in a ragged breath of damp air. This was turning out to be the weekend from hell. After losing her nerve, Dad catching her *not at it* and then finding a guy dead, pissing off Michael was just the icing on the cake. Wasn't it enough that there'd been a fatality?

They turned into M staircase and Poppy wearily climbed the stairs behind Michael. He opened the door to the corridor and let her go first. One of the lights embedded in the ceiling was on the blink. It flashed on and off like a strobe, giving the corridor a strange vibe. There was no sign of life, but on the floor outside the door to what must be Ria's room, someone had left a note. Michael bent over and pushed it closer to the door and then took his time opening the door to their rooms. Even when he nodded for her to go ahead of him, he didn't look at her.

She threw the plastic bag she was carrying to the floor, turned to him and kissed him. She was afraid he would push her away, but he didn't. His lips were hot against hers and as he relaxed into the kiss she reached under his jacket, tugged at his shirt, freeing it from his trousers, and slid her freezing cold hands around his back. He jumped, broke from her lips and grinned.

'You're going to pay for that,' he said running his hands over her hair.

'Really?'

'Uh huh.' An arm hooked around her back, pressed her to him and with his other hand he tickled her side. She squirmed against the assault. Was this his idea of getting his own back?

'Agh! No, no! Stop it! Not fair!'

'Shhh! You're making too much noise,' he whispered, kissing her, drowning out her squeals. There was only one way she could think of to get him to stop. She slid her hand to the front of his trousers.

He gasped and threw back his head. 'Shit!'

Poppy couldn't help grinning. 'Going to stop that now?' she asked.

'Depends. Are you going to stop that?'

'Do you want me to?'

For a minute he stared at her as if struggling with the answer. His chest rose and fell against hers in short quick breaths.

Her throat tightened and her head filled with a strange whooshing noise.

Michael shook his head and pushed her away. 'This is so screwed up.'

'*What?*'

'I'm not going to sleep with you.'

Now she really did feel sick. 'You don't want to?'

Michael ran a hand through his hair. 'No. *You* don't want to. You're only doing this because we argued and you think it'll be a shortcut to making everything OK. That's not a good reason for us to sleep together.'

Was he serious? Anger hummed through her veins. 'Don't talk to me like...like I don't know what I want...like you know me better than I know myself. I want this. I want to have sex with you. There, I've used the word and everything!'

Michael laughed but he wasn't smiling. 'Then I'm really sorry that you're not going to get what you want. Go it solo if you want, but for now my trousers are closed for business.'

What? Her mouth dropped open. Then her cheeks flared hot.

'Oh my God!' She took a step back.

Now he was smiling, damn him. She turned away from him and headed for her room.

'Where are you going?' he called.

'I'm going it solo! *You* are not invited.'

Michael grabbed her elbow just as a terrifying scream echoed through the building.

CHAPTER ELEVEN

It sounded like an animal being slaughtered. Poppy's heart raced, all her muscles locked tight and she could do nothing but stare at Michael. Then, like someone had opened a release valve, both of them ran at the door.

He got there first and yanked it open.

Several feet away a girl was kneeling. Her long blonde hair spilled over her back and shoulders and onto the floor. In the flashing light she seemed to rear up in slow motion. She threw her head back, her shoulders shook and the noise that came from her was like nothing Poppy had ever heard before. She flopped forward again, clasping her chest like it hurt too much to breathe.

Poppy pushed past Michael and kneeled in front of the weeping girl. She squeezed her shoulder, not wanting to frighten her.

The girl looked up. Poppy almost didn't recognise her as the beauty who'd worn that red dress and had two guys hanging off her every word. Her face was too twisted by pain and grief.

She set an arm around Ria and pulled her close. Ria's head settled heavily on her shoulder at the same time as a sheet of notepaper fluttered to the floor, slipping in and out of view as the corridor light flashed on and off.

'Call Dad,' she whispered to Michael.

He nodded and headed back to their set.

Ria sniffed loudly and pulled out of Poppy's arms.

'Sorry,' she muttered.

'It's OK.'

The girl's eyelids were so red with crying that her irises shone unnaturally blue in the flashes of light. 'You look like him,' she whispered, hoarsely.

'Who?'

'Jim.'

Poppy shrugged a shoulder. 'Less stubble.'

The girl's lip curved in the beginning of a smile that was stopped in its tracks when her gaze fell on the piece of paper. Poppy reached out a hand to pick it up but the note was wrenched from her fingers so swiftly that it almost tore.

'*It's private*,' Ria snapped, pressing it to her chest. Her fist tightened and the paper scrunched like a fan. She was shaking. Properly shaking.

'Can I make you a drink? Tea or something?' Poppy asked.

Ria laughed. 'Yes, tea will make it all better, won't it?' The girl wiped the tears away with the back of her hand and shakily pushed herself to her feet. She was wearing a long black dress that billowed at the sleeves and looked like something you'd wear at

Halloween...if you were dressing up as a witch.

Relieved to get away from the flashing hall light that was starting to give her a headache, Poppy followed Ria into a room that stank of cheap incense and candles.

'I heard it was your boyfriend who died,' Poppy said. 'I'm sorry.'

'Don't feel like you have to try to make me feel better. You didn't know him and I can't stand fake sympathy,' the girl barked back without even looking at her.

'It wasn't fake. If something happened to my boyfriend I – well, I don't know how I'd feel, but I'm guessing it would feel like shit.'

The girl ran her hand over her long white-blonde hair and sniffed. 'Shouldn't have been him. Of all of us... It shouldn't have been him.'

All of who? The society they belonged to?

Poppy's gaze drifted over the Afghan rugs, messy bookcases and empty wine bottles to the corner by the window where a low table had been draped in a black velvet cloth that bore an embroidered silver star within a circle. It wasn't the usual pentagram – the symbol beloved of all brands of Pagan belief – this one was upside down. A chill ran up Poppy's spine. On top of the table the burnt-out stub of an incense stick poked out of the mouth of a snarling dragon. Next to that was a small bowl containing what looked like burnt bits of paper and beside that a deep red unlit pillar candle. It was an altar. And if she had to guess, she'd say someone had been practising ritual magic... of a sort.

Ria caught her looking at the altar just as Michael came through the door.

'Don't tell me you're in the same God squad as your father?' she said.

'Who, Poppy?' Michael replied. 'You've got to be joking. She lives in a house filled with that kind of thing.' He nodded to the altar. Michael had hung around her house enough to spot a bit of magic when he saw it. Unfortunately, he had no clue about the differences.

She turned back to see the girl eyeing her with much more interest. Ice slithered down her spine. There was something about this girl that set her nerves on edge, and it wasn't just that she looked a bit like Michael's ex. 'Should I make some tea?'

'No. I'll do it.' Ria grabbed a kettle from the floor and disappeared next door.

'Your dad's just getting out of something. He said he'd be over soon as he could,' Michael said, quietly.

Poppy wandered over to the altar. She wondered if her dad had ever been in here and seen this. She could make out fragments of writing on the burnt pieces of paper. She'd never really been into ritual magic – but her Goddess-loving mum had dragged her to all kinds of workshops, one of which had been on spellcraft. She knew some people wrote their spells and then burnt them with incense. One of the scorched fragments had the letters CON printed on it in black ink. CON? What could that be? Unless it was the beginning of a name...like Conal.

'What's wrong?' Michael asked.

'I'm not sure,' she murmured.

Next to the dragon incense burner there was a screwed-up piece of paper, the only one untouched by flames. It was the note. Poppy glanced at the bedroom door. She had no right to look at it – like Ria said, it was private. But with everything that was going on... She unfurled the paper and read:

Danny was the first to be fitted for his wings.
Who will be next?

A knock at the door made her nearly jump out of her skin. She dropped the note back onto the altar, just as both Dad and Ria walked in through different doors.

Dad nodded to Poppy and then turned to Ria.

'How are you doing?' he asked.

Ria sighed and looked away. 'You don't need to be here. Danny's dead, end of story.'

'I'm not sure it is the end of the story, though, are you?'

The question sounded weighed down with meaning. Almost like Dad knew about the contents of the note she'd just read. What the heck was going on here?

Dad turned back to Poppy. His hair was sticking out all over the pace and his cheeks were grey and gaunt. 'Poppy, would you mind giving us a moment?'

She shook her head, but actually, yes, she did mind. There was something going on, and she got the feeling he was getting rid of her so they could talk openly about it, not so Dad could be all pastoral and *there, there!*

'Come on, let's go back,' Michael said, heading to the door.

Dad scowled after him and Poppy couldn't help rolling her eyes. *Oh, that's right! You don't want me here, but you don't want me behind a closed door with the guy you've known since he was in flaming nappies either.*

She sighed and, in silence, followed Michael out.

Once back in the study, Michael flopped into one of the brown easy chairs and propped his feet on the ringed and scuffed coffee table. Poppy took the other chair and mirrored his pose. She leaned her head against the backrest and closed her eyes. Her head hurt, she was cold and she couldn't erase the memory of the words on the note.

Who will be next?

She hugged her arms over her chest, tried to beat

back a shudder and failed. She heard movement and opened her eyes to see Michael disappearing into his room. He came back a few seconds later with the quilt off his bed, laid it over her and tucked it in until she was cocooned up to the neck.

'Thanks.'

He smiled, rubbed his eyes and then squinted like he couldn't see properly.

'You should take out your contacts.'

'Yeah. Won't be a second.' He retreated to the bedroom and then reappeared a few minutes later wearing the square-framed tortoiseshell glasses she'd persuaded him to get. They really suited him, even if he did hate them.

He retook his seat and put his feet on the table next to hers. He still had on his interview outfit; navy blazer over the same coloured sweater and white shirt. He hadn't worn the tie his mother had made him pack, as she knew he wouldn't. He even still had on his blue and red striped scarf. And with the glasses... Jesus! Could he get any more preppy? He should have got through his interview on fashion alone.

'What are you thinking?'

She realised she was smiling. 'I was thinking how well you fit in here.'

'There was more to it than that.'

She shook her head. 'Nope, that was pretty much it.'

He smiled, but two seconds later he was looking

serious again. He was going to want to *talk* and she just couldn't. It already felt like there was a pneumatic drill pounding away at her skull. She closed her eyes again.

'Pops?'

She pretended not to hear. Something nudged her feet.

'Hmm?' She reluctantly opened her eyes.

'What were you looking at in Ria's room?'

She sighed, sat up and pushed down the quilt. 'That note that was left outside her room, I think it was from the murderer.'

'What?' Michael's feet slipped from the coffee table, he leaned forward and rested his elbows on his knees. 'What did it say?'

'It said something like, *Danny was the first to get his wings, I wonder who'll be next.*'

'Get his wings?'

'Yeah. What's all the angel stuff about? I just don't get it.'

'Maybe it's something to do with the society.'

Poppy shrugged. She reached under the duvet, grabbed her phone from her pocket, opened the search engine and typed in *Cambridge* and *angels*.

The 3G signal wasn't great, probably because the walls of the college were three foot thick, but eventually her search brought up a list of 10,500,000 results. That wasn't going to work. It would take forever to go through them. She looked through the first few pages.

'Anything?' Michael asked.

'There's a tech company. Could that be it?'

'Not unless it's a student company.'

'Don't think so. I'll try finding information on societies.' She typed into the search engine *Cambridge societies*. That brought up a very helpful directory of university clubs, but how was she supposed to know which one she was looking for?

'There's hundreds of the damn things; African Prisons Project, War Gaming Society...nothing with angels.'

'Try searching *Cambridge, society* plus *angels*,' Michael said, reaching for his own phone.

She entered the search terms and waited.

And waited.

'Damn stupid phone!'

Suddenly, the page loaded. The first hit was a Wikipedia entry on something called the Cambridge Apostles. She opened the page only to be faced with a picture of a familiar domed fountain beyond which was Trinity College Chapel.

'Bingo,' Poppy whispered. Her heart picked up speed and her fingers suddenly felt too big to be able to navigate the small touch screen.

'You on the Wikipedia page for the Cambridge Apostles?'

'Yeah.' She scrolled down and read the text. The Cambridge Apostles were a secret society, sometimes referred to as the Cambridge Conversazione Society, founded in 1820 by someone called George Tomlinson.

The Apostles sounded innocent enough – it was basically an exclusive debating society whose members fancied themselves to be a cut above the rest of the students. When they met someone would give a talk and then the members would vote on a question. The society was nicknamed the Apostles because originally there had been twelve of them.

It all sounded a bit dull, until she got to the bit that said that although the active undergraduate members were called Apostles, those who had graduated were referred to as Angels.

Poppy sat up. 'Michael, old members are called Angels.' The note had said Danny had been fitted for his wings. Was that the biggest graduation of all – death? 'This has to be it.' She continued reading. 'Members swear an oath of secrecy and when they join have to hear a curse read that says they'll die if they ever reveal the identity of the other members.' That couldn't have been taken too seriously over the years, because the Wikipedia entry also contained a list of former members.

'I've heard of these guys,' Michael said. 'That's it. Burgess was a member.'

'Who?'

'Guy Burgess was a student here – he went on to work for MI6 during the Cold War, but it turned out he was a double agent, spying for the Russians along with some of his friends from Cambridge. They called them the Cambridge Spy Ring.' Michael flopped back in his chair like he'd been hit by a sledgehammer.

'What?'

'It could be coincidence, but at my interview I somehow got sidetracked into talking about the Cold War and I made a crack about the Cambridge Spy Ring. Professor Madigan said I shouldn't believe everything that had been said about the subject. It was like she knew something.' He sat up and rested his elbows on his knees. 'Y'know, Conal was being really nice to that Yaser guy. They were planning a trip to a strip club.'

'Nice.'

'Why would he be doing that if Ria thinks Danny was killed because he didn't want this guy at the party?' Michael typed something into his phone. His eyes darted up. 'Shit. Yaser's dad is the Saudi Arabian Foreign Minister. That can't be it, can it?' He laughed. 'You don't think Conal's working for MI6?'

Poppy snorted. 'He can't be. He's only a few years older than us.'

'People get recruited at university all the time. Maybe Conal's been trying to get information out of

Yaser and Danny tried to block it.'

'You really think MI6 had Danny killed?'

Michael shrugged. 'Nah. It's probably just a weird coincidence.'

'I don't think MI6 would send threatening notes.'

'No. Unless Ria's picking up where Danny left off. Trying to block Yaser from joining the Apostles.'

It sounded like something from a film. 'Did you see the bit about the book that contains a list of members? Wasn't Conal going on about a book being missing?'

Michael nodded. 'If the killer has that book it means he knows the names of all the Apostles and all the Angels.'

'This is too weird,' she murmured, skim-reading the webpage again. Her eyes fixed on the word 'whales'.

'The traditional meal at meetings was sardines on toast, nicknamed "whales".'

Whales.

The invitation on Dad's mantelpiece had been for sherry and whales. She stopped breathing. She had known he was involved somehow, and now she knew how. It made perfect sense. He didn't like talking about his days at Cambridge but she knew he was ridiculously smart. Like, genius smart. Add to that his public school background, and he was the perfect candidate for the Apostles. Was he being threatened too? Was that why he was being so cagey?

'Dad's one of them.'

'You can't know for sure.'

'There was an invitation in his room, said that they were serving sherry and whales. He's one of them. He was at the party with them. Remember, he had a dinner suit on. I knew Dad knew something.'

'Something about what?' a voice said.

Dad leaned against the doorway and folded his arms.

CHAPTER TWELVE

Michael wasn't sure how much Jim had heard, but he was guessing he'd heard enough.

'Are you in trouble?' Poppy asked. 'Is someone threatening you?'

'What?' Jim laughed, but it sounded strained. 'No. Why would you think I'm in trouble?'

Poppy pushed the quilt onto the floor and sat forward. 'Ria got a threatening note, and either someone's got a really sick sense of humour or it was from Danny's killer.'

Jim sighed, walked in and closed the door behind him. 'Ria showed me the note. She didn't say that she'd shown it to you too. I suspect it's just a sick joke like you said, but I've told her she needs to talk to the police.'

'And is she going to?'

'I left a friend with her. He's going to call them. Look, I'm really sorry that this has happened. I really wanted to spend time with you, but with everything that's going on, I want you out of here. First thing tomorrow, I'm putting you both on a train home. But tonight you're coming to stay with me, Poppy. Go and get your stuff together.'

Poppy leaped to her feet. 'What? No!'

Michael had expected something like this. There was no way Jim was going to leave them alone for another night. Apparently that wasn't going to stop Poppy from being outraged about it.

Jim laid a hand on her shoulder. 'I'm not going to argue with you over this. Someone was killed last night.'

Poppy shrugged him off and folded her arms. 'But it's OK to leave Michael here by himself?'

Jim winced. His eyebrows drew together. 'Have you been drinking? Michael, has she been drinking?'

Before Michael could answer, Poppy stepped in front of him, drawing Jim's glare back on herself like a soldier drawing rifle fire from the rest of the platoon. 'Excuse me? Why are you asking Michael when I'm standing right here? Women didn't chain themselves to railings so that a hundred years later you could blame my boyfriend for stuff I've done like I'm not responsible for my own actions.'

'I'll take that as a yes,' Jim said, wryly.

'Admit it, you don't want me to stay here because you don't want me and Michael being alone. Like we can't be trusted.'

Jim folded his arms, mirroring Poppy's pose. 'Can you be trusted?'

'*Yes.*'

Poppy and her dad glared at each other. Michael couldn't help smiling. Honestly, the two of them had no idea how alike they really were. Michael quickly straightened his face when Jim glanced in his direction.

'That's not what it looked like this morning,' Jim raised his eyebrows. 'It looked to me like you'd taken advantage of the fact that I didn't know how much your relationship had changed.'

'We've not done anything wrong,' Poppy yelled, her voice rising to fever pitch. 'Besides, what we do is none of your business.'

Jim laughed, but he didn't sound all that amused. 'I see. And just how long *exactly* have you been going out?'

'Four months.'

'Four months. *Four months?* You really think it's appropriate to have sex four months into a relationship? Shit!' Jim swore, rubbing his forehead.

Poppy shifted her weight from one foot to the other, like a boxer waiting to land the fatal punch. 'What? Are you afraid I'm going to show you up in front of all of your holy friends? Are you going to stick me in a convent until I'm thirty?'

'This has nothing to do with—'

'—How long did you know Mum before you slept with her? I thought it was like three weeks!'

Jim put his hands on his hips. 'Do you really want to make the same mistakes that we did? Because you cannot think that I'm going to sit by and watch you ruin your life.'

Michael sat up. That was it. That was why Poppy had freaked out last night. She was afraid that history would repeat itself – that she'd end up pregnant like her mum had when she was a teenager. That's why she was talking about needing to go on the pill…that's what that whole 'fracking' conversation had been about. But that wasn't the only thing that was going on here.

'You're right.' Michael muttered.

'What?' Poppy gasped.

Michael cleared his throat and got to his feet. If Jim was going to punch him for what he was about to say, he at least wanted the option of ducking. 'We didn't have sex, but it did go further than it should have.'

Jim took a deep breath and squeezed his eyes shut. When he opened them again he still looked mad…but less like he was going to put Michael through a wall.

'I'm sorry if we violated your trust, Jim. But you violated Poppy's trust too.'

Jim's eyebrows drew together. 'What?'

She was going to hate him for saying this, but someone had to. 'Every time you make plans to see her and then cancel at the last minute you break her heart.'

He felt, Poppy's cool fingers close around his wrist. 'Michael, don't.'

'She won't say it, because it's easier for her to get angry than it is for her to cry. She thinks I don't notice because she always has an excuse – too much homework

157

or she's coming down with a cold – but every time you cancel on her she holes up in her room for a week and barely speaks to anyone, even me.'

Jim's shoulders sagged. Pain flashed through his eyes. 'Is that true, Poppy?'

'He's exaggerating.'

'No. I'm not.'

'Shit.' Jim ran a hand through his hair and shook his head. 'I never meant for us to… I didn't mean to hurt you, Poppy. I had to cancel last time because there was a hearing and if I didn't show up I'd have lost my job.'

'What?' she muttered, her face full of concern.

Jim shook his head. 'It's fine now. It was a misunderstanding. But if I had known it was going to upset you so much I would never have cancelled my visit. To be honest, you always sounded so relieved when I cancelled that I thought you didn't want me there. I don't like that we don't talk any more. I hate that you're in a serious relationship and I didn't know. I hate that I've missed so much.'

CHAPTER THIRTEEN

Poppy closed the door on Dad and double locked it the way he'd shown her. Michael had flopped back in his seat, eyes closed, one hand pressed against his forehead, and his legs stretched out in front of him.

She stepped over his legs and sat on the coffee table in front of him. After a few seconds he opened his eyes and his lips pulled up into a half-smile.

'So…I think I took your dad's mind off us sleeping together.'

She snorted. 'Yeah.'

Michael sat forward and grabbed her hands. He rubbed his thumbs over her fingers. 'Do you think you can forgive him?'

She nodded. 'Aren't you worried I won't forgive you for—'

'—Trying to fix things?' His eyes were red, and he looked kind of exhausted. He shook his head. 'I'm not worried about that. I think you can understand the impulse to want to fix things…Bob.' He smiled.

Poppy smiled. 'So…you forgive me for talking to Fiona?'

'What do you think?'

She stood up and tugged on his hands. 'Come on. Bedtime.'

He let her pull him to his feet. She walked backwards, leading him to her room.

He laughed. 'If your dad—'

'—I mean to sleep.' She let go of one of his hands and opened the door.

As the door swung open she froze. The entire contents of her backpack had been emptied over the bed and the backpack itself was on the floor.

'Sodding hell! Did you have to make such a mess?' she gasped.

'*Me?*'

She put her hands on her hips. 'Yes, you! Did you have to dump everything out of my bag?'

Michael's eyes widened. 'I didn't.'

She turned back to the bed. 'You really went through everything.'

'Honestly, Poppy. I didn't do this. Everything was still in your bag. Really. I just took what was on top, like you told me to. I didn't empty your bag. Someone else has done this.'

That didn't make sense. 'Someone's been in here. *Someone's been through my stuff*?' She felt sick at the thought of someone going through her things. 'Crap! Where's my computer?' She launched herself at the bed and grabbed at the nightie and T-shirt that lay on top of her pile of belongings.

'It's OK,' Michael said. 'It's under here.' He held up the silver laptop.

'Why would someone go through my stuff... Unless – Dad?'

Michael slumped onto the bed. 'Jim wouldn't do that. You're sure there's nothing missing?'

'I don't think so. Why would someone go through my stuff and not steal anything?'

'I think we should call your dad.'

'No.'

'Poppy, someone's been in here, and with everything that's going on...'

If she told Dad someone had been in her room he'd panic. And besides, there was someone else she did want to talk to. 'I want to call the police.'

Michael's eyebrows shot up. 'Really?'

'If this Cambridge Apostles thing is so secret that Dad won't tell the police about it, then I think we should. If someone's threatening them he's in danger too. Plus, I haven't heard any movement out there. I don't think Ria called the police.'

'You're right, you should call them. You maybe want to leave out the part about MI6 otherwise they'll think you're some weird conspiracy theorist.'

'No kidding.' Poppy felt in her pocket and pulled out her phone, and with it the detective's business card. She hesitated. It felt weird, going behind Dad's back, but if she didn't do something and someone else died, she wouldn't be able to live with herself. And if Dad was in danger...

She dialled the number and pressed the phone to her ear. After a couple of rings a voice barked, 'Dalca.'

'Umm – hi. This is Poppy Sinclair. You interviewed me this morning.'

The detective's voice softened. 'Poppy, yes, I remember. What can I do for you?'

'Has a girl called Ria been in touch with you?'

'I spoke to her this afternoon. Why do you ask?'

'You know she was Danny's girlfriend?'

'Yes, I do know that.'

'She hasn't been in touch about the note?'

The detective was silent for a moment. 'What note?'

'She said she would call the police.'

'What was in the note, Poppy?'

'It said something like...*Danny's been fitted for his wings, I wonder who'll be next.*'

There was a scuffling noise. 'When did she get this note?'

'Just this evening.'

'No one's called that in. I'll go and speak to her now. Thanks for calling me, Poppy. You did the right thing. Can we talk properly tomorrow?'

'Umm...yeah, sure.' Her gaze met Michael's. He nodded in encouragement. 'But there's something else.'

'Go on.'

Poppy took a deep breath. *Tread carefully*. 'Have you heard of a society called the Cambridge Apostles?'

'Go on,' the detective said again. Talk about noncommittal. This woman wasn't going to give anything away.

'I got to thinking about the way the guy was posed – the way the murderer had smeared the blood to look like wings. I thought it must be significant. I know that this is none of our business, but I did a Google search and I found the student society called the Apostles. When the members graduate they call them Angels. Do you think someone could be going after the group? Whenever people talk about Danny, they talk about him like he's a member of something. I...we...could be wrong, but I think he was an Apostle.' Poppy forced herself to stop talking before she said too much.

There was a long silence. Oh God! She braced herself for the bollocking the policewoman was probably going to give her for interfering.

'Hello? Are you still there?' Poppy asked, when she could stand it no longer.

'Yes. Sorry, Poppy. Can we meet tomorrow?'

'Umm – yeah, of course.'

'Great. In the meantime, if you think of anything that might be significant, anything at all, I want you to call me right away.'

'OK.'

'Tell her about someone being in here,' Michael said.

'What was that?' Detective Inspector Dalca asked. 'Who's that with you?'

'It's Michael. Um, this probably sounds a bit weird, but I think someone's been in my room – been through my things.'

'Has anything been taken?'

'Not that I can tell.'

'It could just have been a cleaner but we'll talk tomorrow.'

'OK.'

'Poppy, are you and Michael staying together tonight?'

'Yeah.'

'Good. I've got people round the college so I don't want you to worry, all right? Just make sure your door's locked and try to get some sleep, Thanks for calling, Poppy. I'll see you tomorrow.'

Poppy cut the call and threw the phone on the bed, alongside her other belongings. 'Ria hadn't called. They're gonna send someone out to see her.'

'You did the right thing.'

'Hope so.'

Michael looked at the mess. 'I suppose we should clear this up.' He got up and put the laptop on the desk then fetched the rucksack from the floor.

'I'll do it,' she said, taking the bag from him.

He slumped back on the bed and watched while she stuffed things back in her rucksack. The book on Tarot cards she'd brought was tucked under her maths textbook; she grabbed the two together, hoping Michael wouldn't notice, but as she did, his hand reached out and grabbed the small package wrapped in a piece of red silk.

'Umm…that's just—' She tried to swipe them out of his hands, but he was too fast. Giving her a strange look, he unwrapped the red silk, revealing the Tarot cards. His eyes widened and flashed up to hers.

'Why?' he asked.

She shrugged.

'That stuff you said this morning in the Dean's office about not being atheist any more, you weren't just winding me up, were you? Are you getting into this stuff again?'

She'd been brought up going to Pagan rituals and festivals, and in a house full of statues of Goddesses and Gods of all cultures, but after Dad had left she'd been so angry that she'd pushed it all away…and yes, she'd been kind of rampant in her rejection of religion. Just recently she'd experienced a few things that made her wonder, but she certainly wasn't ready to tell anyone. Especially not Mum…she'd throw a party.

'Poppy?'

'No…I'm…' She sighed. 'It's nothing really. Just something I was curious about.'

'OK.'

'I'm not about to start dancing naked around fires or anything.'

Michael pursed his lips. 'That's a shame.'

She laughed. Michael carefully wrapped the Tarot cards in the red silk and handed them back to her. She quickly shoved them in the bag, hoping that was the end of the discussion.

Out of the corner of her eye she saw him grab something else. 'But these,' he said, waving the packet of condoms. 'These I want to know about.'

CHAPTER FOURTEEN

The scritch-scratching noise sounded like the time a pigeon had got stuck in the chimney at home.

Poppy's eyes flew open. Her hand tightened around the corner of the pillow as she tried to keep her breaths even and forced herself to stay still. Michael's hand slid down her side and rested on her hip. She listened harder, past the soft whooshing sound of Michael's breathing. There it was again. It really did sound like a bird. Maybe they'd left a window open and one had got in. Or it was stuck in the wall somehow.

Slowly, she slid from under Michael's arm. He grunted and turned onto his back, and the arm that had been wrapped around her flopped over his eyes. Nothing looked out of place, and the noise seemed further away now, like it was coming from the corridor. Bugger. That wasn't a bird. It sounded like someone trying to pick a lock – what if someone was trying to get in? Maybe she should wake Michael. No. This was probably her being completely paranoid – she wasn't going to wake him for that.

Nevertheless, her heart pounded in her chest as she crept across the room and, quietly as she could, turned the lock and opened the door. The study was in darkness. She looked from shadow to shadow. There was no one there.

As she edged further into the study, she noticed that Michael's door was open. Oh God, what if someone had got in? She slowly pushed on the door until she could see the whole room. Bed...chair...the light from Michael's computer blinking on and off like a heartbeat. No one there.

She sighed. Maybe she'd dreamed it. Except, there it was again...like fingernails scratching against one of the doors further down the corridor. Her breaths grew shallow as she crept towards the door and wrapped her fingers around the cold brass of the handle. Biting her lip she slowly twisted it and cracked open the door.

All the lights in the corridor were out, all except for one: the broken light. The one that flashed on and off like a nightclub strobe. In the brief flashes she saw that the corridor was empty. She sighed with relief. Yup, she was just being paranoid. The noise was probably rats inside the walls – not a pleasant thought but a darned sight better than a lurking killer.

She took one last look. The light flashed off. The corridor was soaked in darkness. But in that darkness she saw a human-shaped shadow. She tensed, but when the light flickered on again there was no one there. She rubbed her eyes. Just a trick of the light. Jesus! What was wrong with her head?!

But as darkness fell again, she saw him, clearer

this time, pacing towards her, dinner jacket flapping, blood staining his white shirt. She knew him. But it couldn't be…

Danny?

She stumbled back, sending the door slamming into the wall. This time when the light flicked on he was still there, his eyes wide and desperate, reaching a bloodstained hand towards her.

'*No…no…no!*'

Just as the dead guy's fingers reached her arm, Poppy screamed.

CHAPTER FIFTEEN

The scream echoed through his dreams, shattering sleep like glass falling from a broken mirror. Michael bolted upright, his heart hammering in his chest. It took a second to realise it wasn't a dream – someone was screaming. *Poppy.*

He leaped out of bed but his foot caught in the duvet and he crashed to the floor. He grunted as pain shot through his hip. He scrabbled to his feet and darted into the study.

Silhouetted against the light flashing in from the corridor, Poppy punched at the air, screaming like she was fighting someone off. He slammed on the light and pulled her to him.

'No! No! Let me go!' Her fist crashed into his chest, her other hand just missed his face.

'Hey – hey!' he said, grabbing her arms and pressing them to her sides. 'Poppy, wake up! You're dreaming.'

Her eyes connected with his at last, wide with terror. Her head swung back to the corridor and then her gaze darted around the study. 'Where did he go?'

'Where did who go?'

Down the corridor a door swung open. Michael instinctively hugged Poppy to him, but it was Ria who came running down the corridor wearing the same black silk robe he'd seen her in before, looking panicked. Conal raced after her.

'What the hell's going on?' he shouted.

Poppy squirmed out of Michael's arms. She looked like she was on the verge of panicking again and so he let her go. She cleared her throat, gasping for breath, and stared at the floor. 'I'm – I'm sorry. I thought I heard somebody out here and then I saw...'

'What did you see?' Conal demanded.

Poppy shook her head. 'Nothing. I saw nothing.'

'If you didn't see anything, why were you screaming the place down?' he blurted.

Ria shoved Conal and glared at him.

Michael felt his blood pressure rise. 'She couldn't help it. I think she was sleepwalking.'

'Well, can she sleepwalk in your set? Don't you think we've had enough to deal with without her screaming the place down like she's being murdered?'

'Conal, enough!' Ria snapped.

Conal ran his hand through his hair and glanced back down the corridor.

Ria edged closer to Poppy and took her hand.

Poppy jerked against Michael. He wrapped an arm around her and rubbed her shoulder. She was shaking.

'What did you see, Poppy?' Ria asked quietly.

'N-nothing. Michael's right. I must have been asleep.'

'Then what were you dreaming?'

'I saw…' Poppy shook her head and turned her gaze back to the floor.

Michael didn't believe that she didn't remember, and by the look on Ria's face, neither did she. But Ria didn't push it.

'Will you be OK?' she asked gently.

Poppy nodded. 'I just wanna go back to bed. I'm sorry if I woke you all.'

'Don't think we were meant to sleep tonight,' Conal said. 'Police haven't long gone.'

Poppy's gaze darted up to the older guy, her eyes suddenly alert.

'Come on, Conal, let's go,' Ria said. Letting go of Poppy's hand, she pushed him towards the door.

Then Ria stopped. 'If you see anything you need to talk about, just give me a knock.'

Poppy's hand slipped into Michael's. He squeezed it reassuringly. It was almost as if she was afraid of the girl.

'Night,' Michael said. He tugged Poppy with him to the door, shut it and clicked the lock into place.

'Are you OK?' he asked.

She nodded, but she couldn't seem to stop glancing around as if she expected someone to jump out at any moment. The fingers of her right hand worried the shiny black stone that hung around her neck, the one that the Native American medicine woman had given her. The small piece of obsidian was meant to protect her – if you believed that shit – but as far as he could see it did sweet fuck all.

'What did you see?' he asked again.

'You're probably right. I was just dreaming. I suppose with everything that happened yesterday… seeing the guy and all… makes sense I'd end up having nightmares.'

It was the logical explanation. But he knew when Poppy was lying.

'What did you dream?' he asked, playing along.

She shrugged, still not looking at him.

'Poppy, tell me. It'll help. Break the dream and all that.'

Her eyes searched his as if unsure how he would react. 'I heard a noise. I thought someone might be trying to get in here, or break into Ria's room. When I opened the door there was no one there, but then…' she blinked and shook her head. 'Was I really dreaming? Felt like I was awake.'

Michael ran a hand over her tangled strawberry blonde hair and brushed his fingers over her cheek. 'What did you see?'

'It was him. The dead guy. He was coming at me.' She turned her face up to his and shook her head. 'I must have been asleep. Must have been.'

CHAPTER SIXTEEN

Poppy felt Michael's finger trace lazy shapes on her cheek as they lay, waiting for morning. Spirals and stars. Letters and symbols. It was something they'd done since they were four or five and they'd seen a deaf woman. Michael had been fascinated by her sign language, but the thought of either of them going deaf had terrified Poppy so much that she'd cried. They didn't know sign language. How would they play? How would they talk? Michael had taken her hand in his and with a grubby finger he'd drawn letters on her palm. 'That's how we'll talk,' he'd told her.

She'd never have guessed that eleven years later he'd be lying in her bed, sharing her pillow, still talking in their secret language. She closed her eyes and concentrated on the tickling movements of his finger.

I ♥ U

The fact that he'd said it before didn't stop the breath from catching in her throat. She smiled and moved her hand from where it was tucked against his chest and drew on his T-shirt:

I ♥ U 2

Michael pressed a kiss to her forehead, glanced at his watch and sighed. 'It's probably time to get up.'

She didn't want to. They'd been awake most of the night and now her whole body ached like she'd run several marathons. She just wanted to stay there with Michael. Warm and safe.

NO, she drew on his chest.

'OK, but if your dad finds us in bed together again you know there'll be trouble.'

He had a point.

After some cajoling by Michael, she got up, splashed some water on her face in hope of waking herself up. When Michael went back to his room she took the opportunity to dress in as many layers as she could find in her rucksack. There was no way she was having a shower. She'd rather smell skanky than risk the chance of a Psycho-type nightmare in the bathroom down the hall.

The sound of voices in the study made her stop still. Dad must have arrived. She wrapped her arms around herself, not wanting to go out there. Seeing him so upset last night had made her realise how horrible she'd been to him. Yes, he'd got stuff wrong, but so had she.

There was a soft tap on the door.

Poppy took a deep breath before opening it.

Dad's eyes were red. Bronze stubble shadowed his chin and cheeks. Clearly he hadn't slept either. But today he was wearing jeans, walking boots and his old black all-weather jacket. He looked more himself. He looked more like her dad than the stranger she thought he'd become.

His lips pulled up into a sad side-smile and his brow wrinkled. 'Hey, Pops.'

Poppy smiled, but her throat was too tight to respond.

Dad pulled her into a tight hug and kissed the top of her head. 'I hear you didn't have such a good night.'

Oh God. Michael had told him what had happened. But what version? The one where she'd sleepwalked, or the one where she'd seen a dead guy when she was wide awake?

He rubbed her arm. 'Come on. Food, shot of caffeine, and then there might be time for me to show you the sites of some of my misdemeanours before your train.'

She pulled out of his arms. 'Misdemeanours? I thought you were the model student.'

He smiled, but lines of tension were drawn around his eyes and mouth – he looked about as worried as she'd ever seen him. Was someone threatening him? Had he had a note like the one Ria was sent?

'Got your keys?' he asked.

She patted her jeans pocket. 'Yeah.' She grabbed her phone from the bedside cabinet, shoved it in her other pocket, hooked up the scarf Dad had lent her and followed him out.

Michael smiled and held out his coat to her. 'I know it'll drown you, but it's better than nothing.'

'I'm OK. I've got, like, four layers on,' she said, tugging at the bulge beneath her hoodie.

'Where's yours?' Dad asked.

'The police still have it.'

'Oh. Yeah. Well, let me get you a new one. There's an outdoors shop round the corner from where I thought we could go for breakfast. We should have time to pick something up.'

The three of them trooped into the hallway and waited in silence while Michael locked the door.

'It's icy out there this morning,' Dad said as they traipsed down the stairs. 'So watch yourself.'

When Poppy stepped out of the archway into Great Court, a sharp wind whipped the breath out of her lungs. She buried her face in Dad's scarf and concentrated on placing her feet between the patches of ice. They had got almost to the corner of the quad when someone started screaming.

All three of them stopped and stared around.

Poppy's pulse picked up speed. 'Where's it coming from?'

'I can't tell,' Dad said.

On the other side of Great Court, two porters were running along the path, away from the lodge, towards the steps that led to Nevile's Court.

'What's going on?' Poppy asked.

Dad shook his head. 'I don't like the look of it.' He squeezed her shoulder. 'You two wait here.'

Dad set off at a pace and followed the two porters up the steps and disappeared in through the archway. Poppy darted after them.

'Poppy, wait!' Michael shouted.

She couldn't stop. She ran up the steps, almost tripping on the last one, and darted past a couple of shocked-looking students, through the wood-panelled walkway, and out the other side.

She caught sight of Dad heading between the pillars of the cloister to the left and chased after him, Michael following close behind.

The cloister opened out onto another courtyard. The much plainer buildings were built in a pinky-coloured sandstone that mirrored the pink and purple sky of the new morning. Most of yesterday's snowfall had melted, but at the centre of the lawn a cushion of perfect, untouched white encircled a massive tree. Hanging high in its branches wasn't a birdfeeder or Christmas lights, but a full-sized bicycle.

Lucy was sobbing into the chest of the guy they'd seen with Ria and Conal that first night when they'd arrived at the college. He stroked the girl's back and whispered into her hair. Dad ran a hand over his face and stalked over to them.

'Go away, Jim!' the guy said.

'Devon, I'm...'

'She doesn't need a priest right now. None of us do,' the guy said.

Poppy couldn't work out why Lucy was crying – the bike in the tree was weird, but hardly something to get upset about. Then two of the porters moved, revealing a snow angel. It seemed that someone hadn't been able to resist making their mark on the snowy lawn after all. Where the wings had been carved out, bright red paint had melted the snow, right the way back to the grass leaving what looked like pools of blood.

Michael's arm slid around Poppy's shoulders. 'That's a really sick joke.'

But was it a joke, or a warning?

Dad wandered over to them and sighed. 'I'm sorry, guys. It looks like I need to deal with some stuff here. Can you go and find breakfast yourselves and I'll catch up with you in a little while? Your train's at eleven.'

CHAPTER SEVENTEEN

Michael glanced at Poppy. Her hand felt like a small block of ice in his. She really wasn't dressed for the weather despite having said she was fine. She was so lost in thought that as they walked through the passageway back to Great Court he had to steer her around the fluorescent yellow cone warning of the growing puddle left by people traipsing in snow. He wondered what had her so consumed. After last night she was too tired and strung out to be thinking clearly about anything.

He still wasn't convinced that what he'd seen had been a straightforward nightmare. He'd have known if she'd experienced something like it before. He was almost certain that if Poppy hadn't told him then her mum would have mentioned it. And as far as he knew, sleepwalking wasn't something that started when someone was nearly seventeen.

They passed groups of students in a hurry to get to hall before breakfast ended, out of the passageway and down the steps into Great Court. Poppy's eyes flicked up and caught his.

Her cheeks reddened. 'What?'

He let go of her hand and wrapped his arm around her shoulders. 'I didn't know you sleepwalk.'

She blinked and turned her eyes to the icy pavement. 'I don't normally.'

'So it's never happened before?'

She shook her head.

'You're sure?'

'I'm pretty sure, but I suppose I would have been asleep at the time, so maybe I don't remember it.' She grinned at him, but it was half-hearted.

He wasn't buying it. 'You didn't look asleep.'

She stepped out of his hold and glared at him. 'I don't know what you want me to say, Michael!' After a second her face fell. She sighed and shook her head. 'I'm sorry, I didn't mean to shout.'

He watched the struggle going on behind her eyes. Any second now she'd try and change the subject but he wasn't done yet. 'Last night you didn't seem all that sure that you were asleep.'

She ran her hand through her hair. 'But I must have been. You've had dreams that feel real, haven't you?'

'Yes.'

'That's all it was.' Her fingers slipped beneath the college scarf that was wrapped around her neck and, although he couldn't see it, he knew that she was fiddling with the small black stone that hung there.

He got the feeling she didn't think she had been asleep at all. He got the feeling she thought she'd seen a ghost. Except, he didn't believe in all that stuff, and for the last few years, neither had she. But working on the principle that ghosts didn't exist, that could only mean that the *ghost* had been a product of Poppy's imagination. He didn't know what it took to get someone to the point of seeing things, but he was sure it wasn't exactly normal.

'Come here,' he said, slipping his arms around her waist.

She resisted at first, but then her body moulded to his and she tucked her head under his chin as he wrapped his arms around her. His mind turned over possible causes. Stress? Mental illness? She nearly drowned a while ago, what if that had left her with some kind of brain damage or epilepsy? He needed to persuade her to see a doctor.

'Can we just go back to the room?' she murmured.

'Sure.'

As she stepped out of his arms he caught hold of her hand. 'I'm worried about you,' he said, quietly.

She tried to smile. 'Don't be. It was nothing. I'm OK.'

The problem was, every time she said that, he believed it a little less.

CHAPTER EIGHTEEN

Poppy washed her hands in liquid soap that smelled like it ought to be put down toilets rather than onto skin, and dried her hands on her jeans. She hadn't actually needed the loo; she'd just wanted a couple of minutes away from Michael's worried glances. He hadn't actually seen the dead guy, but he seemed even more freaked out about it than her. She opened the bathroom door to the sound of more voices than she'd ever heard on the corridor.

'I was just there…it was so horrible!' said a voice with a French accent. 'Who would do such a thing?'

As Poppy eased into the corridor, all four people turned and looked at her. Ria, wearing the long black dress with billowing sleeves again, was draped over Conal like a cat on a hot rock. Lucy was still being comforted by the same guy as before.

So here they were – the Apostles, or at least some of them.

Ria straightened up and brushed her hair back from her face.

'This is Poppy, Jim's daughter.'

The guy with Lucy cocked his head to one side, flipped the tail of his bright green scarf over the shoulder of his fitted blue hacking jacket, and gave her a long hard look. 'You're right, she does look like him. Same eyes. And that's just how Jim's hair would look if he ever went Highlander.'

'Actually, he had long hair for quite a while,' Poppy said. 'I think he thinks he needs to look more respectable now.'

'He may *look* more respectable…'

'Devon!' Lucy warned.

At that moment, the door at the other end of the corridor opened and out came Michael.

'Hi.' He threw Poppy an uneasy look.

'Well, it looks like we have ourselves a wake. About time we gave Danny the sendoff he'd have wanted,' Ria said, opening the door to her rooms. 'Come along, everyone. Poppy, as you were the last person to see him, you will be our guest of honour.'

'I don't think…' Michael began to say, at the same time as Lucy said: 'I'm sure they have other places to be.'

'Actually, why not?' Poppy ignored Michael's glare. Was he kidding? This might be their one chance to get to know something about these guys from the inside.

Ria's room seemed to have collected even more empty bottles than the last time Poppy had been there.

'Conal, get the chair from my bedroom while I make tea,' Ria said.

Conal saluted and disappeared into the bedroom.

'I'm afraid there still won't be enough chairs. You'll have to sit on the floor,' she said to Devon.

'I don't mind a bit. I'm sure Michael won't mind sitting beside me.'

'Oh, yeah, OK,' Michael said.

Lucy touched Poppy's arm. 'You'll have to excuse Devon.' She winked and her wide green eyes sparkled with humour.

'Don't listen to a word she says,' Devon said. 'In fact, you should come and sit beside me too. I want one of you sweet young things on either side.'

'That wouldn't exactly be a first,' Conal said, heaving a slightly ratty brown velour armchair out of the bedroom. He dumped it beside the desk and flopped down into it.

Ria rolled her eyes. 'It wasn't for you, arsehole.'

'Come, come, lovelies. Sit with Uncle Devon.' Devon waved Poppy and Michael over to where he'd sprawled on a pile of cushions next to the makeshift altar in the corner.

This guy was a hoot. She glanced at Michael and he shrugged.

They sat on either side of him and Devon put his arms around them like they were bosom buddies. 'Did I hear mention of tea, Ria? A Darjeeling special, I hope?'

'It's coming.' She turned to Conal, who had grabbed

his gangster hat from the desk and tipped it over his eyes as if he intended taking a nap. 'Arsehole, get up and let Lucy sit down. For heaven's sake, do something useful and give out the cups.'

Conal slumped out of the armchair, onto his knees in front of Ria. He tipped his hat back and stared up at her. 'I am your humble servant, mistress.' He grabbed Ria around the waist and buried his face in her stomach...either biting or kissing, Poppy couldn't tell which.

Jesus! Were they...together? She thought Ria was meant to have been going out with Danny.

Ria cuffed Conal over the head. 'Get up!'

'Yes, mistress, anything you say, mistress.' Conal bowed, his hands pressed together like he was paying homage to a goddess.

Ria rolled her eyes and went into the bedroom, leaving Conal to get on with giving out delicate china cups and saucers, the kind that made Poppy very nervous. The same kind that she habitually broke whenever she visited her very snobby grandparents.

Poppy took the cup and saucer and placed it carefully on the floor in front of her. Nothing bad could happen to it if she wasn't touching it.

Michael caught her eye and smirked.

'Now, what's going on between you two?' Devon asked, squeezing them to his sides. 'We'll have none of your young lover secrets here.'

'It's nothing,' Poppy said.

'Poppy doesn't have the best record with bone china,' Michael said, tossing his cup in the air, and catching it one-handed.

Show-off.

'Then we'll be sure to keep an eye on her. And what a pretty eyeful she is.'

Poppy almost laughed when she saw the look on Michael's face. Really, he couldn't possibly be bothered by a comment like that from Devon. Surely he understood which of the two of them Devon was more likely to be interested in.

Ria came out of the bedroom with a teapot in each hand. As she poured for Lucy, Poppy could have sworn she heard a fizzing noise. When Ria got to her, she held up her cup and saucer. She nearly dropped them when she realised that the teapots did not contain tea.

Ria gave her an amused look. 'What's the matter? Afraid Daddy won't approve?'

In defiance, Poppy raised her cup to Ria. When the cup had been filled she downed the contents in one, wincing as champagne bubbles fizzed up her nose.

'That a girl,' Ria said, refilling her cup.

As Ria continued, Lucy smiled at Poppy from across the room. 'So, Poppy, are you applying for Cambridge?'

'Umm, no. I think I want to go to Manchester, but I

'don't have to decide just yet.'

'Good redbrick, Manchester,' Devon said, nodding his approval.

'But I thought you were visiting...' Lucy looked confused.

'Michael has applied to King's for History. He's the smart one.'

'Don't listen to her,' Michael said, giving her an exasperated look. 'With her grades, she'll be able to go wherever she wants the year after next.'

Lucy smiled. 'Does that mean you're only...what? Sixteen?'

For some reason Poppy felt herself blushing.

Devon gasped dramatically. 'Sweet sixteen and never been kissed! I'd be honoured to put that right.' He puckered up.

'That's already been taken care of,' Michael said.

'I bet it has,' Devon replied, squeezing Michael's knee.

Poppy couldn't help laughing at the stunned look on Michael's face.

Ria tapped a spoon against a teacup, getting everyone's attention. 'To Danny,' she said, raising her teacup. 'Wherever you are, we miss you.'

'To Danny,' everyone echoed, taking a sip of their drink.

'If you're all third years, do you know what you're doing next year?' Michael asked, when their cups had been refilled again. Poppy hid her smile behind her hand. She knew where he was going with this one.

'We're all doing postgraduate degrees,' Lucy said. 'Me and Devon are going to Harvard.' She shot Devon a big grin. 'Ria's staying here. Only Conal's joining the real world.'

'Oh yeah?' Michael pressed. 'Have you got a job to go to?'

'Me?' Conal glanced up as if he hadn't really been listening to a word anyone had said. 'Yeah, I've got a job with the Foreign Office.'

'Sounds interesting,' Michael said lightly, as Ria scowled at Conal.

Poppy stole a glance at Michael. He scratched his forehead to hide his raised eyebrow. So Conal was a spy. Wow. He didn't look very James Bond-y, although he had the kind of eyes that gave very little away.

Seeing as they were all feeling so chatty Poppy thought she'd try her luck. 'Are you guys all members of some kind of club?'

Conal coughed and spat an entire mouthful of champagne over Ria. Poppy bit back a grin. Maybe he should consider a different career after all.

Lucy frowned at Conal before turning to Poppy. 'Why do you ask that?'

Poppy shrugged. 'Someone said something about Danny being a member of a society, but I didn't catch what it was.'

She looked up and caught Ria staring at her. The expression in her eyes would make a glacier look warm. Ria poured herself another cup of bubbly and downed it in one. She cleared her throat. 'I know what we should do. We should have a séance.'

'No,' Lucy said, sighing, as if this was a regular suggestion.

'No!' added Conal with a little more force.

'What do you say, Devon?' Ria asked. 'You're normally up for a bit of table tapping.'

'It does seem a little distasteful, Ria, dear.'

Ria laughed. 'Oh, so just because Danny's dead we're meant to suddenly become good children and live by the rules, is that it? Do you think he'd want that? Do you? Imagine if he was trying to get in touch with us and we didn't even try to open an channel.' Her gaze fell on Poppy. 'What if he's trying to find a way to talk to us?'

Poppy's breath caught in her throat. Did Ria know what she'd seen? How? She felt a pressure on her shoulder. It was Devon, using her and Michael's shoulders to push himself up. He stumbled over to Ria and pulled her into a hug. 'Dearest, don't be getting all screamy in front of the young ones; you'll scare them.'

Devon stepped away from Ria, smoothed down her hair and smiled. Then he turned to the rest of them. 'Up, everyone. Let's move the furniture back so we have plenty of space.'

Poppy could feel Michael's stare before she turned to him.

'Can I speak to you for a moment?' Michael said – his voice low and threatening. 'Out there.' He nodded towards the door.

'Fine. We'll be right back,' Poppy said, shooting the others a smile.

She followed Michael to the door. He held it open and then followed her out onto the corridor. Thankfully, someone had fixed the freaky light, but with her head a bit fuzzy from champagne, she couldn't help shuddering and glancing around just to make sure there were no dead people lingering in the hallway.

'Don't do this,' Michael said, capturing her eyes with his. 'This is crazy, Poppy. Ria's upset, she's not thinking clearly, and – just so we're straight – neither are you.'

Poppy took a step back. His eyes were bit unfocused, but he was serious. Worse, he was really mad with her.

'Why are you so angry with me?'

'I'm not angry with you. I just think we should go. Your dad said the train was at eleven. We can still make it.'

'No. We haven't seen the detective yet. I said we'd be here. Plus, these guys might know something. They're getting pissed in there. They're bound to slip and say something.'

'Is that really why you want to stay in there? Or do you want to stay because you think this séance thing might work?'

'Of course not.'

'Look, you had an awful shock yesterday. It was bound to screw with your head. And if you really think…if you've changed your mind about all the supernatural stuff, then I'm OK with that. You know I'll support you whatever. But don't do this.'

'Nothing's going to happen. It's just a game, Michael.'

'For them, maybe. What is it to you?'

'I don't know what you mean.'

Michael took a deep breath and looked away. He shook his head. 'You need to talk to someone.'

'What?'

He took hold of her hand and squeezed it. 'Your mum. Maybe Jonathan.'

Jonathan? Her stepfather was a psychotherapist. Jesus! He thought she was losing it because of last night. 'That's ridiculous!'

'Last night you were so scared.'

'It was a nightmare.'

'You're lying to me.'

'I'm not.'

His hand slid into her hair and tugged her head back so that she had no option but to look at him. His wide eyes held her gaze fiercely. 'I thought you trusted me.'

'I do.'

He kissed her, gently...teasingly, until her head felt as if all the champagne bubbles had collected there. She felt dizzy and with each breath he sucked in, she felt like she was losing another tiny bit of her soul to him.

Her heartbeat ticked in her throat, getting quicker and quicker.

She pushed her hand against his shoulder and tried to push him away, but he wasn't giving in, and the longer he kissed her, the more she wanted to give into the kiss herself.

He spun them around until her back was pressed up against the wall and she was pretty sure that his mouth and the wall were the only things keeping her upright.

Michael stepped back and stared into her eyes. His chest heaved in and out, and she could tell he was nearer to losing control than he had been when they'd been naked in his bed.

'Don't go back in there,' he pleaded.

'Why don't you want me to do this? It's just pretend. You don't believe in this and neither do I.

Nothing's going to happen.'

'I think you believe in it more than you're willing to admit to me, and I think it's screwing with your head.'

'I grew up with this stuff. I think any screwing that was going to be done must have already happened.' She thought about what she'd just said and grinned. 'Wow, that came out wrong, huh?' She laughed, hoping he'd laugh too. He didn't.

'I don't trust them.'

She couldn't bear to look into his angry blue eyes any longer. She turned away. 'You mean you don't trust *me*.'

'Not at the moment, no. Talk to your mum, talk to your dad. Just talk to someone before you do something like this.'

She shook her head.

Michael sucked in a deep breath and stepped back. Shit! Why did that one move tear the flipping heart out of her chest?

'Don't be angry,' she said, her body automatically following his down the corridor towards their set. He took the key from his jeans pocket and opened the door.

'I can't help how I feel, Poppy. If you're going to go through with this charade then go and do it. But don't expect me to like it or watch it.'

'Michael, don't be like this,' Poppy whispered.

Part of her screamed to follow him through that door and pick up where they'd just left off. But what if Danny was trying to get in touch? She'd seen him twice. If it wasn't his ghost…if the things she was seeing weren't real…

She had to find out.

Poppy shuddered as she walked back into the study. Ria had pulled the curtains closed and lit the candles on the makeshift altar. A strong heady incense was burning and if she wasn't already feeling slightly disorientated after Michael's very worthy attempt to persuade her not to do this, she would have felt dizzy after a lungful of whatever was smoking out the room.

Her head felt hot and heavy. She unwrapped Dad's scarf from around her neck and fingered the small piece of obsidian at her throat. This was going to be OK.

Everyone except for Ria was sitting on the floor around the edge of the room, leaning against furniture. Conal was picking at his nails, looking bored. Devon looked like he was trying to perfect his lotus position.

'No Michael?' he asked, sounding more than a little disappointed.

Poppy shook her head.

Lucy was sitting next to Devon, fidgeting with the

fraying seam of her jeans. She looked up and gave Poppy a tight smile.

'Come and sit down here, Poppy.' Ria had moved the coffee table from the middle of the room. She sat down cross-legged on the rug and indicated for Poppy to sit opposite her at the centre of the circle.

Poppy hesitated. Hold on a minute, why was she in the centre? If this was a magical ceremony, the guys on the edge of the circle would be feeding power into the centre. The centre was not a place she wanted to be. She looked back at the door, wishing Michael were there. Nonetheless, she sank down to her knees and clumsily crossed her legs.

'Now give me your hands,' Ria said, holding out her own hands, palm up.

Poppy took a deep breath and took the girl's hands.

'Close your eyes, Poppy, and try to relax. They can't speak to you unless you relax.'

'They'll be speaking to everyone else too, right?' she said, with a nervous laugh.

'Ria, I think Poppy should sit with me,' Lucy said.

'Don't be silly, Lucy. Poppy is our guest of honour. It's only fair that she gets the best seat in the house.'

Right. Nausea curdled her stomach. She closed her eyes and took a few deep breaths. Just as she settled uneasily into the silence, the door slammed open.

Poppy's heart shot into her mouth. She gasped and snatched her hands back from Ria.

Michael towered over them and he wasn't looking happy. Nonetheless, he sat down beside Lucy.

'You can't be here,' Ria said.

'Why not?' Michael asked, just as testily.

'You don't believe in this shit. You'll fuck it up.'

'You're right, I don't believe in this shit. But as long as she's here, so am I. Deal with it.'

An amused smile spread across Ria's face.

'I do like a man who can take charge,' Devon whispered, like a naughty schoolboy.

The muscles in Poppy's chest contracted and her eyes watered. She blinked quickly before moisture could turn into tears. She had no idea why she'd want to cry, but the fact that he was still willing to be here with her set the strangest pain deep in her heart. But she was happy. How could happiness hurt like that?

Ria rolled her eyes. 'If you're going to stay, you have to keep quiet, whatever happens. Bringing someone suddenly out of a trance state can be dangerous.'

Trance? No one had said anything about going into a trance. She'd never been in a trance, apart from maybe that one time in the Native American sweat lodge, and then all hell had broken loose.

Ria grabbed her hands again. 'Close your eyes, Poppy.'

Damn, she should have asked more questions before

agreeing to this. Michael was right – with Ria in charge anything could happen.

Ria raised an exasperated eyebrow.

Too late now. She'd have to go along with it. She just had to make sure she stayed awake. No trances. No nothing. She took a deep breath and forced her eyes shut. But now her heart was racing so fast that she thought it might vibrate its way out of her ribcage.

'Take slow, deep breaths,' Ria said in a whisper.

Ria squeezed her fingers in a slow pulsing rhythm, and before long, Poppy realised that her breath had conformed to the pattern and she was starting to drift again. No!

For a second she panicked, but then she remembered that Michael was sitting a couple of feet away. This was all a load of rubbish. She couldn't talk to the dead. Michael was right. She was in shock. Didn't mean there was something wrong with her. Her psychotherapist stepdad was always treating people for shock.

Poppy concentrated on slowing her breathing again. Even if she didn't believe in this crap, she had to make it look like she was making an effort.

After a while, the slow breathing and the darkness became weirdly hypnotic. She felt herself slipping deeper inside herself, until Ria's hold on her hands didn't feel real any more, nor the floor beneath her or the air she was breathing. The only thing that felt real was this free-floating part of herself that seemed to strain at the boundary of her skin. She hovered there for a while but nothing happened. She could see nothing and hear nothing, except for the whooshing of air.

Then something snapped.

Lights rushed by her, like she was speeding through a tunnel or falling. Was she falling?

A picture formed before her – confusing as a badly pixelated TV, it flickered on and off, giving her glimpses of colours...green, brown and a deep black that pulled her in. It was water...lake water...she was drowning...

No! Please, no!

The picture shifted and suddenly she was in a different place. It was dark except for the moonlight that flooded in through the arched windows somewhere up above. She was running – her shoes squeaking against a tiled marble floor.

She was in a chapel. Oh God...Oh God, no!

Pain blinded her and she fell. She forced herself onto her back in time to see eyes filled with despair and pain, anger and betrayal.

'I am his avenging angel!' a voice hissed.

Pain bloomed in her chest...it was too much! She was dying. She was really going to die this time.

She became aware of hands stroking her hair and a familiar voice just out of range of her hearing.

'Poppy? *Poppy!*'

She opened her eyes. It was still dark, and she could still feel the pain like a hot poker had been driven into her heart. She gasped at the air, but couldn't seem to force enough of it into her lungs.

'Poppy, look at me!'

The eyes staring down at her were different from before. These eyes were familiar and full of concern.

'Call someone. Call her dad.'

'No. Just give her a minute. Poppy, you can come back now. Come back to us.'

Slowly, the room came into focus: the flickering light of candles, the swirling screensaver on the computer screen, and Michael's worried hands stroking her hair and face.

'Poppy?' he whispered.

'Hi,' she said, her voice hoarse, like she'd been screaming for hours. Had she screamed? She didn't remember screaming.

Michael sighed, leaned down and pressed his forehead to hers. His warm breath brushed against her cheek.

'How do you feel?'

Floaty…like she wasn't quite inside herself…like a part of her was somewhere else.

'I need air.' She felt as though she might hover out of the room rather than walk.

'What did you see, Poppy?' Ria asked.

'Is she all right?'

Poppy tried to sit up, but Michael's arms tightened around her shoulders.

'Poppy?' another voice prompted.

'Leave her alone,' Michael growled. 'Don't you think you've done enough?'

Poppy shifted until she could see Ria, kneeling beside them.

'What happened?' Ria asked. 'What did you see? I know you saw him last night...you were calling his name.'

Poppy pressed her hand to her ribs where the pain still ached. Her head whirled with the mixed-up memories, not sure what was real and what had happened in her head. Tears bled down her cheeks. What was going on? Why was she crying?

She pushed at Michael's arms until he let her go and stumbled to her feet.

Lucy caught her arm before she could fall. The French girl stared at her like she was some kind of monster.

Michael's hand grabbed her other arm. 'You need to sit down for a minute.' Even in the poor light given out by the flickering candles she could tell Michael was scared shitless. What had happened? What had she said?

No matter. She needed out of there. She needed air. She couldn't breathe with all this incense clogging her lungs.

She headed for the door, Michael's hand holding her steady. Ria got there first, blocking the way. Her eyes were wild. She looked like a tiger preparing to pounce.

'You *have* to tell me what you saw, Poppy. Did you see him? Did you speak to my Danny?'

'What did you do?' Poppy shouted. The words slid from her throat like they weren't even hers – like her body had been hijacked by another mind. 'What did you do, Ria? How could you do that? How could you…'

Ria's mouth dropped open. 'I'm sorry, Danny,' she gasped. 'I'm so sorry.'

Ria reached for Poppy's face, as if to take her cheek in her hands. Poppy staggered backwards, away from the stretching fingers, the blood-red nails.

Michael lunged, shoving Ria away from the door.

'Don't you touch her!'

'But…?'

'I mean it.' Michael stepped forward, advancing on Ria. For the first time the older girl looked scared.

'Hey!' Conal said, putting himself between Michael and Ria.

Michael threw the guy a disgusted look, then turned back to Poppy. He put his arm around her shoulders, opened the door and pushed her out into the corridor. The bright light made her squint. The floor wobbled beneath her feet as another wave of agonising pain cut through her stomach. It felt so real. She pressed a hand to her sweatshirt to make sure she really hadn't been stabbed. There was nothing there, so why could she feel it? She bent over and tried to breathe through the pain.

Michael forced her upright. His eyes searched her face. He was terrified and looking for her to tell him what had happened. But she had no answers to give him.

'I just need some air,' she gasped.

He nodded.

Before they got to the door leading to the landing, Poppy heard a slam and the sound of footsteps.

'How is she?'

They turned to find Lucy had come after them. She squeezed Poppy's shoulder, her eyes creased with worry.

'Your friends are idiots,' Michael said.

'You're right. It was a stupid thing to do.' Lucy's hand slid down Poppy's arm and took hold of her hand. 'Poppy, there's something I need to tell you. Something about your father; can we talk?'

Poppy wondered what this girl could have to tell her about her dad. 'Um—'

'—Not now,' Michael said, before Poppy could agree. 'Can't you see what a state she's in?'

Lucy dropped Poppy's hand and nodded. 'Of course. I'll find you later.'

Michael opened the door and helped Poppy down the stone steps of the stairwell.

As soon as she felt the chill of winter air against her cheeks she started to feel like she could breathe. It was such a relief that she began crying again. She could see the pure white snow beyond the pathway. She wanted that cleanness...she wanted to feel like that, to feel unblemished by blood and hurt and pain.

She collapsed down to her knees and buried her hands in the snow, not even minding the cold that bit at her fingers.

'Poppy, you'll freeze.' Despite her protestations, Michael crouched down beside her and tucked her head against his chest.

Quick footsteps headed in their direction.

'What's wrong? Is she ill?' a man's voice said.

'I'm not sure,' Michael replied.

'I'll get someone to call her dad.'

Poppy dragged her fingers through the snow, tracing patterns that her numb fingers could no longer feel. That was what it had felt like – to be there, but not there; to feel things, but not feel them.

But it was all in her head, right? Did that mean she was going crazy?

Michael caught hold of her fingers and folded them within his own. His skin burned against hers.

She looked up into eyes, clouded with worry, and suddenly she realised where she was and what she was doing. She was sitting on snow! Freezing cold water had seeped through her jeans and was freezing her ass off. 'Oh God!' she muttered and pushed herself up from the ground. 'My jeans are soaked.' She strained to see the big wet patch covering her bum. 'I look like I've wet myself.'

Michael was watching her; his hands stretched out ready to catch her. Was he afraid she'd fall or run?

Blood rushed to her cheeks as she realised just how badly she'd freaked out.

Someone was shouting. Shouting her name, in an American accent:

'What's going on? Poppy, what's wrong?'

CHAPTER NINETEEN

Michael realised Poppy was staring at his outstretched hands. He shoved them in his jacket pockets.

'Poppy, what's wrong?' the Dean repeated.

Poppy's eyes, red from crying, darted up to his, looking for help. He had to resist the automatic urge to cover for her. They'd been making up excuses for each other since they were kids, but not this time. He was just as keen as the Dean to hear her explanation of what had just happened.

Bea took hold of Poppy's arm. 'Poppy, you're soaking. Come on, come inside.'

'We need to find Jim,' he said. Her dad needed to see how freaked out she was. If he didn't, Poppy would twist the story until it sounded like nothing. And whatever had happened back there was not nothing – no matter what she said. There was something badly wrong with her, and he wasn't about to sit back and watch.

'What? No. Don't bother Dad,' Poppy protested. 'I'm fine.'

'You're not *fine*.' He had to take a breath to give him time to even out his tone. 'You passed out in there. That's not fine.'

She glared at him, and for the first time in a long

time, he saw real fear in her eyes. 'You're totally overreacting.' She shook her head. 'Honestly, I think I just got too hot…and maybe you're right. Maybe it's stress or something.'

Oh, so now it's stress. Could she hear herself? Shit. He really shouldn't have let her go back in there after what had happened last night.

'I'll go and find you something to change into,' he said, as she began walking with Bea.

She spun around. 'No. I don't need anything. This'll dry.' Her eyes pleaded with him. She knew him too well. She knew what he really planned to do. But he wasn't giving in to her this time.

'I'll be two minutes.'

Bea guided Poppy into the staircase that led to her office before she could make any more objections.

Michael waited until they'd disappeared through the archway before he pulled out his phone and called the only person who might get through to her.

'Michael? Is everything OK?' Poppy's mum asked, the second she picked up.

'Hi, Meg, we're fine, I'm just…What am I saying? We're not OK. I'm worried about Poppy.'

'What's wrong? I thought you'd be on the train by now.'

Michael ran a hand over his face. How was he meant to explain what had just happened? 'We're still in Cambridge. Poppy got pulled into doing some kind of séance type thing. This girl, the student whose boyfriend died, she got it into her head that Poppy could contact him. I tried to stop it, but you know what she's like. The thing is, she freaked out really badly. She just wasn't there any more, Meg. It's not the first time. She was seeing stuff that wasn't there last night. She said she saw the dead guy. I don't know what to do.'

'Where's Jim?'

'I don't know. He had some work to do.'

'Never mind. I'll call Jonathan; we'll hit the road just as soon as he gets back.'

Some of the tension in his stomach unknotted. 'Good. Thanks. I'm sorry to…'

'I'll talk to you in a bit. Just…just take care of her, Michael.'

'I'm trying.'

CHAPTER TWENTY

Poppy wandered around the study while the Dean put the kettle on. Her hands were still shaking from the cold and she couldn't seem to keep still. The photograph of her dad and the Dean's son caught her eye. She headed over to it.

'How are you feeling, Poppy?' Bea asked.

'I'm fine.'

Bea's face cocked to the side. She raised an eyebrow. 'What happened out there?'

Poppy shrugged. Was that what a panic attack felt like? Or was it…? *No, not going there!*

'How did your son die?' she asked, quickly, before any more questions came her way.

Bea's mouth dropped open. 'What?' She sighed. 'Lance was… He…he took his own life.' Her voice was muted. But when she looked up and caught Poppy's eye, the Dean's face was stiff with old, unending pain. 'How did you know he was dead?'

That was a good question. How did she know that? 'Someone must have said something.'

For a moment, the Dean stared at her in confusion. Then it was gone.

'Sit down,' she said.

'I don't want to get anything wet.'

'It's only water, Poppy. Sit down before you fall down.' She did as she was told and slumped into one of the armchairs.

The Dean finished making tea and put a mug into Poppy's hands. After the snow, the hot china scalded her fingers. The tea slopped over the side, splashing her knee and burning her. She jumped and dropped the mug. It landed on the carpet in one piece, but the tea seemed to go for miles.

'Oh, Poppy,' Bea said, grabbing handfuls of tissues from the box on her desk.

'I'm so sorry,' she gasped. 'Let me.'

A firm hand held her in the chair. 'It's only tea, Poppy.'

She could do nothing but sit there while the Dean blotted her jeans with tissues and then made her another cup of tea. This one, Bea put on the table next to her.

'There. Now what were we talking about?'

'You were saying about your son.'

'Oh yes...Lance.' Bea wandered over to the window and looked out over the college. 'He came here desperate to fit in. More than fit in. He wanted to be in with the in crowd. He'd read Evelyn Waugh and seen *Chariots of Fire*, and he wanted to live a life that only really existed in novels and in his head. Champagne tea parties and punting down the river, talking about great art and literature. When he first arrived – he was so happy to finally be in England, to be in Cambridge, he'd call me at Yale, where I worked back then, and tell me all about the wonderful time he was having. But then part way through his first year, things started to go wrong for him. There was a boy I think he had a bit of a crush on and he desperately wanted to be like. But then that boy was initiated into a new group of friends and Lance felt left out.' The Dean shook her head and sighed. 'Such small things make or break a life. Lance was broken by shattered dreams.'

'Have you forgiven him?'

The Dean spun around and for a second stared at Poppy with some of the same desperation she'd seen in Ria's face. 'That's a very perceptive question, Poppy. Yes. I have forgiven Lance.' Her expression darkened. 'I find it harder to forgive those who caused his pain, but I'm...trying. In the end forgiveness and justice is all there is.'

'Do you think he's happy now?'

Bea's face crumpled with pain but she nodded. 'I do.'

Poppy picked up the mug of tea and carefully rested it on her knee. 'Do Christians believe that you can talk to people after they've died?'

Bea's mouth dropped open.

There was a loud knock at the door that made Poppy jump, again spilling tea over her jeans.

'Come in,' Bea called.

Michael's head appeared around the door. He was

looking calmer than before, which meant he'd spoken to her dad. 'Sorry about that,' he said, looking at the Dean, and very definitely avoiding eye contact with her.

'I thought you were going to get me a change of clothes,' Poppy said.

'Oh, er…yeah, sorry. I forgot.'

'Then what were you doing?'

'Nothing,' he said quickly. Too quickly. He sat down in the chair next to hers and muttered thanks to the Dean when she passed him a mug of tea.

Poppy glared at him. 'What did you do?' She knew what he'd done, but by God she was going to make him admit to it.

'What do you mean?' He turned to her, and she could see the guilt there in his eyes. He swallowed. 'If you won't talk to me, I'm going to make sure you talk to someone about what's going on.'

'It was nothing!'

He shifted in his seat until he was facing her. 'Like hell it was nothing.'

'Would someone care to enlighten me?' Bea asked.

There was another knock on the door. It was flung open and her dad rushed in, eyebrows creased with anxiety. Poppy sank deeper into the chair's upholstery. Dad strode across the room and crouched in front of her.

'What's going on, Pops?'

She shook her head.

Dad looked over his shoulder at the Dean. 'Bea, would you mind if I had a moment with Poppy? Sorry to chuck you out of your own office.'

Bea glared at him, but then nodded. 'Come on, Michael. I'll take you for a tour of the old part of the college.'

Poppy kept her eyes on the rippling surface of her tea as Michael and the Dean left. As soon as the door shut, Dad took the mug from her hands and put it on the table.

'Poppy, what happened?'

'I'm just tired, Dad.' She stared at the floor.

Dad put his finger under her chin and raised her face to his. 'Who were you with?'

'Ria and a couple of her friends.'

'Which friends?'

'Lucy and Conal and Devon.'

At their names, Dad's eyes narrowed. He cleared his throat. 'I don't think hanging around with them is such a good idea.'

'OK. I won't do it again.'

'I also don't think it's such a good idea to be mucking around holding séances when you're drunk.'

'I wasn't drunk.'

'No?'

'I didn't have that much.'

Dad squeezed her hand. 'Tell me what happened.'

'Obviously Michael's already told you.'

'Actually, your mum told me. So far, I've only had it third hand. I'd like to hear it from you.'

'He called Mum?' She'd kind of known that Michael would try to find Dad, but why had he called Mum?

'Stop avoiding the question, Poppy.'

'I just freaked out, that's all.'

'Like you freaked out last night?'

She took a deep breath and nodded.

'Has this happened before?'

She hesitated. 'No.'

'Poppy, why are you lying to me?'

'I don't believe in…the supernatural. You know that! This is yours and Mum's thing, not mine.'

'That's what I thought. So tell me what happened.'

Poppy shrugged. 'I think I might have fallen asleep. Ria had the curtains closed and incense burning and I was tired. I think I just fell asleep and started to dream. I must have been thinking about what happened to Danny. That's hardly a surprise, is it?'

He frowned, his eyes still sceptical. 'You always did have very vivid dreams.'

'That's all it was, Dad: a nightmare.'

She could tell by the worry in his expression that he didn't believe her, but he took a deep breath and nodded. He took his phone out of his pocket. 'You go and find Michael. I'm going to call your mum.'

Despite feeling like she'd been run over by a bus,

Poppy sprang out of the chair, glad to be given permission to leave the interrogation room.

She got almost to the door when Dad said, 'Poppy?'

She turned to face him.

'Don't hold this against Michael. He's worried about you. If it were him, you'd have done the same thing.'

The problem with this damn college was that there were no benches – nowhere to just hang around and wait. Poppy stared around Great Court; the golden-coloured stones seemed to hold their own kind of heat, because despite the biting edge to the wind she was so hot she felt sick. And even though she knew that there were plenty of ways out of the college, the place felt sealed off from the rest of the world, as if once you stepped through the Great Gate, the ancient buildings claimed you for themselves. The weight of all that history was just damned oppressive – she had no idea how Dad could work here and stay sane. She'd only been here a couple of days and already she felt like she was losing it.

Poppy wandered slowly around the pathway, towards the chapel with its dark windows and castle ramparts. There were no police guarding the entrance now, but the doors were firmly shut. They couldn't keep it closed indefinitely, but she couldn't imagine that when they finally let people back in there they would be thinking about God as they walked across the threshold. They'd more than likely be looking for blood-smears on the marble floor… and the boy whose eyes had been wide with terror and pain.

She swallowed back the sudden nausea that accompanied the memory of that pain…that feeling of utter hopelessness…of not being able to do anything but to give in to the gaping black hole that was death.

'Poppy, are you OK?'

She realised her eyes were squeezed shut. Poppy forced them open and nodded.

The organ scholar, Chrissie, was beside her. She squeezed Poppy's arm. 'What's wrong?'

'I just keep seeing him,' Poppy said before she could stop herself.

'That's understandable.' Chrissie gave her a sad smile. 'You know, sometimes it helps to go back to a place and see it as it is, without…without the death.'

It made a kind of sense, but she didn't know if she could go back in there. What if it triggered worse memories?

'Let me talk to the porters and see what they say about people being allowed back in there.'

'You don't have to do that,' Poppy said, stepping away from Chrissie. The alarm in her voice caught the attention of three Italian tourists and their guide, who were now eyeing her like she was part of the tour.

'It's no problem. I won't be a minute.'

She watched Chrissie hurry away down the path and disappear into the porter's lodge. She could leave – just walk away. Some time by herself would be good. She could probably get her head together if people would stop asking her if she was OK.

Too late. Michael and Bea turned around the corner of the clock tower. She hadn't even noticed that there was a break in the buildings there. They were deep in conversation and it took a moment for them to notice Poppy.

'Hey.' Michael walked forward and caught hold of her hand. He squeezed her fingers but his face remained serious and he didn't even pretend to apologise for going behind her back to her parents.

'Where's your dad?' Bea asked, looking around.

'He'll be down in a minute. He just needed to make a call.'

The Dean nodded. 'Ah, Chrissie, what can I do for you?'

Chrissie's face filled with colour. 'I've just asked if one of the porters can open the chapel so Poppy can go in there.'

Michael let go of her hand and turned to face her. 'Why would you want to go in there?'

'I don't... I didn't...'

'I'm sorry. That's out of the question,' the Dean said, glaring at Chrissie.

Chrissie folded her arms and stared at the ground. 'I

just thought it might help,' she muttered.

'I think Poppy can do without that kind of help.'

Poppy got the impression that she'd unwittingly become a blade of grass in a long-running turf war.

'There's your dad,' Bea said, nodding to the opposite corner of the court. Weird. She'd left him in Bea's office, how the heck had he come out over there? They waited in silence as Dad took the central path that led directly to the chapel steps.

'I've got quintet practice tonight, but maybe after that you and Michael could come out for a drink with me?' Chrissie asked Poppy, shooting Bea a cold smile.

'Umm…yeah, maybe,' Poppy replied.

When Dad reached them, he immediately put an arm around Poppy and smiled.

'Hi, Chrissie. How are you?'

Before the girl could answer, they were distracted by two porters bolting down the path from the lodge to the archway where Dad had just come from.

'What on earth is happening now?' the Dean said, beginning to walk in that direction.

They all followed. When someone screamed, Dad let go of Poppy and began running. She followed, straight across the snowy lawn. At the archway, Dad whirled around and pointed a finger at her.

'Stay there!'

Poppy nodded, but the second he disappeared into shadow, she darted after him.

The archway led onto a corridor that had various doors off it. She spotted daylight to the right and ran towards it.

'Poppy! Wait!' It was Michael, hard on her heels.

She ignored him and ran on. A doorway opened onto another court, smaller and less grand than the one she'd just come through. Two paved levels were divided by ten or twelve steps and surrounded by what looked like modern halls of residence. Lying at the bottom of the steps was a girl.

Her long red hair looked dull in comparison to the scarlet blood pouring from the holes where her eyes used to be.

The air was punched out of Poppy's lungs. Her knees buckled. 'Lucy!'

'Michael, get her out of here now!' Dad ran and kneeled beside the girl.

She was alive? Poppy didn't know whether to be relieved or horrified.

Lucy cried and punched out at Dad, but he put a hand on her head and tried to hold her still. Oh God, she was awake…and feeling everything. Poppy's stomach churned.

'Sweet Jesus!' the Dean gasped, stopping beside them. 'OK, anyone who doesn't need to be here, get back to your rooms!' she shouted, to the growing crowd of people pouring out of doorways.

'Let's do as she says,' Chrissie said. She tugged at

Poppy's arm.

But Poppy couldn't move. She couldn't look away.

Someone ran past them.

Poppy recognised the blue hacking jacket and green scarf.

'No! No!' Devon wailed. 'Not Lucy! No!' He fell on his knees.

Dad tried to put a hand on Devon's shoulder, but he pushed it away. 'Get off me!' he screamed. 'She's my friend. She's my best friend.'

Lucy's bloodstained hands reached out at the sound of his voice.

'Talk to her, Devon. She needs to hear your voice,' Dad said to him.

Michael tugged Poppy's arm, and pulled her back through the doorway they'd come through, passing more porters on the way.

It had happened. It had really happened.

The threat contained in Ria's note had been carried out – the murderer had tried to kill another Apostle. Why Lucy? Of all of them, Lucy was... Her feet stopped moving – her legs seemed to have gone numb, but Michael urged her forward, out into Great Court.

The sound of an ambulance siren echoed around the walls. Poppy automatically reached for Michael even though he had an arm around her. He squeezed her hand and hugged her tightly.

'Come on, let's go inside,' he said, tugging her in the direction of M staircase.

Poppy planted her feet. 'I want to wait to see if she's OK.'

Michael sighed and gave her a look, but he didn't try to persuade her.

Poppy watched as two paramedics ran through the courtyard carrying packs of equipment. The sirens had brought faces to some of the windows, and a few students ventured into Great Court, huddled in coats and cardigans. Like a pack of wolves, they somehow knew that another of their own had been taken.

No one spoke above a whisper. It was as if the whole college was holding its breath, waiting to hear what terrible thing had happened within its walls today.

After five minutes more, several uniformed police officers bolted from the lodge to the same doorway everyone else had gone through. Then another two paramedics hurried across the court, wheeling a stretcher between them. They were followed by yet another group of people, one of whom she recognised at Detective Inspector Dalca. The woman's shoulder-length blonde hair streamed out behind her as she hurried to the new…murder scene? Could anyone survive those injuries?

Michael tugged her hand again. 'You're going to freeze if we stand around out here. Your dad'll come and find us when he's done.'

She nodded, and was about to give in to the tugging on her hand when the paramedics reappeared, wheeling the now occupied stretcher. She saw bandages and a flash of red hair.

That was good, right? If they were taking her to hospital, it meant Lucy was still alive.

Dad reappeared, escorted by Detective Inspector Dalca. The two of them headed in their direction.

'What happened?' She dropped Michael's hand and ran to meet Dad and the detective.

Dad was as white as a sheet. 'Poppy, I want you and Michael to go home now.'

'Actually, I need them to stay,' the detective said. 'You're welcome to move them elsewhere in Cambridge but this is a major investigation and Poppy is a witness. In fact, Poppy, I'd like to talk to you again now, if that's convenient?'

'You can come back to my rooms,' Dad said. 'But then I want them out of here.'

The detective eyed her. 'Why don't I buy you a coffee? You look like you need a warm drink.'

'I was just going to take them, you'd be welcome to join us,' Dad said. He moved ever so slightly into the detective's eye line, as if trying to draw the detective's gaze from her.

The detective shook her head. 'Thank you, Reverend Sinclair, but if you have no objections, I'd like to talk to Poppy alone.'

Dad looked like he was about to blow a gasket. 'I suppose…if it's OK with Poppy…'

'It's fine,' Poppy said, widening her eyes at Michael, who looked like he was about to lodge an objection. 'Really. I'll call you when I'm done.'

Dad and Michael glanced at each other. Neither of them was happy, but neither seemed able to muster a reason why she couldn't go.

'Seriously, guys. I'm going to have my very own police escort. I'll be fine. I promise I'll call you the minute I'm through.'

Dad sighed. 'OK. But I don't want you hanging around here by yourself. Call me the second…'

'I promise.'

'Are we allowed to leave?' Dad asked the policewoman.

'Yes. Officers have closed Angel Court until we can establish where the attack happened.'

At the word 'angel' Poppy gasped. Dalca's eyes darted to her, as did Michael's. Neither of them looked pleased.

'Reverend Sinclair, I'd like to talk to Poppy now. I'll return her to you very soon.'

'Fine,' Dad said. 'Come on, Michael.'

Poppy waited until Dad and Michael had reached the corner of the court before she blurted, 'There's an

Angel Court? Didn't you guys have people in there? So obvious.' She ran a hand through her hair. Why hadn't she remembered that there was a part of the college called Angel?!

'As a matter of fact we have a quite a few officers undercover. But we can't be everywhere, Poppy. I wish we could.' The woman touched her arm. 'Come on.'

The detective led her out through the porter's lodge where there were several uniformed officers, onto the street. They turned right, past the massive bookshop and various boutique windows all snazzed up with tinsel and baubles for the holidays. Poppy stuffed her hands into the pockets of her hoodie to stop them from freezing.

The policewoman stopped when they reached what looked like a church stuck between the shops. The sign said Michael House Centre and Café.

'It'll be quiet in here at this time,' she said.

Poppy followed her into what was obviously a converted church. Modern-looking tables and chairs were spread out across the floor and next to the till there was a wrought iron spiral staircase that led up to a balcony where there were more tables. Brightly coloured oil paintings of poppy fields were hung on every wall – it seemed to be some sort of exhibition – and to the right, behind glass doors, there was what looked to be a chapel.

'What would you like to drink?' the detective asked.

'Oh, umm, coffee, please.'

The woman smiled. 'Go and have a look around while I get the drinks.'

Poppy walked between the mostly empty tables, looking at the pictures. Weird that all the paintings were all of poppies, especially in a place called Michael House. She was actually kind of fond of poppies, despite her name rather than because of it, but seeing all that red only reminded her of Lucy's bloody eyes. She gravitated towards the chapel part and looked through the doors. Someone had lit candles on the circular stand, making the place look kind of alive, even if it wasn't much of a church any more. A part of her wanted to go in there and light a candle for Lucy; why, she didn't know. Maybe it was the only thing left to do for her. She'd been so nice...so normal compared to the others. Surely this did away with Michael's theory that MI6 were involved. People who worked for the government – even trained assassins – couldn't be that...cruel.

A statue caught her eye; it was of an angel, presumably the Archangel Michael. He had golden wings and held a sword against his chest. The whole of Cambridge seemed obsessed with the winged creatures. Why, when it felt like they flew around all the towers and steeples waging war against humanity?

The detective came up beside her holding a tray. She

nodded to the furthest corner.

'Let's go out of the way.'

Poppy slumped down on a chair. Detective Inspector Dalca put a steaming hot cup of coffee in front of her, as well as a plate of toast and jam each.

'Thanks.'

'No problem. Go ahead and eat.'

She wasn't sure whether the churning feeling in her stomach was revulsion or hunger pangs. She hadn't eaten all day, but... 'I don't think I can.'

'Try. You need to get your sugar up after the shock.'

Reluctantly, Poppy set about buttering her toast. The first mouthful stuck in her throat, but she added a dollop of strawberry jam and after that, it seemed to go down OK. She wiped the stickiness from her lips with a napkin and looked at the detective who was making short work of her toast.

'Do you know what happened? Was she conscious?'

The detective snorted. 'I shouldn't tell you anything.'

'But you're going to?'

'All she managed to tell us was that she was attacked at her room. When she came to she couldn't see. She managed to make it out of the building, but she fell down the steps and that's where she was found.' The detective's gaze dropped to Poppy's jam on toast.

The bottom fell out of Poppy's stomach. She dropped the toast back to the plate and pushed it away. Strawberry jam had been a big mistake.

'Is she going to be OK?'

'I'm not sure. She'd lost a lot of blood and she'd fallen unconscious by the time they took her away. We'll know in a couple of hours.'

'She's an Apostle.'

'How do you know that?'

'She's friends with Ria and Conal. I – me and Michael – got invited to the wake they were having for Danny this morning.'

'This morning?'

'Yeah. It was all very weird,' Poppy said, not wanting to go into the details of the special tea and séance.

The detective nodded. 'I can imagine. What can you tell me, Poppy?'

'I don't know. I would lay bets on Ria and Conal being Apostles. And there's a guy called Devon. He was the one with Lucy. But there must be more of them. Why did the killer gouge out Lucy's eyes? Why not just…kill her?'

The detective shook her head. 'I really don't know.' She sipped at her cup and then very purposefully put it back on the saucer. 'Poppy, your dad was a student here, wasn't he?'

'Yeah.'

'I think he knows something he's not telling me.'

Shit! Was this why she wanted to talk? She wanted her to inform on her dad? 'You have got to be kidding me.' Her voice echoed around the café.

'He knows something, Poppy. And I need to know what that is. Do *you* know what it might be?'

'*No.*' Damn. She'd said it too quickly, too defensively.

Detective Inspector Dalca picked up the teaspoon from her saucer and stirred the last dregs of her coffee. 'He was seen coming out of the chapel at about the time that Danny died.'

He was? 'He *works* there.'

The detective's phone rang. She touched the screen and held it to her ear. 'Yeah – really?' Her gaze flicked up to Poppy. 'Now that *is* interesting – Abdul's still on him? Then bring him in. Do me a favour and give Messenger a heads up.' She ended the call and slipped the phone back into her coat pocket.

Messenger? That was the person Dad was trying to get Conal to contact. 'Who's Messenger?' Poppy asked.

'He's the Chief Constable.'

This just kept on getting weirder and weirder.

'Why do you ask?'

Poppy shrugged. 'The name's familiar.'

Just then, Poppy's phone started buzzing. As she reached in her pocket to turn it off, the detective leaned forward. Her gaze caught Poppy's and held it.

'I'm just doing my job, Poppy. The best way for you to help your dad is to tell me everything you know.'

'What?' Her stomach clenched. Dalca made it sound like Dad was in real trouble. Serious trouble. Poppy frowned, breaking eye contact, and grabbed her phone out of her pocket. It was Michael.

Something had happened. She knew it. 'What is it?'

'Poppy, where are you?' Michael asked. The line was crackly as if he was facing into a storm.

'What's going on?'

'They – the police – they just arrested your dad.'

CHAPTER TWENTY-ONE

Poppy cut the call and jumped to her feet. Her hands were shaking. It wasn't fear, though, it was anger. Her attempt to stay calm lasted a split second.

'What kind of game do you think you're playing?' she shouted at the detective. 'There is no way my dad has anything to do with Danny's murder. You know what I think? You let Lucy get hurt and you feel bad about that and now you're getting desperate.'

'A witness saw your dad arguing with Lucy yesterday.'

For a moment she was stunned. It was true. Lucy was the girl who'd been with Conal when he and Dad had that spat yesterday afternoon.

'That doesn't mean he'd hurt her!'

'If he's innocent, he and you have nothing to worry about, Poppy. We just want to ask him some more questions.'

'You didn't have to arrest him to ask questions. Everything you have is circumstantial. What is it you're not telling me? And hold on a minute…you said Messenger is the Chief Constable?'

The detective frowned. 'I don't see what that has—'

'—He went to Cambridge?'

'I believe he did.'

'Trinity, by any chance?'

'St John's College, I think. What are you getting at?'

'Maybe you should take a look in your own backyard, Detective. I think you might find your boss is up to his neck in this.'

Poppy felt a tiny pang of satisfaction as she watched the woman's face go blank with confusion. She raised her chin and gave Dalca one last blazing look before whirling around and barging out of the café.

As soon as she got outside, the cold air stole her breath away. She stared around as people passed her by: students laughing and joking about, shoppers hunting for bargains. The snow had all but melted on the streets, leaving patches of black slush between the dirty brown cobbles. For a moment, none of it seemed real, as if she'd stepped back into that strange waking dream state of the night before. She felt dislocated, lost. She had to find Michael, but she couldn't remember where he'd said he was.

'Poppy,' a voice said, as a hand grabbed her arm. It was Dalca.

'Go away!' Poppy tried to shake the woman off.

The detective's brow was furrowed. 'Come with me,' she said, gently.

'Are you arresting me too?'

Detective Inspector Dalca let out an exasperated sigh, as if *she* was being awkward. 'No, of course not.'

'Then get your hands off me!' Poppy shouted,

drawing the attention of the passing shoppers.

Detective Inspector Dalca glanced around at the staring faces. She let go of Poppy and stepped back, a frown of frustration on her face.

Poppy turned and marched down the street.

'Where are you going?' the detective shouted after her. 'Poppy, you need to be somewhere safe.'

Poppy ignored her and ran.

Michael watched as the two coppers put Jim in the squad car. They had the lights flashing and everything. He felt utterly useless. He'd called Poppy just as soon as he'd realised what was happening, but now he didn't have a clue what he should do. He thought about calling his dad. Jim clearly needed a solicitor and his dad could probably help with that. Not that his dad liked Jim all that much – he'd heard him call Jim a hippy layabout waster before he'd gone and got himself a job at a Cambridge college. Soon as his dad heard that, he'd magically changed his mind about Jim. *Nice bloke. Always liked him.*

Michael's phone buzzed in his hand. He hit answer and pressed it to his ear.

'Where are you?' Poppy's voice was panicky.

'In front of the entrance to King's.'

'I'll be right there.'

He looked up and almost at once spotted Poppy

running down the street towards him. She had seen the police leading Jim to their car and was sprinting like an Olympian.

'No! Stop!' she shouted.

Michael grabbed her before she could do something stupid like drape herself over the police car.

'There's nothing you can do,' he said, tightening his hold as she struggled to break free. 'For fuck's sake, Poppy, calm down. This isn't going to help.'

Swearing seemed to have the desired effect. As the police car moved away, dodging cyclists and pedestrians, Poppy stopped struggling and instead rested her head on his chest. He hugged her.

'It'll be OK. He didn't do anything wrong, Poppy. He'll be fine.'

'They've got stuff tying him to the victims,' she said.

'What?'

She lifted her face to his and although her eyes were glazed with tears, they had that determined look that scared the shit out of him.

CHAPTER TWENTY-TWO

'We should probably find the Dean,' Michael said as they passed the three uniformed police guarding the main entrance to Trinity. Poppy nodded. She was so pale – it was as if she was fading away right in front of him.

Spotting them through the crowd, an old guy with a weatherworn face and white hair sticking out from under a bowler hat stopped them and ushered them into the porter's lodge.

'We've not met. My name's Mr Seddon, I'm the head porter.' The old guy shook hands with him and then Poppy. 'The Dean asked me to keep an eye out for you, so if you don't mind waiting here, I'll give her a call.' The porter went around the desk and picked up the phone.

'Poppy, what's going on? Where's your dad?' a voice asked.

It was Chrissie, the girl who'd been talking to Poppy before.

Poppy shrugged and glanced up at him. 'Umm… he…'

'I heard he'd been arrested. Is it true?'

Poppy nodded.

The girl snorted. She shook her head. 'Oh God.

That's ridiculous! Jim couldn't hurt a fly, let alone kill people!'

'Chrissie, I think it best if you keep your voice down,' Mr Seddon said, as he put the phone down. 'There's enough gossip flying around college without us adding to it.'

'Yeah, you're right, Charlie,' the girl said, her face crumpling. 'I just can't believe it.' She turned to Poppy. 'He has got a solicitor, hasn't he?'

'I don't know.' Poppy's voice suddenly sounded wobbly. It was hitting her.

Michael grabbed Poppy's hand and squeezed it. Her eyes sought his and he made himself smile reassuringly. 'We're just about to sort that out.'

'Do you need some help finding one?'

'We're waiting for the Dean. I'm guessing she'll know what to do.' Michael tried to give Poppy an encouraging look, but she was obviously deep in thought and not really listening to a word either of them was saying.

Chrissie was frowning. 'The Dean? But she hates Jim. He's always going on about her stymying anything he tries that's new or different.'

A figure appeared in the doorway, tall enough to almost block out the light.

'Master, is there something I can do for you?' the head porter asked.

The man standing in the doorway had steel-grey

hair. His eyes were alert and his shoulders filled out his suit jacket like he was twenty years younger and spent half of his life running laps around Great Court. The way the guy looked them over, like they were some lesser beings, made Michael stiffen. He'd met this type before, usually among his dad's business friends. The man's gaze stalled on Poppy. He twiddled the ring on the little finger of his left hand and smiled.

'You must be Poppy.'

Poppy nodded.

'I've spoken to the police,' the man announced, 'and I'm confident that we can get this horrible mess cleared up very soon. My solicitor is on his way to the station.'

'Thanks,' Poppy murmured.

'Now what are you going to do until we can get this matter sorted out?'

'Ummm…'

'I can look after them,' Chrissie said. 'They can come to my room.'

'Actually,' the porter said, 'I believe the Dean is on her way over here.'

As if on cue, Bea squeezed past the Master into the already full lodge.

'Sir John,' she said, nodding respectfully to the Master.

'If you have no objections, Dean, I'd like to give Poppy and Michael afternoon tea.' It wasn't a question so much as a statement.

'Oh, umm, of course, Master. I'm sure there's nothing they'd enjoy more.' Michael thought he heard more than a hint of sarcasm in her voice. 'I just didn't want them to be left floundering.'

'How thoughtful of you, Beatrice. Come along,' he said, catching Michael's eye. 'It's too cold a day to be standing around in here gossiping.' He gave the Dean and Chrissie a steely glare before turning and walking out of the door.

The Dean let out a noisy breath. 'That bloody man. You'd better run along,' she said, squeezing Poppy's arm. 'But just as soon as he lets you out, you come and find me.'

'OK,' Poppy said.

'What's a master?' Poppy whispered, with an incredulous look on her face, as they hurried to catch the guy up.

Michael imagined the monologue she was bound to come out with about old white men and their love of titles that make them feel like they are master of all they survey.

'He's the head of the college. Kind of like the principal.'

'Did Bea just call him Sir John?'

Michael nodded. 'Trinity's a royal foundation. The Master is appointed by the Queen. He was probably already a knight.'

'How do you know all this?'

'It's in the prospectus.'

Poppy shook her head. 'I'm just going to call you *geek* for the rest of the day.'

'Works for me.' He shot her a smile. At least she was making jokes again.

But her attempt to recapture something like normal didn't last. As they walked past the chapel he noticed Poppy staring at the door. She had that weird look in her eye again, the same one she'd had last night when she'd woken from her supposed nightmare.

The Master carried on straight past the chapel, around the corner, and stopped in an archway set back into the opposite wall. He reached into his pocket and then opened the door, turned and waited for them.

He didn't smile as they approached, merely waved them in.

'Come in, come in,' he said, smartly.

They squeezed past him, through a hallway and into a huge study that made the Dean's look like the servants' quarters. Michael glanced at Poppy. She was staring at the ceiling, her head crooked back and red-blonde curls spilling down her back. The sight made his throat tighten. He wanted to help her…to make her safe. And he felt so helpless. If anything happened to Jim…

He glanced up too. The white plaster ceiling was

emblazoned with gold swirls and even a coat of arms. The room was like something from a royal palace.

'Don't feel like you have to stand on ceremony,' the Master said, following them in. 'Take a seat and let's see if we can get some food in here.'

Michael felt a tug on his hand and Poppy led him towards a red sofa. They sat down and watched while the Master went to a desk in the corner of the room and used the phone.

'Hello, yes, I know it's a bit late, but could you sort out afternoon tea? For three. Thank you so much.'

He put the phone down and wandered over to them. He slouched down into an armchair, crossed one leg over the other and looked at them, a slight smile on his tanned, lean face.

'Really, don't worry about this business with your dad. We'll have him home in a jiffy.'

'I hope so,' Poppy replied.

'Actually, I'm glad to finally meet you. I've heard a lot about you from Jim. I know he misses you an awful lot. Took quite a bit of persuasion to get him to take this job. He wanted to go to some terrible parish in Cumbria so he'd be nearer you. But he'd have been terribly unhappy – wasting away up there.'

Beside him, Poppy stiffened. Michael felt like ripping into the guy, even if he was the bloody Master of this place. Could he not hear himself?

'Why did you want Dad to come here?' Poppy

asked, lightly, but Michael could hear the held-back emotion.

'I've known your father since he was a boy. Your grandfather is a great chum of mine, we were at school together.'

'The old boys' network.' Poppy chewed on her bottom lip, as if trying to hold back all the things she wanted to say.

The Master laughed. 'Just like your father. He could never stand the thought of getting anything he hadn't worked for. I always rather respected him for that.'

'He took this job.'

'He took a fair amount of persuasion – and there was some objection raised by one of the fellows. He was what we needed, though. I'm just so sorry that he's having to go through all of this. The police are being idiots, of course. Most of them really don't understand how an institution like this one works. I imagine it's all a bit of a mystery to you too.'

'Actually, Michael's a bit of a Cambridge geek – he's going to King's.'

Michael almost groaned. 'Actually, I've only applied, I haven't got in yet.'

'King's, eh? And what is wrong with Trinity?'

This, again? 'Nothing. I'm applying for History, so...'

'I see. And Trinity is only interesting to Maths and Science bods? That's a misconception we're trying to get away from. We're not all mathematicians.'

The Master talked for a little while about the college until he finally let slip that he'd been Jim's tutor.

'You taught my dad?' Poppy asked.

'Yes. He was an incredibly bright young man, something of a polymath. Could turn his hand to any subject that caught his eye.'

'Was he an Apostle?' Poppy asked, as simply as if she'd asked if her dad had played rugby.

A slow smile spread across the Master's face. 'Now then, what would make you ask a thing like that?'

Here we go, Michael thought. The Master really didn't know what was about to happen. He could almost enjoy this.

Next to him, Poppy shuffled and crossed her legs – settling in for a spot of questioning.

'Was he?' she persisted.

The Master stared steadily back at her. 'The membership of the Apostles is a closely guarded secret.'

'Doesn't seem to be. Seems to me that most people know that Danny was a member. And if Danny was a member I'm guessing Lucy is too, and Ria, and Conal, and Devon.'

The Master was doing a good job of remaining expressionless but surprise registered in his steel-grey eyes. 'Who told you that?'

'I worked it out, just the same as the police have worked it out.'

241

'Clever girl. You've inherited your father's analytical brain, I see.'

'Actually, I get that from Mum!'

Michael half winced, half grinned. Poppy's voice was acid. She was barely keeping her temper in check. He hoped the Master had a storm shelter handy.

The Master smiled and nodded, as if humouring her. Michael caught his breath. The man would regret that.

'I can't speak for the Apostles—'

'—Is that because you were one too?' Poppy interrupted. 'So that would make you an Angel, right?'

'You really have done your homework.'

'Wikipedia is a great resource.'

'Not always accurate, though.'

'What did I get wrong?'

The Master chuckled. 'As I said, I can't speak for the Apostles. But I will tell you that I've spoken to a representative of the society to express my concern.'

'Current, or former member?'

'Former. He's a contact between the college and police. An emissary, you might say.'

'You mean a...*messenger*?' Poppy asked.

Michael turned to look at her properly. He had no idea where she was going with this, but he was dying to know, and the excitement in her eyes told him she had something up her sleeve.

'Isn't that what angels are in the Bible? Divine messengers.' Poppy was watching the man like a hawk.

The Master was positively grinning now, and Michael got the feeling he was missing a whole chunk of what was going on.

'That's precisely what they are.'

'Funny thing to call a Chief Constable. I bet he doesn't appreciate being your messenger boy.'

The Master stopped smiling and his jaw dropped open. He stared at Poppy like she was some kind of freak. 'How do you know that?'

Poppy shrugged. 'People say things. I listen. It really wasn't that hard to work out. In fact, for a society supposedly made up of the brightest and the best Cambridge has to offer, you're all pretty crap at keeping secrets.'

At that moment there was a knock on the door, and in came two waiters in uniforms bearing silver trays of finger sandwiches and cakes.

The Master rapidly changed the subject and began talking about his last visit to see Poppy's grandparents, but Michael got the feeling that he wanted them gone as quickly as possible.

After a very rushed afternoon tea, at which Michael and Poppy ate barely a thing, the Master herded them out of the study and towards the door.

The Master held it open, but stopped in the doorway, blocking their way.

'Poppy, I hope you'll be sensible about who you talk to about the Apostles.' His face held a threat, even if his voice remained even. Michael rested a hand on her back, half warning, half supporting; but she didn't break eye contact with the man.

'There are staff and more than a couple of students who feel that membership of the society was their birthright and yet failed to meet the mark. The last time someone tried to leak the names of the Apostles things got very messy. I hope, for your father's sake, you'll keep out of whatever's going on.'

Michael groaned. He looked at the older man in disbelief. The Master clearly had no idea what he'd just done. Now Poppy would never stop digging.

CHAPTER TWENTY-THREE

'I wonder what he meant about things getting messy the last time someone tried to out the Apostles,' Poppy thought aloud as they walked back through Great Court towards the Dean's study. 'Who would know about something like that?'

'I've no idea. But I'm not sure we should try to find out. The Master's an important guy around here, Poppy; you could get your dad into serious trouble.'

'Trouble? I'd think being suspected of murder pretty much covers that.' Poppy glanced at Michael.

He nodded. 'Why don't we wait for your dad to get back from the police station and talk to him?'

'He could be hours. And there's no guarantee that the Master's solicitor will be able to get him out of there.'

'And there's absolutely *no* guarantee that you will succeed where the police seem to be failing.'

Poppy stopped walking. He seriously expected her to stay out of this – even with Dad being accused of murder?

Michael didn't seem to notice she'd stopped. He just kept on going. 'Is the Chief Constable really an Angel? How the hell did you work that out?' When she didn't reply he spun around, looking for her.

Poppy's pocket started ringing. She grabbed her phone hoping it was Dad, but the screen said *Home Calling*. She took a deep breath and accepted the call.

'Poppy, is that you?' Mum said.

'Mum, you called my phone, just who did you think it would be?'

'What's going on? I can't get hold of your dad.'

'Umm…' If she said Dad was at the police station, possibly being charged with murder, all hell would break loose. 'He's busy.'

'What's going on with you?'

'I'm fine. *Really*,' she said, giving Michael the serious look meant for Mum. He shook his head, flipped up the collar of his jacket and kicked at a pile of snow.

'Michael said that you took part in a séance. And that you…had some kind of episode.'

Some kind of episode? She narrowed her eyes at him. He didn't even blink.

'Mum, it was a crazy thing to do. This girl, she wouldn't take no for an answer. But I'm fine. It just freaked me out a bit. You know I don't like that kind of thing, right?'

'That's why I was so surprised. Pops, Dad told me how upset you got last night. I'm really worried about you, sweetheart. You don't sound yourself.'

'I'm fine. Dad and Michael are freaking out over nothing.'

'OK, but me and Jonathan are going to drive down

there and pick you guys up.'

'No!'

'This isn't something we're going to discuss.'

'Like hell it isn't! Meg, I'm totally fine. We have return tickets and we know how to use them. It'll be loads quicker than you driving. Trust me. If there was something wrong with me I'd tell you. I just got a bit stressed – seeing Dad and stuff.' It was pretty low, but at this point she wasn't above playing on Mum's lingering guilt about the divorce.

'I want you on a train today.'

'OK – OK, today. Actually, it's kind of late; it might be tomorrow now. I can't leave and not say goodbye to Dad. Just promise me you'll stay there.'

'I want to hear from Dad which train you're getting.'

'Fine. Please, don't worry. I'll get him to call you. I promise, everything will be OK. Love you, Mum.'

She waited for Mum to say goodbye, put the phone back in her pocket, then took a deep breath and folded her arms.

Michael put a hand on her shoulder. She shrugged him off. 'Don't.'

'I know you're angry with me…'

'You shouldn't have called Mum.'

'I didn't know what else to do.'

'You could have talked to me.'

Michael huffed out a laugh and turned his face to the clouded sky. 'Excuse me? But don't you think I've tried talking to you? What happened at Ria's wasn't normal, Poppy. You really scared me.' He stepped closer and slid an arm around her waist. She resisted, but was no match for his strength. She rested her hands on his sides and leaned her forehead against his chest. Everything was slipping out of control.

'Hey,' Michael murmured.

'What…what do you think's happening to me?' she whispered.

She took a deep breath and turned her face to his. For a second he didn't look at her. He focused over her head and bit his lip. When he finally looked down at her his serious blue eyes searched hers. 'What do *you* think is happening?'

Poppy swallowed, her throat dry. 'I don't know.'

'Don't you want to know?'

Did she want to know if she was seeing ghosts or going crazy? That was a big question – one that she didn't have an answer for.

'Poppy?' His thumb grazed her cheek.

'I'm scared, Michael.'

'I know.'

They arrived at the Dean's study, not speaking but holding tightly onto one another's hand. Admitting to Michael that she might be going crazy had drained Poppy of every last drop of energy. She just wanted to hide somewhere. Go to sleep for a hundred years until everything was normal again.

The Dean ushered them in and set about making yet more tea. The thought of drinking any more of the stuff made her feel physically sick.

Bea looked between the two of them and frowned. 'Has something happened? What did the old bastard say to you?'

Poppy glanced at Michael, hoping he wasn't going to bring up what they'd just been talking about. She really couldn't handle that.

Instead, he turned to Bea and asked: 'What do you know about the Apostles?'

The Dean fingered her clerical collar as if it had suddenly become too tight. 'I – uhh – I know that over the years the society's caused some trouble.' She let out a laugh, and rolled her eyes. 'What am I saying? It's a pernicious influence, responsible for more trouble than people will admit. Personally, I'd ban all secret societies. They cause so much hurt. Why are you interested in them?'

'I read something about them in that history of Russia I was telling you about.'

'Oh yes,' Bea mused. 'Some of the Cambridge Spy Ring were members. Back in the States there are fraternities and sororities. There are a fair few secret societies too, but they don't seem to cause the same amount of trouble as they do here.'

Poppy felt her pocket vibrating as the ringer sounded. She half expected it to be Mum again. She was about to reject the call when she saw it was Dad. Quickly she pressed *accept*.

'Dad? Where are you?'

'Poppy, are you OK?' he asked down a rubbishy line.

'I'm fine. What happened?'

'They've almost done with me, I've just got to finish up some paperwork. I hope to be back in about an hour. Pops, I've had your mum on the phone again. She wants you on a train, and so do I.'

'If they're letting you go, does that mean they know it wasn't you?'

At that, Michael looked at her. He leaned a little closer as if trying to hear what was being said.

'It means someone believes me,' Dad said. 'I'm not so sure the detective in charge of the case is convinced. Do me a favour and let me speak to Michael for a minute.'

Her grip on the phone tightened. 'Why?'

'Because I want to talk to him.'

Her breathing quickened and her jaw tensed. 'Why?'

'You know why, Poppy, now put him on the phone.'

Poppy's eyes flicked up to Michael. He gazed steadily back, lips tight.

'Poppy, if you don't put him on then I'll just call him.'

They'd made up their minds. They thought she was having an 'episode'. They were watching her like an experiment gone wrong. Suddenly the room was too hot. Sweat prickled on her forehead. She needed to get out of there...get some air. She handed her phone to Michael and got up.

'Hold on a minute, Jim.' Michael sprang up and blocked her path. 'Where are you going?'

'Just the bathroom.'

She saw the struggle behind his eyes. He didn't want to let her leave but couldn't think of an excuse to keep her there. He stepped aside.

'There's one just a floor down,' the Dean said.

'Thanks,' Poppy murmured and left.

CHAPTER TWENTY-FOUR

Poppy ran down the stone steps. She didn't even pause when she reached the floor with the loos. She just needed ten minutes by herself to think. She kept going, out of the archway and into Great Court, along the icy pathway until she reached M staircase.

By the time she reached their set, her legs were shaking with the exertion and her lungs burned, but she couldn't stop. She had about a minute before Michael would come looking for her and, right now, she didn't want to be found. She needed to be alone...get her head together. She unlocked the door to her room, grabbed her purse. Her gaze stalled on her laptop; she grabbed that too, stuffed it into her backpack and heaved it over her shoulder. Then she ran, down the corridor past Ria's set. She swung open the door onto the staircase and crashed into a solid body, at least a foot taller than her. Michael?

'Bugger!' she gasped.

'What's the hurry?' Conal stepped forward, forcing her back into the corridor.

Behind her the door to Ria's set opened. 'Poppy?'

'I have to go,' Poppy said, trying to step around Conal.

'No, grab her!' Ria shouted. 'She knows something

and it's about time she shared.'

Poppy felt Conal's hand close around her upper arm.

Panic ripped through her; she jerked her arm, but he wasn't letting go. His dark eyes narrowed and suddenly he looked cruel. Cruel enough to kill?

The next second, Ria was in her face. She pushed Poppy against the doorframe, almost knocking the air from her lungs. 'What did he tell you?'

'I don't know what you mean,' Poppy gasped.

'Don't play with me. What did Danny tell you?'

'Nothing. I didn't see anything, OK?' But she had seen something: those eyes so full of pain and hatred. Could they have been Conal's eyes, or Ria's? The note could have been a fake – Ria could have written it herself. Why would Ria be so determined to know what she'd seen if she was innocent in all of this? And there were those words that had slid from Poppy's mouth, almost as if someone else was speaking them... *What did you do?*

Ria glared. 'That's a load of shit. You know it. I know it.'

'I tried,' Poppy said, trying to keep her face neutral, to not show the fear that was zipping around her body. 'I tried but I can't do that...contacting the dead thing.'

Ria laughed. 'Oh, I think you can, Poppy. I think you're a natural. But if you're not in the mood to share, how about I share a few things with you? Let me start by telling you that your father is seeing a student. How do you feel about that? Him seeing someone a couple of years older than you. Maybe that's why he left your mother. Maybe she got a bit old for him?'

'That's not true.' Poppy shoved Ria away, but she couldn't as easily push away the image of Dad and Chrissie sitting together on the sofa in his rooms – the way he'd draped his arm behind her like it was a normal thing to do.

Ria studied Poppy, her eyes alive with power. Ria was enjoying this – towering over her like a playground bully. 'You knew. You knew it already. Think they've done it in the chapel, Poppy?'

Poppy shook her head. 'That's crap.'

'And you might want to ask him about his time of experimentation when he was a student. Quite the wild child, from what I hear. Sex…drugs…magic. I hear they arrested him for Danny's murder. Wouldn't be the first death he was responsible for, but if I find out he…I'll kill you both.'

'Ria,' Conal warned.

Ria smiled, coldly. 'Maybe you don't know your father as well as you think you do.'

Poppy pushed Ria away from her and barged past Conal. She ran down the stone stairwell, Ria's laughter echoing around her.

The wind had grown meaner. Her jeans were still damp and every icy blast cut through her like a knife. Darkness fell with surprising speed along with a swirling mist that clung to the ground like dry ice. It was going to be another foggy night. Poppy kept her head down and folded her arms over her chest as she walked out into the courtyard. She half expected to run into Michael but no one stopped her until she reached the porter's lodge.

Standing outside, bundled up in a big overcoat was the porter they'd met when they'd first arrived. He smiled at her. 'Where are you off to?'

'I'm just running to the shop.'

He gave her an assessing look and then his red, weatherworn face frowned like he thought that there was something wrong with her too. 'Where's your friend?'

'He's with the Dean. I've gotta go.' She gave him what she hoped was a reassuring smile, before slipping out the gate and onto the bustling lane.

She took a left off the main street and followed a cobbled side street until she hit what appeared to be another of the main shopping streets. She turned right again and followed the lane until she found a coffee shop with free Wi-Fi. Poppy bought a bottle of water and slumped into a chair at the table furthest from the door.

For a moment, she could do nothing but sit there

and breathe. But then the things Ria had said played over and over again in her head. *Your dad's seeing a student... Danny's death's not the first he's been involved in.*

No! Dad couldn't be seeing Chrissie. He wouldn't do that, would he? She swallowed back the tight feeling in her throat.

She tried to put it all out of her mind but the fact was, this trip had proved to her that Dad had a whole other life that she knew nothing about. Maybe she didn't know him at all. She didn't even know herself any more, for God's sake. What was she thinking, running away from Michael like that? She hadn't run away since she was ten years old and protesting the imposition of bedtime. All she'd done was prove him right. She was acting like...like a crazy person.

She had to go back there. But she needed some space and after this little stunt Michael wasn't going to let her out of his sight. She closed her eyes and tried to think beyond the pounding in her head.

She thought back to the séance. The horrible sense of being apart from herself lingered worse than a memory. God, if she'd explained that to Michael he really would think she was losing it. She'd felt like she'd been torn out of her body, and not in a nice floaty, how-great-to-have-an-out-of-body-experience kind of way. She shuddered. Maybe her imagination had got the better of her. The eyes that had stared down at her and the sharp burning pain in her chest – that could all be the product of her mind. Why had it felt so real? Her hand rubbed her stomach through the layers of T-shirts and sweatshirts.

Beyond the windows of the coffee shop, snow had begun to fall again – big fluffy flakes blown by the wind like feathers caught in a storm. The window of the bag shop opposite caught her eye. Fairy lights twinkled and right in the centre of the bay window was a large renaissance angel dressed in a blood-red gown, with golden hair that fell around her shoulders in graceful curls. She was beautiful. But how could Poppy ever think of angels in quite the same way again? Instead she imagined a terrifying creature flying high over the town, its huge feathery wings brushing the steeples and towers of the colleges...just waiting to collect more souls...more murder victims.

Was it an Angel doing all of this? Even if the murderer now had the book, he or she must have known Danny was an Apostle before. And why would someone try to set Dad up? Was that the point of all this? Were people getting hurt so Dad would get into trouble? What possible motivation could they have for that? Did someone want his job? Or maybe he'd upset someone. No. She was pretty sure the motive was revenge. The memory of that terrifying voice echoed through her mind.

I am his avenging angel.

She unscrewed the top off the bottle of water and took a long gulp. *That wasn't evidence!* She had to stick with the facts, *only* the facts. Except, what if there was some truth in what Ria had said? What if Dad had been involved in a death and now someone was out for revenge?

She unzipped her backpack and pulled out her laptop. After a couple of minutes of messing around on a registration page, Poppy was able to connect to the internet. The only possible crime that would provoke murder was another murder. And the only death she knew of connected to Dad and Cambridge was that of the Dean's son. Bea had said it was suicide but she'd made it sound like she thought that someone was responsible. Plus, she hated the Apostles. Why?

Poppy opened a new search page and typed in: *LANCE SUICIDE CAMBRIDGE.*

She scrolled through the search results. There weren't many – after all, Lance had died before the Internet had taken off – and most of them had nothing to do with the Dean's son, but then she found one local newspaper report that just said that Lance Tillman had been found dead in a punt floating near Grantchester Meadows. He was believed to have taken a cocktail of drugs and alcohol. The police weren't looking for anyone in connection with the death.

The Dean had said that Lance had developed a crush on someone. Could that someone have been Dad? Ria had said… No! Everything Ria had said was crap. She'd been trying to goad her. In fact, Poppy was beginning to think that the girl had a guilty conscience.

Danny had been Ria's boyfriend, but she'd hardly been playing the grieving widow apart from that one time she'd lost it in the corridor. Maybe that was for show. In fact, she was never apart from Conal. It wouldn't be beyond the realms of possibility that Ria and Conal were more than just friends, and if they were secretly seeing each other, maybe they wanted Danny out of the way?

But then there was the Dean. What if she somehow blamed Dad for her son's suicide? Chrissie had said that the Dean had it in for Dad. Why, if she wasn't bearing a grudge?

Poppy groaned. None of it made any sense.

She had to go back to the crimes themselves. The way the murderer had killed his first victim had pointed her to the Apostles. But what about the second crime? Why the hell would someone gouge out a person's eyes? That had to be significant.

Poppy searched: *EYE GOUGING.*

By the time she'd read an article about it, a whole new wave of nausea crashed over her. It seemed that the biggest issue with eye gouging happened on the rugby pitch, which confirmed everything she already thought about the guys on the school team. Very helpful – *not.* She needed to be more specific than that.

What happened if she added Lucy's name?

As soon as she hit the return key, she knew she'd found what she was looking for. The first result was a Wikipedia entry about Saint Lucy. The accompanying image showed a painting of a young woman holding a golden bowl containing two eyes. It seemed that Saint Lucy was said to have had her eyes gouged out and was tortured before being killed for the crime of giving away her dowry to the poor and refusing to marry some guy who thought she had beautiful eyes. Her feast day was the 13th December. Christians really did pick the strangest things to celebrate.

Poppy glanced down at her computer's calendar. It was the 13th December today.

'You're kidding me,' she muttered. The murderer seemed to have gone to a lot of trouble to point to St Lucy...but why?

Poppy carried on reading, finding it harder and harder to concentrate. St Lucy appeared in Dante's *Inferno*, and her feast day was often called the shortest day of the year, which was crap because the winter solstice was the 21st December. Having been brought up a good Pagan, Poppy had known that bit of useless information since she was five years old.

She sighed, squeezed her eyes shut and massaged her aching forehead with her fingers. This was no good. She was no closer to knowing who the murderer was or what they wanted.

Except, a little voice whispered, Dante was the subject of Dad's PhD thesis.

That just meant that there was no doubt about it – someone was trying to set him up. They knew him, they knew his interests and they were trying to make it look like he'd done these terrible things but, unfortunately for the killer, she knew her dad and she knew it wasn't possible. He could never hurt anyone. *Never.* Not...purposefully.

This was so messed up. All of it.

She needed to text Michael and tell him she was OK. He was going to be so pissed off with her. She felt in her pocket for her phone. It was gone. Bugger! Then she remembered handing over her phone to Michael. No wonder she hadn't had a million phone calls.

She was about to close the laptop when she spotted there were new emails sitting in her inbox. She clicked on the email icon and froze.

Subject: Want to play a game?
From: TheAvengingAngel@cantab.net

CHAPTER TWENTY-FIVE

Michael took the stone steps two at a time. He'd given Poppy ten minutes before heading down to the women's toilets to find that she wasn't there. He should have known that she'd give him the slip after he'd gone behind her back to her parents. But what option had she left him with? She clearly wasn't going to talk to him about what had happened in Ria's room. For a minute in there, he'd thought she was having some kind of fit, and it wasn't like he was worrying over nothing – she'd fallen unconscious!

He ran down the path towards M staircase, nearly crashing into an elderly academic.

'No running!' the man growled, shaking his stick at Michael.

'Sorry...sorry...' he muttered, without stopping.

He bolted up the steps, unlocked the door onto the corridor and headed for their set. The main door was open.

'Poppy?'

He strode across the empty study and pushed open the door to her room. She wasn't there, but on closer inspection he couldn't see her bag or her laptop.

'Sodding hell, Poppy!'

He stared around the room again. His gaze stalled

on the bundle of red silk sitting on the bedside table. Tarot cards. If she'd just kept away from all that stuff… Anger rushed through him like a tidal wave, until his muscles were tight with the need to throw something. He grabbed the package and hurled it at the wall. The cards spilled out of the red silk and fluttered to the floor.

He squeezed his eyes shut and tried to think where she would go. She'd taken her laptop. Had she gone looking for an open internet connection? The only way she'd get one of those was in a café. Which would be a great start if they weren't in the land of the flaming coffee shop. He'd just have to do a tour of them all.

He headed back out into the study. It was then he saw the note on the coffee table, simply addressed: *Michael.*

CHAPTER TWENTY-SIX

You and I are going to play a little game.
Tell anyone and we'll see how
nice your boyfriend looks with wings.

Poppy stared at the screen. At any moment a message would pop up saying *Just kidding!* It didn't.

Shit!

She closed the laptop, stuffed it back in her bag and made a race for the door. Straight into a guy carrying a tray-load of drinks. Cups smashed against the floor as the guy tried to jump back, away from the splashes of coffee and hot chocolate.

'What the hell do you think you're doing?' he shouted, brushing at his now coffee-stained jacket.

Automatically she crouched down to start cleaning up the mess. What was she doing? She didn't have time for this! She had to go and find Michael before the killer did. She shot back to her feet.

'I'm sorry,' she said as she edged around him. 'Really, I'm sorry.'

She ran out of the door into an oncoming flurry of snow to the sound of the guy shouting for her to stop.

The streets had almost emptied. Only students returning to their colleges and die-hard shoppers remained, bustling through the streets with their heads down, not looking where they were going.

Poppy darted back up the street, the way she had come. When a double-decker bus rounded the corner and she almost stepped right into its path, she realised that she must have gone wrong somewhere. She spun around. Shops, a weird-shaped church – none of it was familiar.

'Damn!'

Poppy grabbed a passing student. The girl looked up in alarm.

'I'm looking for Trinity.'

The girl pointed to the left.

'Thanks.'

Poppy took off again, nearly impaling herself on some scaffolding. She pushed through a cluster of shoppers, ignoring the angry words shouted after her.

By the time she reached the porter's lodge she was breathing so hard she thought her lungs would explode. One of the old guys she'd spoken to before came around the counter, frowning.

'Miss Sinclair, your dad's looking for you. Are you all right? You look like you've run a marathon.'

'Dad's here?' she gasped. Thank God!

The porter frowned as he moved towards her. 'Why don't you come and sit down and I'll give him a call.'

Poppy edged back out of his reach. 'What about my friend, Michael?'

The porter shook his head. 'I've not seen him, but I've not long come on duty.'

'He was with the Dean.'

'The Dean went out about twenty minutes ago.'

With that she backed out of the lodge, ignoring the Porter's protest, and sprinted into Great Court. Now that the big gates had been shut and only students were allowed through, the court was almost deserted. There were, however, three uniformed police standing at the corner by the entrance to Angel Court.

She couldn't afford to be noticed or stopped. Images of the French girl, her eyes pools of blood, sent a sickening shiver through Poppy. She couldn't let that happen to Michael. Poppy quickened her step. She instinctively put her head down as she passed the police, feeling like some kind of criminal.

As soon as she reached M staircase, she ran up the stairs and grabbed the keys out of her pocket. Her hand was shaking so much that she struggled to get the key into the lock.

'Damn it!' she swore, jiggling the key with frozen fingers. Finally, it turned.

The door swung open and any breath left in her lungs was knocked clean out. She pitched to the side and had to cling to the doorpost to stop herself from tumbling back down the stairs.

Six feet away, lying on the floor, was Conal. Both hands clutched his chest. He lay in a nest of large white feathers, like a pillow had exploded over him. Feathers had attached themselves to his hands and shirt, fixed there by the scarlet blood seeping through his fingers.

She darted down the corridor, dumped her bag and fell on her knees beside him.

A wet, gurgling noise was coming out of his mouth. He was still breathing, or trying to. His dark eyes turned to her.

'It's going to be OK.' She squeezed his shoulder gently, not wanting to hurt him further.

She had to call for an ambulance. Bugger! She had no phone. Maybe he did. She leaned over him and felt his pockets, but Conal had no phone either. She'd have to leave him, go and get help. There were police down in the courtyard.

She looked into his eyes. 'I'm just going to call an ambulance. Hold on, OK?'

His lips were moving, but she couldn't make out what he was trying to say.

'I'll be right back.' She tried to push herself to her feet.

'Nooo,' he hissed. A hand wet with blood caught hold of her arm. He was mouthing something, but she didn't understand. Shit! There wasn't time. She had to get him help.

'I can't hear you, Conal.'

His face crumpled with pain. He sucked in a rasping breath and tried again.

The words came out as a husky whisper. 'Too late.' His shoulders jerked as he tried to cough. 'St…st… sta—'

'Stay? You want me to stay with you?' Oh God! She couldn't.

His head tipped forward a little.

'I need to get help. I'll only be a minute. We need to need to get you to a hospital. You're going to be OK.'

His sticky red hand found hers and clung to her with surprising strength. And in the dark eyes that had intimidated her more than once she saw real fear. He was scared. Suddenly, she knew he was dying. It was in his eyes, the colour of his skin, his breathing. It was too late. She had to stay – she couldn't leave him alone.

'OK.' She nodded. 'I'm not going anywhere. I'm right here.'

His shoulders dropped a little and the muscles in his face relaxed but his eyes remained on her, like she was his anchor in this world. But the chain connecting them was buckling and breaking. Soon it would snap.

Her heart raced at the thought. She couldn't do this. She had no idea what to say. Even if it was hopeless, shouldn't she be doing some kind of first aid? She glanced down at his chest. Something had torn through his shirt, leaving tattered bloody edges. He'd been shot.

Oh God! This couldn't be happening. But it was. And she had to see it through.

With her free hand she stroked the damp hair away from his forehead, brushing away the awful feathers that clung to his skin. When a single tear streaked down his cheek, pain slid into her heart. What was she supposed to do? If there were right words to say, she didn't know them. There should have been someone else here – someone who knew how to comfort him… someone who really believed in something beyond this life who could tell him that death was a doorway into…something else…something better. Her nose started to run, and as tears clouded her vision she did the only thing she could think to do: she leaned down and kissed his forehead. When she pulled back his lips had lifted almost into a smile.

She did her best to smile back at him. 'Don't be afraid. I'm here. You're not alone.'

His gaze remained fixed on hers but she wasn't sure he saw her. He seemed to be looking through her to something else.

She continued to stroke his hair until the hand holding hers fell slack, his face relaxed and the noise of his gurgled breathing gave way to silence. The strangest feeling of peace filled the corridor, blanketing out the blood and horror like a layer of freshly fallen snow. He was gone. The pain and fear were over. It was OK… He was OK now. Her mind cleared and the terrible ache in her chest subsided.

She forced herself to lay Conal's hand down by his side – to let go of him. She had to leave him now and go and find help.

Then a terrible thought hit her, and her peace was shattered. What if Michael had been in their room when the killer came? She stumbled down the corridor and pushed open the door to their set. She almost collapsed with relief when she found the rooms empty. She should have asked Conal who'd shot him. How could she have been so stupid as not to ask that question?

She ran back down the corridor and had to fight back the wave of hysterics that threatened to swallow her when her foot caught on Conal's hand.

She grabbed her bag, and tried to slow her breathing as she made it out of the door and onto the landing. Clutching the handrail she staggered down the stairs and out into the night air.

'Help! Please! Somebody help!'

Heavy footsteps beat the pavement. She swung around to see tall black shadows pelting towards her.

'What's wrong?' a policeman gasped before they even reached her.

'There's… Someone's…' She couldn't bring herself to say *dead*. 'Someone's been hurt.'

'Shit!' one of them swore, before swerving past her and heading up the stairs, shouting into his radio.

'Wait right there, somebody will be with you in few seconds,' the other policeman said to her, before chasing after his colleague.

Her brain was full of static. She couldn't seem to pull one clear thought out of all the chaos except *Michael*.

Someone had Michael.

She couldn't stand there waiting for the police. She needed to find Dad.

She ran straight across the thickening snow covering the lawn, up the steps leading to the walkway through to Nevile's Court. She looked back as she reached the door. Police swarmed out of every archway, all heading towards M staircase.

She slipped through the door and jogged along the walkway, past the doors open to the servery, wafting food smells, and out the other side into Nevile's Court. Her hands were sticky; she rubbed at them without thinking, looked down, saw Conal's blood, dark smears on her palms. Her stomach lurched. No time to wash. She thrust her hands in her pockets, clenching sticky fists.

What would she do if Dad wasn't there? She couldn't go back to the police. She'd just run from a crime scene. For God's sake, she had blood on her hands! No: she couldn't go to the police. And what if the killer was watching her? If the bastard saw her talking to the police, Michael could get hurt. He could die.

271

Her legs turned to rubber as she jogged up the worn steps to Dad's rooms. Before she reached the top step she saw the note pinned to his door bearing her name.

She tore it down and unfolded the paper.

The note read:

Danny, Lucy, Conal…all Angels now.
They gave their lives to keep the Apostles' secret but they're not the only ones. Others had their lives taken from them – innocents.
Tell the world, Poppy, or your father will be the next to die.

CHAPTER TWENTY-SEVEN

Poppy hammered on the Master's door and then stuffed her bloodstained hands into the pockets of her hoodie. She couldn't stop shaking. If the Master wasn't in she had no idea who else she could tap for information. Maybe one of the porters, but that would risk her being handed over to the police – she had, after all, run away from a crime scene.

Panic took over and Poppy pounded on the door again. Just when she thought her heart would explode, a light illuminated the mottled glass. The next second the door swung open.

The Master was no longer in a suit, but wore a pink sweater over his grey trousers and white shirt.

'Poppy? I thought your dad was home.'

'H-he is,' she lied. 'I need to ask you something.'

The Master frowned, but he stepped back as if to usher her in.

'No, I'm sorry, I don't mean to be rude but I don't have time.'

'Then you'd better spit out what it is you want to know.' He folded his arms and squared his shoulders.

She took a deep breath: please, let him help her. She didn't know where else to go.

'You said that there'd been trouble that last time someone tried to out the Apostles. When did it happen?'

'Young lady, I thought I told you not to get involved.'

'You don't understand…' Exhaustion flooded through her. 'With all due respect, it's a bit late for that, Saint John…I mean, Sir John.'

He smiled, but then a thought visibly passed over his face and he took a step towards her. 'Are you in some kind of trouble, Poppy?'

Poppy shook her head. 'No, but Dad could be. Please…'

'I could call Messenger.'

'That really wouldn't help.'

'OK.' His lips thinned but he nodded. 'Well, I don't remember too much about it, it was just before my time. I've only been here since the beginning of term. Much of it amounted to nothing more than childish pranks.'

'Who was going to expose them?'

The Master shook his head. 'I don't remember, as I say, it was before I was Master here. I think it was a student. Someone who worked for the student paper… not the official one, the other. *The Student Room*, I think it's called.'

'That's all I needed to know. Thanks.' She turned to walk away.

'Poppy, wait!'

She turned around. He was walking towards her, frowning.

'Poppy, let me see your hands. What have you...'

She stumbled back.

'Poppy, stop!'

She ran, leaving the Master's voice echoing off the walls of Great Court.

The police were everywhere, but there were plenty of civilians too. Drawn by more sirens, people had spilled out into Great Court. That, combined with the icy fog that blurred outlines and faces so that no one would recognise anyone unless they were up close, meant that she could slip through the crowds undetected until she found a wrought iron gate that opened onto stone steps descending to an unlit passageway.

'What's down there?' she asked a passing student.

His eyes narrowed, then he shrugged, adjusting the bag on his shoulder. 'It's the passageway under the road. Goes through to another court.'

'Thanks,' she murmured as he walked away.

She was never going to get past the porters on the main gate, and there had to be another way out on that side of the campus.

She edged slowly down into the gloom, until her feet fell into the pattern of the steps. At the bottom she jerked to a stop and grabbed at the damp stone wall to steady herself. She began moving again, staying close to the wall, and eventually, as her eyes adjusted to the darkness, she could make out the faint light up ahead, and the outline of steps going up. Gaining in confidence, Poppy hurried towards the light and up the uneven steps. At the top, she pushed the wrought iron gate open and emerged into another court with a snow-covered lawn at the centre, and a tall stone building surrounding it. She spotted what looked like a gate. She'd made it. She glanced down at her hands; they were still stained with Conal's blood. She had to do something. She couldn't walk around the streets looking like this. She looked like she'd committed…murder. She glanced around. There were no signs pointing to toilets and she didn't have time to go looking. Finding a heap of cleared snow piled up against a wall, she crouched down and plunged her hands into the piercing cold. By the time she'd finished washing her hands she was shaking hard and the snow had turned pink. She covered the stain as best she could, dried her numb hands on her jeans and cautiously headed in the direction of the gate.

There was a smaller porter's lodge next to the entrance, but the porters didn't even come out as she opened the door. She stepped over the threshold and emerged onto the street, almost opposite the Great Gate of Trinity College, from where the statue of King

Henry looked on, along with a couple of uniformed police.

Now she had to find somewhere open with Wi-Fi, or a copy of *The Student Room*, and she had no idea where to find either. She decided to see if the coffee shop she'd used before was still open, although it was already nearly seven – most of them would be shut. Shit. What if she was barking up the wrong tree? What would happen to Michael and Dad? Maybe she should just go to the police and tell them what had happened. But she couldn't risk it. This killer meant it: Danny, Lucy, Conal. They wouldn't hesitate to hurt Michael and Dad. It was up to her. There was no one to help. Tears burned her eyes.

She jogged down what she hoped was the same cobbled lane she'd walked down earlier that day. But in the fog, everything looked different. Lights glowed from the windows of the buildings, creating strange sheens in the air that she couldn't see beyond, and huddled figures hurried by – nothing more than ominous shadows. Poppy shivered. She tugged her hoodie closer, but even the ridiculous amount of layers she was wearing couldn't keep out the damp cold that gnawed at her bones.

The cobbled lane opened out onto the main street. Ahead was the gate to what she assumed was another college. Silhouetted against the warm light pouring through the open door was a man who looked like he was on door duty. Dodging the cyclists who speeded ahead, despite the thickening fog, Poppy crossed the road and headed right for him.

'And what can I do for you?' the porter asked, smiling when she stopped in front of him.

'This might sound like a daft question, but I don't suppose you have a copy of *The Student Room*, do you? Or know where I can get one?'

'Nahh… Sorry. Not my kind of reading. But I do know where you'll find someone who writes for them.'

Poppy almost hugged him. 'That would be great.'

He nodded to the college. 'Come on in out of the cold and I'll give him a buzz.'

Poppy followed the porter past a sign saying *Sidney Sussex College Closed to Visitors,* into a lodge that was tiny in comparison to the lodge at Trinity. But it was bright and there was a blow heater that she huddled beside, careful to keep her hands in her pockets in case she hadn't got all the blood off.

The porter rubbed his hand over his bald head while he looked down a list of numbers. 'Here we are,' he said and began to dial.

'James, it's Brian down at the lodge. I've got a young lady here wanting a copy of your rag. I thought you might be able to help. Oh yes, she's definitely worth your time.' The porter rolled his eyes at Poppy while at the same time grinning. 'Good man.'

He put the phone down. 'On his way.'

'Thanks,' Poppy said. 'I really appreciate the help.'

She had to squeeze against a partition wall as a couple more porters crowded into the lodge rubbing their hands together and complaining about the fog. A minute later a tall guy with blond hair and a hopeful smile walked into the lodge. His eyes landed on her and brightened even more.

'Hi, I'm James.'

'Poppy,' she said, shaking the hand he offered before quickly slipping hers back in her pocket.

'What can I do for you?'

'Actually, I wanted to know if you could point me in the direction of the person who was writing a story on the Cambridge Apostles a couple of years ago. I believe the story didn't run but—'

'—Hold on a minute. Who are you? Why do you want to know?' His eyebrows pulled together.

'Please,' she said blinking back the tears collecting in her eyes. 'It would really help for me to know who that was.'

'Umm – hey, don't get upset,' he said, glancing around as if he expected the porters to blame him for her tears.

'Please,' she begged.

'It was a guy called Nick Bradwell.'

'How can I get in touch with him?'

'You can't.'

Her heart sank. Her last chance had just vanished. Michael and Dad's last chance.

'What! Why not?'

'He's dead. He died a couple of years ago. A car crash.'

CHAPTER TWENTY-EIGHT

The only place still open was a Starbucks. Poppy found herself a quiet corner, and after buying a coffee, she opened her laptop and Googled Nick Bradwell.

Nicholas Bradwell from Sunderland had been a second year student at Trinity College when he died tragically in a car accident on the A12. There was lots of stuff about the road being a death trap, but not a lot about Nick himself.

Poppy fingers shook as she opened her email inbox. It was there. Another from the Avenging Angel. All it said was:

Tick-tock.

Bastard! Poppy hit reply.

Is this about Nick Bradwell?

She waited. Hit refresh. And waited some more. Every second she waited, her heart picked up speed.

'*C'mon!*' she muttered, drawing looks from the people around her.

Just when she was about to give up, an email popped into her inbox.

Yes.

That was it? Poppy tried to type a reply, swearing every time her fingers hit a wrong key.

I don't understand what more you want me to do! Where are Michael and my dad? Please let them go. Whatever you think happened to Nick, they've done nothing wrong!

How was this supposed to end? What was she supposed to do now? A tear escaped down her cheek. She brushed it away only for it to be replaced with another. She had no phone, her laptop battery was running low, and she had nowhere to go and no one to turn to.

Poppy fished in her pocket; beside a tissue, she found Detective Inspector Dalca's business card.

Another email pinged into her inbox.

I'm not sure your dad is entirely innocent. What about Lance Tillman?

Shit! Was the killer the Dean? Did Bea have Dad and Michael? She'd said she hadn't forgiven those people she blamed for Lance's suicide. But that had been a suicide – the Dean had admitted that. And this Nick's death had been a road accident. How could Bea blame the Apostles for both deaths? Did she know something the police had never found? If it *was* Bea. But what connection did the Dean have with this Nick guy?

Poppy squeezed her eyes shut and rubbed the heels of her hands into her burning eyes. *Think, Poppy, think!*

This could go on forever. OK, it was suspicious that Nick had died right before he could out the Apostles, but nothing in the searches she'd done suggested that anyone ever thought his death was anything more than an accident.

Unless it never made it into the news.

Poppy stared at her laptop screen, not seeing it. OK. She'd reached the end. She wasn't going to play this game any more. She was done with being ordered around by a crazy killer. If they had Dad and Michael, surely they couldn't be watching her...

She had no choice, she had to take the risk and call Detective Inspector Dalca.

CHAPTER TWENTY-NINE

Where had all the telephone boxes gone? It took asking three people and ten minutes of walking in circles to find one. Then the first two times she tried the DI's number, she didn't pick up. Finally, on the third attempt Dalca answered.

'Poppy, where are you? Are you with your dad?' The detective's voice was as close to frantic as she'd ever heard.

'No—'

'—It was you who found Conal Preshoe, wasn't it?'

'Yeah. I'm sorry I ran away, but I've got a good reason. Please, please, just listen.'

'Talk.'

'I need you to look up an old case file. It was a car accident; a guy called Nick Bradwell died.'

'Yeah, that came up when we cross-referenced Trinity College through our computer system, but we couldn't see a link.'

'It's there. Maybe Messenger deleted something, or covered something up. Could he do that? The murderer is someone connected with Nick.'

'Poppy, where are you?'

She glanced around, afraid someone might be watching. 'I'm at a phone box. You can't come after me, though; they've got Dad and Michael.' Her voice sounded funny. She was having to squeeze words past the big lump that was stuck in her throat.

'Shit! Poppy, now you need to listen to me. You can't do this by yourself.'

'I have to. The note said that if I contacted anyone…'

'If the murderer contacted you, he or she wants to be found. And I don't like that, Poppy. Because I'm not sure what the end game is. So we need to work together.'

'They'll find out.' She whispered the words into the handset, feeling like she might faint.

'This person is smart, but you and me? We're a hell of a lot smarter, OK?'

Poppy breathed. Were they smarter? Were they really? If this went wrong, she could lose the two people she loved most in the world. 'OK,' Poppy said at last.

CHAPTER THIRTY

Michael tugged at the electrical tape binding his wrists and ankles. There wasn't a chance he'd break free, but just struggling against his bonds eased the sense of helplessness. Plus, somehow he needed to get over to Jim.

Even with only the light from the streetlamps bleeding in through the windows, Michael could see the pool of blood circling Jim's head like a black halo. He was pretty sure the older man was still breathing, but he couldn't be certain.

He couldn't believe he'd fallen for the note trick. What kind of an idiot was he? But he wasn't the only one.

'Hello?' a voice called, echoing around the curving stone walls.

Here came the next sucker.

Michael shouted, but the electrical tape over his mouth smothered the sound to a muffled grunt. Footsteps got louder. Whoever it was was heading in his direction.

'Hello? Ria, are you there? For fuck's sake, quit pissing around will you! Didn't you hear? Lucy's in hospital, I haven't got time for this.'

Shit, it was Devon, and he had no idea what he

was walking into. Michael renewed his struggle; if he could warn him somehow – get his attention – maybe Devon could get out – get help. But the bitch hadn't only taped his wrists and ankles together, she'd attached his bound wrists to the carved oak pew with rope.

'Ria? What are you doing?' Devon asked. A pause, then, his voice a pitch higher, disbelieving: 'Is that a gun? You're kidding me.'

'Get down on your knees.' Ria's own voice was hoarse and shaking.

'What? No!' Devon gasped. 'What's this about?'

'Don't question me,' Ria snarled. Michael could hear her panting as though she'd been running. Like she was about to lose it. 'Just do it! Unless you want a bullet in your brain.'

'No!' Devon protested. 'I'm getting out of here.'

The sound of the gunshot almost deafened Michael. His chest constricted and his heart hammered in his throat. There wasn't enough air – he couldn't get enough air in through his lungs. Tears blurred his vision and the calm that he'd managed to maintain was gone. His nose started to run, the mucus backed up into his throat and he was choking.

'OK, OK!' he heard Devon scream. 'Just put the fucking gun down.'

He wasn't dead. The bitch had snared another victim in her web, but Devon wasn't dead yet.

OK, calm down. Michael focused on slowing his breathing. He had to keep it together if he ever wanted out.

CHAPTER THIRTY-ONE

The baristas hovered around her like flies waiting for a sheep to drop dead. There was five minutes before the Starbucks closed, and she was damned if she was moving until then.

Poppy refreshed her email.

Nothing.

Damn it, what was taking so long?

Detective Inspector Dalca had told her to sit tight – she was going to send through what she had on the Bradwell case in the hope that something would leap out at Poppy. She tapped her nails on the laptop, unable to sit still. She was pretty sure that she was running on nothing but adrenaline now, which explained the almost constant shivering and dry throat.

Finally, an email pinged into her inbox. It had a massive file attached – no wonder it had taken so long. Poppy clicked on it and watched as the download progress bar filled with blue.

'I'm sorry, we're closing now,' said a young woman with an impressive array of piercings.

'Just one more minute,' Poppy begged.

'Sorry, but we have to close up.'

'Shit!' Poppy glanced down at the progress bar, but it was only halfway done.

'Miss?' The girl's voice had gone up in pitch.

Poppy groaned. She glanced up at the woman. Nothing. She had to go. Poppy stood up, shoved her backpack over her shoulder, picked up the still-open laptop and slowly shuffled towards the door, her eyes glued on the progress bar.

75%...

78%...

Too slow! She had to stall. Poppy slid her backpack off her shoulder and swung it towards a table where the chairs had been piled on top. The chairs teetered, and she had to jump back to avoid the computer being smashed as one slid off and crashed to the floor.

'Oh God, I'm so clumsy!' Poppy slid the laptop down onto the counter that held all the napkins and packets of sugar, and crouched to grab a chair. 'Here, let me help you.'

'That's OK, we can do that,' the girl snapped. She was staring at Poppy like she was a nutter.

She had *no idea*!

'I must. I really don't want to create more work for you guys right at home time.' Poppy took her time putting the chairs back up on the table, glancing every now and again at the progress bar.

She needed more time but the girl was glaring, looking for reinforcements.

'Goodnight,' Poppy said. And walked towards the door.

'Hey, don't forget your laptop,' the girl said.

Poppy spun around and slapped her forehead. OK, she wasn't going to win any prizes for acting but it was all about killing time.

'I'm not only clumsy, but really forgetful,' Poppy said. She picked up her laptop and slowly walked back towards the door.

98%…

99%…

Bingo! 'Thanks so much.' Poppy grinned and headed out of the door.

Back outside, holding the computer in one hand, she scrolled through the document with the other. It was a computer-generated report spewed out by something called HOLMES.

There were several sections. One was the coroner's report on the death of Nicholas Bradwell, but another section contained details of a complaint that was made by the Bradwell family about Trinity College's handling of their deceased son's belongings. They claimed that someone had tampered with them.

Poppy scanned through the names of the people who'd given statements.

Mr Simon Bradwell. Mrs Rachel Bradwell. Miss Christina Sharrock.

Oh, God! Chrissie!

Poppy snapped the computer shut, shoved it in her bag and started running. Her legs were wobbly and her lungs felt like they would give in any second, but she had to keep going. She had to get to Trinity.

The road seemed to have lengthened since the last time she'd slogged up it, and no matter how hard she pushed herself, her legs wouldn't take any more punishment. She slowed to a walk and fought the burning pain in her thighs. She had to keep going.

She was almost there, she could just about see the Great Gate looming through the fog, when a figure stepped out of the shadows and grabbed her arm. Poppy screamed.

'Shhhh!' a voice hushed her.

It was the detective, and not far behind her was her bouncer.

'I know who it is,' Poppy whispered.

'Yeah. We do too and we think we know where they are. Poppy, my sergeant's going to take you back to the lodge and stay with you until we get Michael and your dad out of there.'

What? 'No. *NO!* I have to go there. She's expecting me. If she thinks I've talked to you she'll kill them.'

'That's not going to happen. The team know how to handle these things. Thank you for getting us this far. But your part in this is over.'

'Where are they, then?'

'She'd booked a room, in a building out towards the

river. We think they're there. It's one of the places the Apostles used to meet so it seems likely.'

Chrissie had booked a room? Somehow, that didn't feel right. How was Poppy meant to have found out that she'd booked a room?

'Come on.' The detective put her arm around Poppy and pushed her on towards the gate to Trinity. 'Sergeant Lachlan's going to look after you now,' she said, squeezing Poppy's arm. The woman's face softened. 'Don't worry, it's going to be OK.'

Funny, those were the exact words Poppy had said to Conal.

As the detective walked away and joined a shadowy group of people, just a little way up the street Poppy nearly collapsed.

Another hand on her shoulder startled her.

It was the sergeant. 'Come on, Poppy, let's get you somewhere warm.'

The heat of the lodge came as a shock after the freezing fog, as did the ten or so faces who all turned to look at her. Among them she recognised the weather-beaten face of the head porter. He edged past the others, around the desk and stopped in front of her.

'Am I glad to see you,' he said, with a kind smile. 'Your mum's on her way. The police are bringing her and your stepdad down from Cumbria.'

She tried to smile, but her cheeks were frozen.

'Hey, your dad's going to be just fine. I've known that lad since he was here as an undergraduate, and I reckon the number of scrapes he got himself out of were all good training for this.'

She really hoped so. Dad was smart and so was Michael. They'd know what to do…just as long as they were still alive. They had to be. Had to be.

'I think she could do with a sit-down and a hot drink,' the sergeant said. 'She looks like she's about to keel over.'

'Frank, get a seat out here for Poppy,' the head porter called. 'And put the kettle on while you're about it. Won't be a minute.' He scuttled off, back behind the counter.

For a moment, Poppy almost let herself relax. But then her heart began to thud. Her brain ached as she struggled to think. There was something. Something was wrong. Dacla had got it wrong.

The room-booking thing. It was bugging her. There was just no way that someone who'd got away with murdering three people would be that careless. Chrissie had wanted *her* to find them, not the police. Poppy squeezed her hands into fists and forced her mind to quieten. If Chrissie really wanted to find her, surely she'd have told her where she was eventually.

'Can I borrow your phone?' she asked the sergeant. 'I'd like to call my mum.'

'Oh, yeah, of course.' He handed her a smartphone; there was a burst of static and then a crackly voice. The sergeant frowned and pulled a radio from his pocket. 'Receiving. Excuse me a minute.'

Poppy nodded as he walked away. She looked around the lodge. Everyone seemed occupied with something or other. No one would notice if she went somewhere quieter to use the phone.

Poppy edged back until she was almost at the door, then before anyone could notice, she'd hopped out of the side gate onto Trinity Street and set off down the cobbled lane. Spotting a shadowy shop doorway, she slipped inside and leaned against the tiled wall. Her hands were shaking and the phone was a model she'd never used before, so it took her a couple of minutes to find the web browser and open her email account. As she'd suspected, there was a new message from the Avenging Angel.

Time's running out, Poppy.

She quickly typed a reply.

They killed him and then covered it up. I get why you're so angry, Chrissie. I would be too. Where are you? We need to talk.

She sent the message, closed her eyes and prayed.

Killing once must be hard enough – even when someone was blinded by grief and anger. Killing three times had to mean that Chrissie had dropped off the edge into... what? Madness? But what did she want? The truth? Could she even hear the truth now?

Poppy refreshed the browser page. Chrissie had replied.

The Round Church. Come alone or I'll kill them all.

Poppy jogged up the lane, following the flashing red dot on the phone's GPS. The Round Church lived up to its name. Built of a dark-coloured stone it looked something like a beehive topped with a conical roof and a smaller round tower. A faint glow emanated from the windows in the turret as if someone was burning candles in there. She pushed the phone into her pocket and squeezed her trembling, cold hands into fists. Slowly, she approached the main door. A white piece of paper flapped around the studded oak – a notice cancelling a quintet practice. God! How normal that seemed – a music rehearsal. Another world. She glanced around. Bushes and trees marked the churchyard with shadows, and although she could make out shadowy figures drifting past the gate, she was sure no one would see her. Taking a deep breath, she slipped her hand through the freezing iron loop and pulled. The door made a creaking noise but didn't shift. There had to be a back door.

She couldn't do this. What if she got it wrong? This wasn't a game – Dad and Michael could die. She thought about calling Dalca. Went as far as pulling out the phone and finding her number in the address book. But what would they do? Would they send in armed police? A hostage negotiator? What possible bargaining chips would they have? She'd heard of too many of these situations going badly and she couldn't lose Michael or Dad. She'd rather die herself. She had to try – convince Chrissie to let them go. She had to try.

She wouldn't phone. She couldn't afford the time for a conversation; the risk of the policewoman convincing her to do nothing, to wait for the pros. But...just in case something went wrong...

Poppy's numb fingers stumbled as she texted Dalca:

She's at the Round Church.

Poppy tucked her head down into her scarf, scrunching up her tense shoulders to try to ease the constant shudders that racked her body, and followed the path that ran around the curving wall of the church. Stuck onto the back was a square building, and set into the wall was a door. She tried it and it opened.

The room she stepped into was in darkness, but in

the gloomy light coming in from the streetlamps she could make out the outline of a desk and filing cabinets. She quickly crossed to the only door she could see. It opened onto another very dark, very confusing area. She felt around the wall, past shelves and rows of books. Her toe hit something and she tripped, sending something clattering to the floor. Well, that took care of her plan to make a quiet entrance. She edged forward again until she found another door. Taking a deep breath she creaked it open, half expecting someone to leap out at her.

'Come in, Poppy,' a voice called.

She felt beneath Dad's scarf and pressed the small piece of obsidian between her finger and thumb. If ever she needed protecting, it was now.

She edged out of the darkness and into the flickering circle of light created by the candles burning in various recesses and corners. To the left, at the square end of the church there was an altar and rows of pews facing in towards the aisle. But to her right, through the arched columns that circled the heart of the church, she saw a girl with long white-blonde hair and eyes that no longer looked angry or defiant, but scared and uncertain.

Ria raised her hand. In it she was clutching a gun.

CHAPTER THIRTY-TWO

Poppy froze. Ria? Not Chrissie after all? Had she got it so wrong?

Ria had the blank look of a robot that hadn't yet received instructions on how to respond. She didn't seem in control of anything. Was that it? Was she was being told what to do? Ria's eyes shifted, almost imperceptibly. Poppy followed her gaze to the altar. There was nothing there, except, wait…what was that shadow on the tiled floor?

Poppy started towards it.

'Poppy, stop,' Ria said, but there was no power to her voice. Ria wouldn't shoot her. She'd meant for her to go over there. The person really in charge of this scene didn't want her dead – not right away anyway.

Her footsteps echoed as Poppy darted towards the altar. As she drew closer, she saw that the shadow wasn't a shadow at all, but a boot sticking out around the edge of the carved oak pew. The boot was connected to a leg, and the leg belonged to…

'Dad!' she gasped. Oh no! Not him…no…please!

Poppy fell to her knees. Dad's hands and ankles had been bound with tape and dark blood had dripped from his forehead onto the tiled floor.

'Dad? Dad!'

His eyes flickered open. The breath flew out of her chest with a cry. He was alive. There were muffled noises behind her. She spun around. Lying face down in the pew was Michael. His hands and ankles were taped together and there was a rope looped around his arms, tying him to the pew so that he could hardly move. His gaze connected with hers. Someone had done this to him…to both of them. If it was Chrissie, she would…

Poppy scrabbled towards Michael, blood pounding in her head.

'That's enough. Leave him,' a voice said. This time it was the voice she had expected. Fury filled her heart. And fear.

Poppy pushed to her feet. Her whole body was shaking. She looked between the columns: standing behind them, several metres away, in the centre of the round chapel, was Chrissie.

Burning anger surged through Poppy's veins. She ran at the girl.

'Stop!' Chrissie thrust out a gun, aiming it at Poppy's face.

Her pumps squeaked against the tiles as she skidded to a halt. Poppy's heart thrashed in her chest as she sucked in short sharp gasps of air. 'You bitch!'

'Unlike Ria's gun, this one isn't for show,' Chrissie said. The girl brushed a strand of her bobbed brown hair away from her face and she steadied her stance as if preparing to fire.

Just to the right of Chrissie, Ria slumped to the ground; the gun she was holding clattered down beside her and she wrapped her arms around her legs and buried her head in her knees. She'd given up. She was waiting to die.

Chrissie would kill them all. She had to delay, string her along until the police got here. She licked her lips, tried to stop shaking with fear and hatred.

'How did you get them all here? That was clever.'

Chrissie huffed out a laugh and her gun arm dropped to her side. 'It was stupidly easy. Michael kindly met me here as per the note I left him. Then once I had your mobile phone, it was just a process of texting really. And collecting more phones, until...' Chrissie spread her arms wide.

Poppy had seen Dad, Michael, Ria...were there more? More dead people. She shuddered harder.

'What did you do to my dad?'

'He wasn't cooperating.'

Anger bubbled up from her stomach, this time it felt like hot lava. Without thinking, Poppy took two steps towards Chrissie before the gun was once again levelled at her face.

'Don't be stupid, Poppy. You don't want to die... not for Jim. After all, he left you. He's one of them, Poppy. He stands there in that chapel, preaching about

301

us all being equal before God and yet he's one of them: a group who think they're so much better than everyone else.'

'And what about Michael? What crime did he commit?'

Chrissie frowned, looked confused, but then swallowed and raised her chin. 'Nothing yet. But can't you see? He's going to come here and become another one of them. And then he'll leave you too.'

'No, he won't.'

'Don't you get it, Poppy? I'm saving you the pain. In another year he'll be here and you'll be at home. He'll meet someone else and he'll rip your heart out. Better to lose him now.'

'Is that what Nick did?' Poppy asked. 'Did he come here and find someone better?'

Chrissies face flushed with anger. 'No! Nick was different. He loved me.'

A laugh echoed through the stone arches. Ria raised her head and snarled: 'Oh my God, you're so full of crap. Nick had been trying to break it off with you from the minute he got here.'

Chrissie strode across the chapel and backhanded Ria, sending her sprawling on the tiles.

Ria let out a series of grunts; Poppy couldn't tell if she was laughing or crying.

'*They* killed him.' Chrissie pointed the gun at Ria. Her finger tightened against the trigger. 'Her and the rest of them. And they covered it up to make it look like an accident!'

Ria raised her head. 'How many times do I have to tell you, we had *nothing* to do with Nick's death?'

Chrissie turned back to Poppy; her eyes were wild and unfocused. 'We were in love.' A memory seemed to lighten her face and brought with it a faint smile. 'He wanted to be a journalist. He was good, too – everyone said so. Then when he got here he was invited to a black-tie party. He said, "You'll never guess what, I think I'm gonna be invited to join this really famous secret society." Typical Nick, though, he wasn't excited about being asked to join; he was excited at the thought of writing an exposé. He wrote about the silly dinners...and being introduced to all these important people, even the Chief bloody Constable. He started working out who the members were. Then when he was invited to join, he said yes, and went through their silly ritual. That was it – he had enough to write his story. But he had these stupid ethics. Didn't want to turn into a tabloid journalist. And so he made the mistake of telling *them* he was going to write a story about the society.

'That's when stuff started to happen. A dead rat was left on his bed. His bike disappeared and then reappeared up a tree. He complained to the college, but no one did anything about it. I told him – if these people...these *Angels* were as important as he said they were, he had to be careful. But he went ahead and got himself a job with a student newspaper.' Chrissie smiled. 'He was so excited. His first story for them and it was going to be the lead. They'd given him a week to finish up, and that's when it happened. I got the phone call from his mum saying that he'd had *an accident*.'

'That's crap,' Ria, muttered. 'You're telling yourself fairy tales. Nick wasn't going to publish that story. Lucy persuaded him—'

'—Shut up. Shut up!' Chrissie roared. She raised the gun again – this time her hand was shaking and she was breathing so fast she was almost hyperventilating.

Not good. She was losing it.

'So that's why you did it?' Poppy asked quickly, hoping to distract her. 'You wanted to punish them. To be his avenging angel?'

Chrissie's eyes widened as if those words had connected with something inside her. She dropped the gun to her side and nodded. 'No one listened to me. But they're everywhere. I've got the book with all their names in. Politicians...judges...they're everywhere. They had him killed and made it look like an accident. Then they wiped his computer. They think they fooled everyone. But I know what they've done...they're evil. They manipulate everyone and everything. They took my Nick from me. They have to be punished.'

Chrissie reached in her pocket. 'Use this. Get the tape off Devon's ankles and bring him out here.' Chrissie threw a penknife to Poppy. And pointed to the pew where Michael was.

Poppy hesitated. Oh God. Chrissie wasn't looking for answers. This wasn't a trial. This was an execution.

'Now!' Chrissie yelled.

Poppy's legs shook as she forced herself over to the pews. She made herself walk past Michael. There in the next pew was Devon, hands and feet tied together, his mouth taped shut. He looked up at her, terrified.

'Just stay calm,' she whispered. 'We're going to get out of this.' Surely the police would arrive soon. If they didn't... Her hands trembled as she used the knife to saw through the tape around Devon's ankles. Devon caught her eye and nodded to the right where a thin rope had been looped around the pew leg. It was the rope tying Michael down.

Poppy grabbed the rope and started sawing through it.

'Hurry up, Poppy,' Chrissie shouted.

Clipped footsteps rushed towards Poppy. She'd only cut through half of the strands. 'Shit!' Poppy hissed, preparing to abandon the rope. But then there was the sound of scuffling.

'Sit back down, Ria!' Chrissie screamed. 'Don't make me kill you!'

'Why drag it out? If you're going to kill us all in the end you might as well get it over with,' Poppy heard Ria scream back. 'Because I'd rather be dead than listen to any more of your shit!' The Apostle sounded like she'd got some of the fight back in her. 'I wiped Nick's hard drive. I did it. But he was already dead! He'd already decided not to write the story. He wanted to be one of us.'

'No! You're lying!' Chrissie hissed the words. Poppy shuddered: the killer sounded totally crazy.

The last thread of the rope snapped, and while Chrissie and Ria argued, Poppy flattened herself on the dusty cold floor and reached through the gap beneath the pew to Michael. She heard him gasp when her hand found his. His fingers frantically closed around hers and squeezed them. She didn't want to let go...she couldn't let go of him. Tears leaked down her cheeks. This was her fault. She should have waited for the police to get there.

Something nudged her shoulder. She looked up and Devon widened her eyes at her. Footsteps were heading towards them. Chrissie was on her way over here. She quickly pressed the handle of the penknife into Michael's hand and pushed herself to her feet.

She helped Devon to stand and they were out of the pew before Chrissie had made it over to them.

Devon followed Poppy to the round part of the chapel, his hands still taped behind his back. Chrissie shoved him onto the floor next to Ria and the two Apostles glanced at each other, eyes wide with fear. Chrissie leaned down and with her free hand tore the tape from Devon's mouth.

'Agh!' he gasped.

In the flickering candlelight, Poppy saw a fleeting smile cross Chrissie's lips. However this had begun – as a search for answers or just plain revenge – Chrissie was enjoying this. And that scared Poppy, more than the gun.

Devon glared up at Chrissie.

Poppy's eyes flicked to where Dad's boots had been. He'd moved. Maybe Michael had been able to use the knife to get him and Dad free. If they were free, then maybe they could get out. She had to keep Chrissie talking.

'Who did it?' Chrissie spat. 'This is the last opportunity to save yourself. Tell me who tampered with Nick's car and I'll let you all go.'

'Like hell you will, you murdering bitch!' Devon shouted. 'Why did you take her eyes? How could you do that to Lucy?'

'She deserved to die.'

'Why? She was Nick's friend. She'd never have hurt him. And even if you kill us, you didn't get her. Lucy is alive. She's alive! And she's going to be OK.' Devon's voice was thick with tears.

'I've had enough of you.' Chrissie pointed the gun

at him. Her thumb flicked back the safety catch. She was going to do it!

'No! Stop!' Ria screamed. 'If you don't believe us then get Poppy to talk to Nick.'

'What?' Chrissie said.

Ria sat forward. 'Poppy's a medium. She talked to Danny. You can talk to Nick, can't you, Poppy?'

Ria turned to Poppy and widened her eyes, encouraging her to play along.

'Yeah,' Poppy murmured. 'I can do that. I can try and contact Nick for you.'

'You're just stalling,' Chrissie shouted.

'No. It's true,' Ria said, quickly. 'She's a medium. She talked to Danny. She saw him.'

Chrissie turned her gaze back on Poppy, her eyes suddenly filled with desperation. Poppy's mouth dropped open. Yeah – Chrissie was just crazy enough that this might work.

OK. The longer she could spin this out, the more time the police had to get here. Poppy pressed her eyes shut. She had to put on a good show. Do anything to make her believe. She rubbed her forehead to make it seem like she was concentrating. OK…what should she say? That he loved her? That he missed her? What would make her stop this?

A familiar tune slid through her mind – sweet and tragic, but so familiar. It was a piece that Mum played over and over again.

'He misses hearing you play the Bach. That was his favourite,' she heard herself saying. Poppy's eyes flew open.

The arm holding the gun dropped to Chrissie's side. 'How did you...? Who told you?'

Ask her about the text, a voice whispered, like there was someone standing right behind her. 'You...you didn't reply to his text.'

'What?' Chrissie whispered. For a second the girl squeezed her eyes shut and when she opened them again, her face was twisted by some terrible emotion.

Poppy didn't know how, but she knew she was onto something. 'He texted you the day he died. You never replied.'

Chrissie shook her head. 'I was angry.' She groaned. 'I'm sorry...I'm sorry, Nick.' Her voice rose to a wail.

'He wants you to forgive him.'

'Forgive *him*?'

Poppy nodded. The words came more easily now. She just opened her mouth and they were there. 'He wants you to forgive him for...for driving too fast. He knows you hated him driving like...like a whippet that's been shot in the arse.'

At that Chrissie choked out a laugh. She pressed a hand to her mouth as tears flowed down her cheeks.

'He's sorry, Chrissie. He needs you to forgive him.'

'It wasn't your fault, Nick. It was their fault.' Chrissie's eyes were glazed. She spoke to Poppy like she'd become Nick. 'But it's OK, I'm going to punish them. I'll be with you soon.'

What? Poppy looked hopelessly at Ria. This wasn't working. She was still going to kill them. 'He...he... doesn't want you to do that, Chrissie. He wants you to stop this. He wants you to live.'

'I can't. I can't stop now...' She sniffed and aimed the gun at Ria.

'No!' Poppy shouted. 'Chrissie, you have to stop – now. You won't get away with this, y'know? You can kill us all but the police will find you. Or maybe one of them will. If Angels are everywhere like you say they are, they won't let you get away with this.'

Chrissie froze. 'Your dad once told me that in the kabala, angels aren't creatures, they're energies created to undertake a task. And when that task is finished, the angel disappears. That's all I am, Poppy. That's all I have left – to be his angel.' Her once pretty brown eyes were cold and blank, like she'd lost all trace of humanity and become the mythical creature of vengeance she imagined herself to be.

Poppy took a step backwards. It was obvious that Chrissie didn't care about consequences now. She was way past that. As far as Chrissie was concerned, she was already dead. Now she was going to take them all with her.

No. That was not going to happen. Not to Michael. Not to Dad!

'Even if they did what you say they did, you're pathetic. This isn't justice. Me, Dad, Michael; we had nothing to do with Nick's death. You're not an angel. You're worse than they are. What you're doing is evil, Chrissie.'

Chrissie stared at her. 'You think you're so much better than me.' She shook her head. 'You think you couldn't do what I've done, but if you were me you'd be doing this too.'

'No. I wouldn't.'

'Are you really sure about that?' Chrissie's face hardened. 'Then let's see how you feel when it's your boyfriend dead.'

CHAPTER THIRTY-THREE

Michael fought for breath as he tried desperately to saw through the layers of tape, but the damn knife kept slipping and he stabbed his wrists again and again, until the handle became so slippery with blood that he could barely get a gip on it.

Poppy was doing a good job of keeping Chrissie talking, but at this rate, he was going to slice open an artery before he got free. Then a scream echoed through the church. Poppy's scream! Michael nearly dropped the knife. He looked up into Jim's panicked eyes. Jim had regained consciousness and in some yoga move had almost got his whole body through the loop of his arms. He was trying to unpick the tape around his ankles. Their eyes were locked, and Michael could tell they were thinking the same thing: was Poppy hurt?

Fast footsteps headed in their direction. Michael gave up on the knife and tried to wrestle his arms free. Something snapped and the pressure holding Michael's wrists together fell away.

Quickly he grabbed the knife and slit open the tape binding his ankles. He leaped up just in time to look down the barrel of a gun. He stumbled back. The knife slipped from his hands and clattered to the floor.

'Out here,' Chrissie said to Michael. 'Very slowly.'

Behind Chrissie, Poppy was staring at him, frozen with terror.

CHAPTER THIRTY-FOUR

What had she done?

Poppy flew at Chrissie.

'Stop!' Chrissie shouted. Poppy's legs obeyed the command. She fell forward, almost losing her balance completely. She'd done this. She'd put the idea into Chrissie's head. If Michael got hurt it would be her fault. She should have called the police and stayed out of it. And where the hell were they? Hadn't Dalca received the text?

'Move it!' Chrissie shouted.

Michael never took his eyes off Poppy as he edged out of the pew. He was doing his best to appear calm, but Poppy knew those eyes and he couldn't hide his fear from her.

'You touch him and I'll…' Poppy couldn't breathe. She'd forgotten how to breathe.

'You'll what? Kill me?' Chrissie laughed. 'So…we're not that different after all.'

'Don't do this,' Poppy begged.

Chrissie looked at her intently, like she was willing Poppy to see the truth in what she was saying. 'You won't truly understand until you really feel it. Until it takes hold of you and becomes who you are. Until you become pure. Until the fire burns away everything and you become one with it. That's what an angel is, Poppy. '

That's when she knew for certain, this girl wasn't just angry and vengeful…she was insane.

Chrissie slowly edged backwards. Never dropping her gun hand, she reached down into a large canvas bag and pulled something out and threw it to the floor. A knife landed a foot away from Poppy. 'You have a choice, Poppy. Either you do it, or I do it. If you do it, maybe he lives. If I do it he dies now.'

For a second, Poppy didn't understand what Chrissie was saying. Chrissie wanted her to… Her gaze dropped to the floor. The knife blade glimmered hungrily in the candlelight. A butcher's knife, long enough to gut a pig.

Her insides squeezed together. Twisted. She almost threw up. Poppy stared at the knife, then looked up at the pale, intent face of the girl who was going to kill them all.

'No.'

'Pick up the knife, Poppy.'

'*No!*'

'I'm going to start counting down from ten. You know what's going to happen when I get to zero.'

Poppy ran at Michael and landed heavily in his arms.

'Ten…'

He took hold of her shoulders, pushed her away and

levelled his gaze with hers. 'Do it,' he whispered.

'Nine…'

'No!' Poppy cried. Her hands tightened around the folds of his jacket as her heart punched away the seconds.

'Eight…'

Michael's hand smoothed down her hair, he pulled her closer and brushed a kiss against her cheek.

'Seven…'

His fast, uneven breathing whistled in her ear. 'She'll let you live, Poppy,' Michael whispered. 'Do this and she'll let you live. *I need you to live.*'

'Six…'

Poppy jerked away from him. Despite his panic, Michael's eyes were steady. He nodded. 'Do it, Poppy. It'll buy us some time.'

'Five…'

'I can't!'

'Four…'

His grip on her arms tightened. 'You have to. It'll be all right.'

'Three… Get out of the way, Poppy!' Chrissie shouted.

'OK…OK…OK…' Poppy spun out of Michael's hold, darted over to the knife and grabbed it from the floor. The handle felt like a shard of ice.

'Two…'

Michael caught her eye and nodded. Poppy

swallowed against the dryness in her throat. Her heart seemed to slow, slowing time with it. She looked down at the knife meant for Michael and a wave of utter calm came over her, just like that moment when Conal had died holding her hand.

Slowly, she walked towards Michael. Her eyes fixed on his. She stopped a pace away from him.

'It's OK, Poppy,' Michael whispered.

Poppy nodded. It would be OK. She spun around, flung the knife at Chrissie and then pressed her back against Michael's.

'No!' he screamed. 'Poppy, get away from me!'

She reached behind and grabbed handfuls of his jacket. 'If you want to kill him, you have to kill both of us.'

Chrissie edged forward. 'Poppy, move!'

'No. If you want to kill us, fine. But you won't turn me into you. You might think it's OK to kill and hurt people, but I don't. So you can kill me, but you can't turn me into you. You're not an angel, you're just very ill and sad.'

'Police!' a woman's voice shouted.

Poppy landed heavily on the ground with Michael on top of her.

Then, as if in slow motion, Poppy saw Dad appear from behind an archway. He grabbed Chrissie's wrist, forcing it up as a shot rang out. The gun slid from Chrissie's hand as plaster fell from the ceiling in big white flakes. They floated down out of the vaulted ceiling like feathers from a bird – or maybe an angel – shot out of the sky as police in flak jackets stormed the church.

Dad gently lowered the girl who had tried to kill them all to the floor. He cradled her to his chest and rocked her.

'Let me die…I was supposed to die…' Chrissie sobbed over and over again, until her words echoed from every pillar and archway, so loud that even the dead would hear her.

EPILOGUE

The strange metal creature looked like a particularly evil cricket. Its legs cranked backwards and forwards, spinning the golden disc below while its mouth snapped open and shut. Poppy was glad it was behind glass – the thing looked like it would take your finger off.

'What is it?'

Dad smiled. 'It's called a chronophage. A time eater.'

'It's nasty.' The creature's metal eyelid slid closed. 'Ugh, it just blinked at us.'

Dad chuckled. 'It's just a clock.'

'It's freaky. And who wants a time eater around? Really – did someone think it was cute or something?'

'It's meant to remind us that our time here is short, that we never get time back. Once the chronophage eats a minute or a day, it's gone forever.' Absently, he scratched the big plaster that covered the gash in his forehead.

After last night, Poppy didn't need a chronophage to remind her how fragile life was, or how quickly it could come to an end.

Dad sucked in a deep breath and Poppy tensed. She'd been waiting for…

'Last night, when you were talking to Chrissie about Nick—'

'—Dad—'

'—I'm not trying to give you a hard time. But if what you said came from...' He sniffed and looked away as if searching for the right words. 'If you were somehow *channelling* Nick, then don't you think we need to talk about that?'

Poppy toed a pile of slush, shaping it into a mushy pyramid, hoping the chronophage would speed up and chomp away the minutes so that they wouldn't have time for this conversation. But in the silence that followed she realised that Dad was willing to wait her out on this one. She glanced up to see him watching her.

'I'm not even sure it was anything...real. Maybe it was in my head. Or maybe I'd somehow picked up information that I didn't consciously remember.'

Dad nodded. 'Or maybe Nick was somehow communicating with you.'

Poppy shrugged.

'Is it getting more frequent?'

'Look, I know you probably think it's the devil or something—'

'—I don't think it's the devil.'

'But I promise, in the future I'll keep away from everything weird and spiritual. I'll leave that to you and Mum, OK? I'm done. I'm out.'

'Yeah, because that strategy's worked so well for you up until now.' Dad gave her a wry smile that she couldn't help but return. He turned back to the chronophage. 'A while ago I read a paper written by a psychologist at the University of Michigan. He'd done a study on people who'd been through a near-death experience.'

'Let me guess, they all turned out to be mentally unstable?'

'No. He found that people who've had a close call with death are far more likely to experience what we think of as psychic phenomena.'

'You really believe that? Because it sounds like what we scientists call *pseudo-science*. More commonly known as bullsh—'

He turned his gaze back on her. '—Your heart stopped beating, Poppy. The day you had the boating accident the lifeboat crew thought you were dead. And ever since that accident…'

Ever since that accident, Death had followed her around. Always there…in her peripheral vision…like an extra shadow she couldn't get rid of.

Dad took her hand and squeezed it. 'I know what's happening must be scary. Hearing dead people would frighten the fucking life out of me. And to be honest, I don't have any answers for you. Yes, I have colleagues who would say that talking to the dead is wrong, or that some malignant spiritual force is trying to deceive you. Is that what it feels like – like something is trying to hurt you?'

Poppy shrugged. 'I don't think they're trying to hurt me.'

'Good. Then we're just going to have to do what we priests call contextual theology.'

'Contextual theology?'

'It's what we do when we don't have a bloody clue what's going on. But I don't think ignoring what's happening and hoping it will go away is an option. Tonight, you, me and Mum are going to sit down and talk about what we can do to help you make sense of this. And if we can't help, we'll find someone who can. OK?'

'OK.'

He smiled, his golden eyes holding hers. 'Come on.' His arm slid around her and he tugged her across the road, towards the gates of King's College, where Michael was talking with Professor Madigan.

Fiona smiled as they approached.

'Thank you,' Michael said, like a guy who'd just been handed his life back. 'I really appreciate it.' He caught Poppy's eye and nodded.

Poppy launched herself at him. He hugged her tightly and then brushed his lips against hers in the most weak-assed kiss she'd ever known.

She raised her eyebrows at him. 'What the hell was that?'

Michael's gaze slid over to her dad.

'I'm with Poppy.' Dad punched his shoulder. 'That

was pathetic…although that's all you can really expect from a King's man.'

Michael rolled his eyes, but couldn't seem to help smiling.

'We really do appreciate it, Fiona,' Dad said. 'It was good of you to tell him today.'

Fiona tucked a brown curl behind her ear. 'I think after everything you guys went through, you deserved a bit of good news. I just hope what happened hasn't put you off Cambridge.' She widened her eyes at Michael in mock threat.

'After all this, he'd better accept the place,' Poppy said, whacking him with the back of her hand. Michael grabbed the offending hand and squeezed it.

'Right, I'll leave you to it. I'll look forward to seeing much more of you—' Fiona raised her eyebrows at Poppy '—both.'

Fiona touched Dad's arm before heading back through the college gates. Dad stared after her, a wistful smile on his face.

'Don't you think it's about time you asked her out?' Poppy nudged Dad. 'She won't wait around forever. Hear that sound?' Dad gave her a puzzled look. 'That's the chronophage snapping at your heels. You're not getting any younger, y'know.'

His tipped his head back and snorted. 'Come on, my little matchmaker. There's a detective waiting to talk to us.' He slung one arm around Michael, one around her, and they began the walk back to Trinity.

Snowflakes lazily drifted out of the sky, slowly covering the icy brown sludge in the road and making it hard to spot the really icy patches. Christmas shoppers bustled in and out of doorways looking harassed, and every now and again Poppy caught a line of a carol drifting out of open shop doors.

There was one thing Ria had said that was still bugging her. 'Dad?'

'What?' Dad asked, squeezing her shoulder.

'Oh, nothing.'

'Hey, what it is?'

'It's stupid. It's just…Ria said that you and Chrissie were…'

Dad's eyes widened. '*What?* No!' he sighed. 'The hearing I told you about? There was some trouble earlier in the term when a student got…well, got a bit attached. But that wasn't Chrissie, it was Lucy. When I didn't reciprocate her feelings Devon got rather annoyed with me…he told people some stuff. I'd been through something similar before and it had ended disastrously. I was so determined to not hurt Lucy that I ended up handling it all wrong. Bea had me up before a disciplinary committee. It was a mess, but eventually Lucy realised what was happening and she went to Bea to straighten things out. She was very brave.'

'The time it happened before, was that Lance, Bea's son?'

Dad let out an astonished laugh. 'You've only been in Cambridge a few days – how the hell have you found out all of this? Do I have any secrets left?'

'One or two.'

'I wouldn't bet on it,' Michael muttered.

Dad smiled. 'Come on, you two. If we don't get back soon Detective Inspector Dalca might arrest me again.'

'How's Lucy?' Dad asked, holding the teapot over Detective Inspector Dalca's cup to offer her more tea.

The detective shook her head. 'She's doing better. It's going to take some time for her to come to terms with what happened, but I think she'll get there. I popped in on her this morning and she and her friend Devon were talking about Harvard. She seems determined not to change her plans.'

Poppy stared at the detective and couldn't help remembering the girl who'd sat in that exact place on Dad's sofa. The way she had laughed and joked. She'd seemed so normal while all the time her soul was being torn apart by grief and madness.

'How's Chrissie?' Poppy asked, cautiously.

The detective stared steadily back. 'She's in a secure unit. It's unlikely she'll be found fit to stand trial.'

'What'll happen to her?'

'She'll be sent somewhere to get the treatment she

needs. She's in the right place, Poppy.'

Poppy felt Michael's warm hand slip into hers. She looked into his serious blue eyes and shuddered at the thought of what might have been lost.

'I have something for you.' The detective reached into her bag and pulled out an old leather-bound book. She held it out to Dad. 'We found this in Chrissie's room, in an envelope addressed to *The Times*. My boss said that you would return it to its rightful owners.

'Is that the Apostles book?' Poppy asked.

Dad nodded. He took the book and after a moment's hesitation he handed it over the coffee table to Poppy.

Poppy shot a glance at Michael. He sat forward and looked over her shoulder as she opened the crumbling binding. Some pages listed the members, but most appeared to contain the scribbled minutes of meetings – the subject of the Apostles' discussion and the outcome of the votes they took. Some of the votes were on a philosophical topic whilst others were downright ridiculous. Michael pointed to one vote that asked: 'Musicals – are they of the devil?' Apparently, the Apostles thought they were.

'I don't get it,' Michael said. 'There's no great secrets in here, other than the membership.'

'It's the Apostles' silence that has driven people's curiosity about them,' Dad replied. 'At times that silence was necessary to protect members. When Guy

Burgess was revealed to be spying for the Russians the security services instituted a witch-hunt – they assumed that all the Apostles were Russian sympathisers. The group became even more secretive. But really, there was nothing to hide, except maybe a trail of nepotism and that's hardly particular to them. The Apostles is a debating club – nothing more.'

Poppy flicked forward until she found the most recent entries. Weird, but the last question they had voted on had been proposed by Conal: 'Does life continue after death?' She suspected he was the one person who had voted no. She ran a finger over his name, hoping he'd discovered he was wrong.

As her dad walked the detective to the gate, Poppy and Michael waited at the corner of Great Court.

Poppy shivered, no longer sure if it was the cold or just an excess of adrenaline still buzzing through her system. She glanced up at Michael. He was staring at her like he'd never really seen her before.

'Did you insinuate my kiss was lame?' he said, tugging Poppy to him by the front of her new coat.

She grinned as his arms slid around her, pressing her close enough that she could feel the warmth of him against her chest. She glanced over her shoulder. Dad had disappeared into the porter's lodge. She turned back to Michael and wiggled her eyebrows.

'I just call it like I see it, *King's boy.*'

Michael groaned. 'Don't you start that as well.' He rolled his eyes, but he couldn't hide the big cheesy grin.

She smoothed the collar of his coat down and brushed away the snow that clung there. 'I'm so happy for you.'

'If you hadn't been so damned stupid and put yourself in danger like that...' He swallowed and his jaw tightened. 'I should be so angry with you.'

Poppy tucked her head against his chest and hugged him tighter. She was afraid she wouldn't be able to let him go, ever again.

'Poppy,' Michael whispered into her hair. 'How did you know about the text Nick had sent Chrissie? Was it in the stuff Detective Inspector Dalca sent you?'

Poppy bit her lip. It would be so easy to lie, just to keep things normal. But lies hurt, even when you didn't want them to.

She shrugged. 'To be honest, I don't know.'

Michael took hold of her shoulders and eased her just far enough away that he could look into her eyes. He stared at her for what felt like forever, then took a deep breath and raised his eyebrows. 'Looks like you're not the only one who needs to adjust their world view.'

'Let's not rush into anything, huh?'

His expression grew serious again. 'You will talk to someone about what you...saw?'

'Yeah. Dad's already warned me that a conversation's going to happen.'

'Good. I think we both need to do a bit more of the talking thing.'

Poppy nodded. 'On the subject of which, about the…fracking.'

His eyes widened. 'Yeah?'

'I could so easily lose myself in us…*in you*…and a part of me really wants to, but another part of me thinks I have too much going on at the moment to really know who I am or what I want. Everything's moving so fast. And if we go ahead with the… *fracking*…I'm not sure what's next. All I've ever seen is people breaking up and I don't want to break up with you. I don't want that to happen to us. I love you and things are so good when we're not being shot at. I want us to stay the way we are right now…just for a little bit longer.'

His arm slipped from around her and for a second she thought he was going to push her away. Instead, he caught hold of her hand, lifted it between them and turned it palm up.

With a finger, he slowly traced:

ME 2

HISTORICAL NOTE

You might be interested to know that although I fictionalised them, the Cambridge Apostles are a real secret society that exists to this day. If you'd like to know more about their history you can find plenty of information on the internet or in Richard Deacon's excellent book *The Cambridge Apostles: A History of Cambridge University's Elite Intellectual Secret Society*.

And for those who know Trinity College well, you will know I took some liberties with geography and staffing. For my own nefarious purposes I conflated the role of Dean and Dean of Chapel, and to my knowledge, not many priests are taken on as chaplain for their curacy, but in Jim's case, strings were pulled!

ACKNOWLEDGEMENTS

Thanks to Rebecca Frazer and Rosalind Turner for their wise comments and insights, to Thy Bui for designing such stunning covers for these books, and to all the team at Hachette Towers for their help and support. Endless thanks go to Jenny Savill, agent extraordinaire.

Thanks to Dr (!) Jennie Barnsley and my sister, Gillian Swift, for their support. To Rachel Greene, Victoria Johnson, J'annine Jobling, Teri Terry and Liz de Jager – fabulous women all! Antonia Gray, whose passion for writing continues to inspire me and whose comments and critique were priceless. And most of all to Ellen Renner for her patience and diligence and being the best critique partner a girl could ever have. Thank you!

Thanks to the real Ria Mansey and Conal Preshoe for offering their names up as character fodder! Bet you thought I wouldn't do it... Needless to say, to my knowledge the real Ria isn't a member of the Apostles and Conal doesn't work for MI6...although, who knows! And finally, thanks to the staff and porters of Trinity College for their cheerful assistance when I turned up on their doorstep looking for help.

Have you read the first
Poppy Sinclair thriller,

DEAD JEALOUS?

Read on for a sneak peek…

Poppy massaged her tense shoulders and picked her way through the sagging tents, passing a yurt with a door that looked like the entrance to a hobbit house. The dewy grass was slippery beneath her Converse, but was soon replaced by hard pebbles as she reached the water's edge.

Scariswater. The lake stretched out before her like a swathe of shot silk. The ripples reflected all the colours of the morning; inky blacks and burnt oranges. A ghostly full moon graced the sky, even as the sun was stretching its rays from the east. The scene was so beautiful, so otherworldly, that she almost got it – the need to thank someone or something. She let her eyes fall closed and breathed in the fresh damp smells of the lake and hills. But in a flash, gratitude was replaced with terror. She was back there, in that other lake. The freezing water blinding her. Burning in her lungs. Drowning her.

She forced open her eyes and gasped in air.

Air, not water.

Breathe – *breathe!*

The lap of water against the pebbles made a hypnotic swishing sound, the lightest of breezes lifted the hair from the back of her neck, blowing away the memory but not the fear.

She'd grown up in Cumbria. Lakes water pulsed through her veins and she couldn't imagine ever living anywhere else and yet that day, nearly a year ago, a lake just like this one had nearly killed her.

It had been an accident. A freak fricking accident! It wasn't going to happen again.

She leaned down, quickly undid her laces, pulled off her socks and stuffed them into her Converse. She refused to be afraid of something she loved. She just had to get over it. She'd been unlucky that day, that's all.

The pebbles felt like dry ice cubes beneath her bare feet. She hopped around for a moment until she could stand the cold. Her jeans were skinny, and she had to yank the denim to get it past her calf muscles, but with her jeans as high as she could get them, she braced herself and edged into the lake.

The shock of the water made her gasp and then giggle. The water tickled as it lapped over her toes. Freezing, but not too bad. She'd been in colder.

As she stepped out, the feel of the pebbles beneath her feet transformed. They were no longer rough, but slippery, covered by a layer of slime. Poppy tried to concentrate on what her feet could feel instead of the frightened voice in her head telling her to get out of there. Sharp edges needled between her toes; moss tickled.

The bottom of the lake sloped gently down, and by the time the water was above her ankles, she was wondering where the inevitable shelf was, where the ground would disappear and she would find herself plunged waist deep and in need of a change of clothes.

Ahead, darkness swirled beneath the surface. It stretched out towards her like a shadow. Maybe this was it – the drop. But no, she could still see shapes beneath the water. She took another couple of steps forward and stumbled. The water hit the back of her knees, like a slap with a wet kipper, and soaked her jeans. A nervous giggle escaped her throat. Or was it a cry?

It's OK, she told herself. She was safe.

The water was so cold, her feet so frozen, that she almost didn't feel it – the gentle caress against her skin.

Fish?

She peered down into the water and saw something pale move, just below the surface.

Definitely fish.

She shifted her foot, hoping to get a better look and something cupped her leg. Something even colder than the lake.

It was then she saw it: a pale hand gliding towards her.

She screamed, but it was too late. Her foot slid from under her. She plummeted backwards. Icy cold water filled her eyes and mouth.

And the sky disappeared.